Acclaim For the Work of
MAX ALLAN COLLINS!

"Crime fiction aficionados are in for a treat…a neo-pulp noir classic."
—*Chicago Tribune*

"No one can twist you through a maze with as much intensity and suspense as Max Allan Collins."
—*Clive Cussler*

"Collins never misses a beat…All the stand-up pleasures of dime-store pulp with a beguiling level of complexity."
—*Booklist*

"Collins has an outwardly artless style that conceals a great deal of art."
—*New York Times Book Review*

"Max Allan Collins is the closest thing we have to a 21st century Mickey Spillane and…will please any fan of old-school, hardboiled crime fiction."
—*This Week*

"A suspenseful, wild night's ride [from] one of the finest writers of crime fiction that the U.S. has produced."
—*Book Reporter*

"This book is about as perfect a page turner as you'll find."
—*Library Journal*

"Bristling with suspense and sexuality, this book is a welcome addition to the Hard Case Crime library."
—*Publishers Weekly*

"A total delight…fast, surprising, and well-told."
—*Deadly Pleasures*

"Strong and compelling reading."
—*Ellery Queen's Mystery Magazine*

"Max Allan Collins [is] like no other writer."
—*Andrew Vachss*

"Collins breaks out a really good one, knocking over the hard-boiled competition (Parker and Leonard for sure, maybe even Puzo) with a one-two punch: a feisty storyline told bittersweet and wry…nice and taut…the book is unputdownable. Never done better."
—*Kirkus Reviews*

"One supremely satisfying example of a classic, twisty hard-boiled tale."
—*Criminal Element*

"Masterful."
—*Jeffery Deaver*

"Collins has a gift for creating low-life believable characters… a sharply focused action story that keeps the reader guessing till the slam-bang ending. A consummate thriller from one of the new masters of the genre."
—*Atlanta Journal Constitution*

"For fans of the hardboiled crime novel…this is powerful and highly enjoyable reading, fast moving and very, very tough."
—*Cleveland Plain Dealer*

"Entertaining…full of colorful characters…a stirring conclusion."
—*Detroit Free Press*

The slice of moon was painting the overgrown area behind the buildings a deceptively peaceful ivory. Forming a semi-circle, they were in the ankle-high grass, but a thicket of weeds and kudzu and God knew what else was waiting like an all too penetrable wall just a few yards away.

So pale he almost glowed, Dix was smoking, grinning, his mustache riding his sneer like a surfboard does a wave. He had a gun in one hand, a snubby .38. He stood near Dixie, who faced the bouncer and his prisoner. The captor had a roundish head, a stupid face, long brown stringy hair with sideburns, and was beefy verging on fat. His chin sat on another one and his little eyes peeked out from piggy pouches. For a big guy, he didn't look like much trouble to me.

But he was plenty of trouble for the salesman, whose arms he held pinned back...

...if not as much trouble as the big-boobed beehive redhead in the black waitress uniform and the white apron, which was already splashed with blood.

The three places where she had hit him in his bald skull with the hammer were easily visible, ribbons of red trailing from each. The little guy was woozy from pain but the mercy of unconsciousness hadn't come his way yet.

She snarled, "What do you think, Dix? Has our guest learned his lesson...?"

Quarry's
CHOICE

by **Max Allan Collins**

A HARD CASE CRIME NOVEL

A HARD CASE CRIME BOOK
(HCC-118)
First Hard Case Crime edition: January 2015

Published by

Titan Books
A division of Titan Publishing Group Ltd
144 Southwark Street
London SE1 0UP

in collaboration with Winterfall LLC

Print Edition ISBN 978-1-78329-084-0
E-book ISBN 978-1-78329-085-7

Design direction by Max Phillips
www.maxphillips.net

Typeset by Swordsmith Productions

The name "Hard Case Crime" and the Hard Case Crime logo are trademarks of Winterfall LLC. Hard Case Crime books are selected and edited by Charles Ardai.

Printed in the United States of America

Visit us on the web at www.HardCaseCrime.com

For my old musical comrade
Joe McClean —
like Quarry, a road warrior.

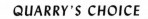

QUARRY'S CHOICE

> "Why do we electrocute men for murdering an individual and then pin a purple heart on them for mass slaughter of someone arbitrarily labeled 'enemy?'"
>
> SYLVIA PLATH

> "I shot a man in Reno just to watch him die."
>
> JOHNNY CASH

APRIL 1972

ONE

I had been killing people for money for over a year now, and it had been going fine. You have these occasional unexpected things crop up, but that's life.

Really, to be more exact about it, I'd been killing people for *good* money for over a year. Before that, in the Nam soup, I had been killing people for chump change, but then the Broker came along and showed me how to turn the skills Uncle Sugar had honed in me into a decent living.

I'll get to the Broker shortly, but you have to understand something: if you are a sick fuck who wants to read a book about some lunatic who gets off on murder, you are in the wrong place. I take no joy in killing. Pride, yes, but not to a degree that's obnoxious or anything.

As the Broker explained to me from right out of the gate, the people I'd be killing were essentially already dead: somebody had decided somebody else needed to die, and was going to have it done, which was where I came in. *After* the decision had been made. I'm not guilty of murder any more than my Browning nine millimeter is.

Guns don't kill people, some smart idiot said, *people kill people*—or in my case, people have some other person kill people.

There's a step here I've skipped and I better get to it. When I came home from overseas, I found my wife in bed with a guy. I didn't kill him, which I thought showed a certain restraint on my part, and when I went to talk to him about our "situation" the next day, I hadn't gone there to kill him, either. If I had, I'd have brought a fucking gun.

But he was working under this fancy little sports car, which like my wife had a body way too nice for this prick, and when he saw me, he looked up at me all sneery and said, "I got nothing to say to you, bunghole." And I took umbrage. Kicked the fucking jack out.

Ever hear the joke about the ice cream parlor? The cutie behind the counter asks, *"Crushed nuts, sir?" "No,"* the customer replies, *"rheumatism."* Well, in my wife's boyfriend's case it was crushed nuts.

They didn't prosecute me. They were going to at first, but then there was some support for me in the papers, and when the DA asked me if I might have *accidently* jostled the jack, I said, "Sure, why not?" I had enough medals to make it messy in an election year. So I walked.

This was on the west coast, but I came from the Midwest, where I was no longer welcome. My father's second wife did not want a murderer around—whether she was talking about the multiple yellow ones or the single-o white guy never came up. My father's first wife, my mother, had no opinion, being dead.

The Broker found me in a shit pad in L.A. on a rare bender— I'm not by nature a booze hound, nor a smoker, not even a damn coffee drinker—and recruited me. I would come to find out he recruited a lot of ex-military for his network of contract killers. Vietnam had left a lot of guys fucked-up and confused and full of rage, not necessarily in that order, and he could sort of… channel it.

The contracts came from what I guess you'd call underworld sources. Some kills were clearly mob-related; others were civilians who were probably dirty enough to make contacts with the kind of organized crime types who did business with the Broker—a referral kind of deal. Thing was, a guy like me never knew who had taken the contract. That was the reason for a Broker—he was our agent and the client's buffer.

Right now, maybe eighteen months since he'd tapped me on the shoulder, the Broker was sitting next to me in a red-button-tufted booth at the rear of an underpopulated restaurant and lounge on a Tuesday evening.

He was wearing that white hair a little longer now, sprayed in place, with some sideburns, and the mustache was plumper now, wider too, but nicely trimmed. I never knew where that deep tan came from—Florida vacations? A tanning salon? Surely not the very cold winter that Davenport, Iowa, had just gone through, and that's where we were—at the hotel the Broker owned a piece of, the Concort Inn near the government bridge over the Mississippi River, connecting Davenport and Rock Island, Illinois.

Specifically, we were in the Gay '90s Lounge, one of the better restaurants in the Iowa/Illinois Quad Cities, a study in San Francisco-whorehouse red and black. The place seemed to cater to two crowds—well-off diners in the restaurant area and a singles-scene "meat market" in the bar area. A small combo—piano, bass and guitar—was playing jazzy lounge music, very quietly. A couple couples were upright and groping on the postage-stamp dance floor, while maybe four tables were dining, money men with trophy wives. Or were those mistresses?

The Broker sat with his back to the wall and I was on the curve of the booth next to him. Not right next to him. We weren't cozy or anything. Often he had a bodyguard with him, another of his ex-military recruits—the Rock Island Arsenal was just across the government bridge and that may have been a source. But tonight it was just the two of us, a real father-and-son duo. We'd both had the surf and turf (surf being shrimp, not lobster—my host didn't throw his dough around) and the

Broker was sipping coffee. I had a Coke—actually, I was on my second. One of my few vices.

The Broker was in a double-knit navy two-button blazer with wide lapels, a wide light-blue tie and a very light-blue shirt, collars in. His trousers were canary yellow, but fortunately you couldn't see that with him sitting. A big man, six two with a slender but solid build, with the handsome features of a sophisticated guy in a high-end booze ad in *Playboy*. Eyes light gray. Face grooved for smile and frown lines but otherwise smooth. Mid-forties, though with the bearing of an even older man.

I was in a tan leisure suit with a light brown shirt. Five ten, one-hundred and sixty pounds, brown hair worn a little on the long side but not enough to get heckled by a truck driver. Sideburns but nothing radical. Just the guy sitting next to you on the bus or plane who you forgot about the instant you got where you were going. Average, but not so average that I couldn't get laid now and then.

"How do you like working with Boyd?" he asked. He had a mellow baritone and a liquid manner.

I had recently done a job with Boyd. Before that was a solo job and then five with a guy named Turner who I wound up bitching about to Broker.

Contracts were carried out by teams, in most cases, two-man ones—a passive and an active member. The passive guy went in ahead of time, sometimes as much as a month but at the very least two weeks, to get the pattern down, taking notes and running the whole surveillance gambit. The active guy came in a week or even less before the actual hit, utilizing the passive player's intel. Sometimes the passive half split town shortly after the active guy showed; sometimes the surveillance guy hung around if the getaway was tricky or backup might be needed.

"Well," I said, "you *do* know he's a fag."

The Broker's white eyebrows rose. It was like two caterpillars getting up on their hind legs. "No! Tough little fella like that? That hardly seems credible. Could you have misread the signs? You must be wrong, Quarry."

That wasn't my name. My name is none of your business. Quarry is the alias or code moniker that the Broker hung on me. All of us working for him on active/passive teams went by single names. Like Charo or Liberace.

"Look, Broker," I said, after a sip of Coke from a tall cocktail glass, "I don't give a shit."

"Pardon?"

"I said I don't care who Boyd fucks as long as doesn't fuck up the job."

Surprise twinkled in the gray eyes and one corner of his mouth turned up slightly. "Well, that's a very broad-minded attitude, Quarry."

"A broad-minded attitude is exactly what Boyd doesn't have."

The Broker frowned at me. He had the sense of humor of a tuna. "If you wish, Quarry, I can team you with another of my boys—"

I stopped that with a raised hand. "I think Boyd is ideal for my purposes. He prefers passive and I prefer active. You're well aware that sitting stakeout bores the shit out of me, whereas Boyd has a streak of voyeur in him."

"Well, that's hardly enough to recommend him as your permanent partner."

"I'm not marrying him, Broker. Just working with him. And anyway, I like his style—he's a regular guy, a beer-drinking, ball-team-following Joe. Fits in, blends in, does not the fuck stand out."

Understand, Boyd was no queen—he was on the small side

but sturdy, with a flat scarred face that had seen its share of brawls; his hair was curly and thick and brown, with bushy eyebrows and mustache, like so many were wearing. Also he had the kind of hard black eyes you see on a shark. Good eyes for this business.

With a what-the-hell wave, I said, "Let's go with Boyd."

Broker smiled, lifting his coffee cup. "Boyd it shall be."

You probably noticed that the Broker talked like a guy who'd read Shakespeare when to the rest of us English literature meant Ian Fleming.

"So," I said, "four jobs last year, and the one last month. That par for the course?"

He nodded. "Your advance should be paid in full by the end of this year. With that off the books, you'll have a very tidy income for a relative handful of jobs per annum."

"Jobs that carry with them a high degree of risk."

"Nothing in life is free, Quarry."

"Hey, I didn't just fall off a turnip truck."

A smile twitched below the mustache. "So, they have *turnip* trucks in Ohio, do they?"

"I wouldn't know. I've never been on a farm in my life. Strictly a townie." I leaned in. "Listen, Broker, I appreciate the free meal…keeping in mind nothing is free, like you said…but if you have no objection, I'm going to head home now."

He gestured like a *Price Is Right* model to a curtain opening onto a grand prize. "You're welcome to stay another night, my young friend. Several nights, if you like. You've earned a rest and a…bonus, perhaps? Possibly by way of a working girl? Something young and clean? Check out the redhead and the brunette, there at the end of the bar.…"

"No thanks, Broker." He seemed unusually generous tonight. "I just want to head back."

"But it's eight o'clock, and so many miles before you sleep."

I shrugged. "I like to drive at night. Why, is there something else you want to go over?"

It had felt throughout the meal that something more was hanging in the air than the question of Boyd as my official passive partner.

He lowered his head while raising his eyes to me. There was something careful, even cautious about it. Very quietly, though no one was seated anywhere near us, he asked, "How do you feel about a contract involving…a woman?"

With a shrug, I said, "I don't care who hires me. Hell, I don't even *know* who hires me, thanks to you."

"Not what I mean, Quarry."

I grinned at him. "Yeah, I knew that. Just rattling your chain, Broker."

He sighed, weight-of-the-world. "You know, I really should resent your insolence. Your impertinence. Your insubordination."

"Is that all? Can't you think of anything else that starts with an 'I'?"

That made him smile. Maybe a little sense of humor at that. "Such a rascal."

"Not to mention scamp."

Now he raised his head and lowered his eyes to me. Still very quiet, as if hunting wabbits. "I mean, if the…person you were dispatched to dislodge were of the female persuasion. Would that trouble you?"

That was arch even for the Broker.

I said, "I don't think it's possible to persuade anybody to be a female. Maybe you should check with Boyd on that one."

"Quarry…a straight answer please."

"You won't get one of those out of Boyd."

He frowned, very disapproving now.

I pawed the air. "Okay, okay. No clowning. No, I have no problem with 'dislodging' the fairer sex. It's been my experience that women are human beings, and human beings are miserable creatures, so what the heck. Sure."

He nodded like a priest who'd just heard a confessor agree to a dozen Hail Marys. "Good to know. Good to know. Now, Quarry, there may be upon occasion jobs in the offing...so to speak...that might require a willingness to perform as you've indicated."

Jesus. I couldn't navigate that sentence with a fucking sextant. So I just nodded.

"May I say that I admire your technique. I don't wish to embarrass you, Quarry, but you have a certain almost surgical skill..."

That's what they said about Jack the Ripper.

"...minimizing discomfort for our...subjects."

"Stop," I said. "I'll blush."

He leaned back in the booth. "Not everyone came back from their terrible overseas ordeal as well-adjusted as you, Quarry. Some of my boys have real problems."

"Imagine that. I'd like some dessert, if that's okay."

I'd spotted a waiter with a dessert tray.

The Broker gave a little bow and did that Arab hand roll thing like he was approaching a pasha. Jesus, this guy. "It would be my pleasure, Quarry. There is a quite delicious little hot-fudge sundae we make here, with local ice cream. Courtesy of the Lagomarcino family."

"Didn't I do one of them in Chicago last September?"

"Uh, no. Different family. Similar name."

"Rose by any other."

Knowing I planned to book it after the meal, I had already

stowed my little suitcase in the back seat of my Green Opel GT out in the parking lot.

So in fifteen minutes more or less, the Broker—after signing for the meal—walked me out into a cool spring night, the full moon casting a nice ivory glow on the nearby Mississippi, its surface of gentle ripples making the kind of interesting texture you find on an alligator.

The Concort Inn was a ten-story slab of glass and steel, angled to provide a better river view for the lucky guests on that side. The hotel resided on about half a city block's worth of cement, surrounded by parking. The lights of cars on the nearby government bridge, an ancient structure dating back to when nobody skimped on steel, were not enough to fend off the gloom of the nearby seedy warehouse area that made a less than scenic vista for the unlucky guests on the hotel's far side. The hotel's sign didn't do much to help matters, either, just a rooftop billboard with some underlighting. Four lanes of traffic cutting under the bridge separated the parking lot from the riverfront, but on a Tuesday night at a quarter till nine, "traffic" was an overstatement.

We paused outside the double doors we'd just exited. No doorman was on duty. Which was to say, no doorman was ever on duty: this was Iowa. The Broker was lighting up a cheroot, and for the first time I realized what he most reminded me of: an old riverboat gambler. It took standing here on the Mississippi riverfront to finally get that across to me. All he needed one of those Rhett Butler hats and Bret Maverick string ties. And he should probably lose the yellow pants.

"Broker," I said, "you *knew* Boyd was gay."

"Did I?" He smiled a little, his eyebrows rising just a touch, his face turned a flickery orange by the kitchen match he was applying to the tip of the slender cigar.

"Of course you did," I said. "You research *all* of us down to how many fillings we have, what our fathers did for a living, and what church we stopped going to."

He waved the match out. "Why would I pretend not to have known that Boyd is a practicing homosexual? Perhaps it's just something I missed."

"Christ, Broker, he lives in Albany with a hairdresser. And I doubt at this point he needs any practice."

He gave me a grandiloquent shrug. "Perhaps I thought you might have been offended had I mentioned the fact."

"I told you. He can sleep with sheep if he wants. Boy sheep, girl sheep, I don't give a fuck. But why hold that back?"

He let out some cheroot smoke. He seemed vaguely embarrassed. "One of my boys strongly objected to Boyd. But somehow my instincts told me that you would not. That you would be—"

"Broad-minded."

"I was going to say forward-thinking." He folded his arms and gave me a professorly look. "It's important we not be judgmental individuals, Quarry. That we be open-minded, unprejudiced, so that our professionalism will hold sway."

"Right the fuck on," I said.

He frowned at that, crudity never pleasing him, and the big two-tone green Fleetwood swung into the lot from the four-lane with the suddenness and speed of a boat that had gone terribly off course. The Caddy slowed as it cut across our path, the window on the rider's side down. The face looking out at us was almost demonic but that was because its Brillo-haired owner was grimacing as he leaned the big automatic against the rolled-down window and aimed it at us, like a turret gun on a ship's deck. A .45, I'd bet.

But I had taken the Broker down to the pavement, even before the thunder of it shook the night and my nine millimeter was out from under my left arm and I was shooting back at the bastard just as a second shot rocketed past me, eating some metal and glass, close enough for me to feel the wind of it but not touching me, and I put two holes in that grimace, both in the forehead, above either eye, and blood was welling down over his eyes like scarlet tears as the big vehicle tore out.

The last thing I saw was his expression, the expression of a screaming man, but he wasn't screaming, because he was dead. And dead men not only don't tell tales, they don't make *any* fucking sound, including screams.

I didn't chase them. Killing the shooter was enough. Maybe too much.

The Broker, looking alarmed, said something goddamned goofy to me, as I was hauling him up. "You wore a gun to *dinner* with me? Are you insane, man? This is neutral territory."

"Tell those assholes," I said, "and by the way—you're welcome."

He was unsteady on his feet.

The desk manager came rushing out and the Broker glanced back and shouted, "Nothing to see here! Children with cherry bombs. Franklin, keep everybody inside."

Franklin, an efficient little guy in a vest and bow tie (more riverboat shit), rounded up the curious, handing out drink chits.

There was a stone bench near the double doors and I sat Broker down on it and plopped beside him.

"You okay?" I asked.

He looked blister pale. "My dignity is bruised."

"Well, it doesn't show in those pants. I killed the shooter."

"Good. That should send a message."

"Yeah, but who to? And if you correct me with 'to whom,' I'll shoot you myself."

He frowned at me, more confusion than displeasure. "Did you get the license?"

"Not the number. Mississippi plates, though."

That seemed to pale him further. "Oh dear."

Oh dear, huh? Must be bad.

"Somebody may call the cops," I said. "Not everybody who heard that, and maybe saw it, is in having free drinks right now."

He nodded. "You need to leave. Now."

"No argument." I had already put the gun away. They weren't coming back, not with a guy shot twice in the face they weren't. Anyway, by now "they" was one guy, driving a big buggy into a night that was just getting darker.

I patted him on the shoulder. That was about as friendly as we'd ever got. "Sure you're okay?"

"I'm fine. I'll handle this. Go."

I went, and the night I was driving into was getting darker, too. But I had the nine millimeter on the rider's seat to keep me company. That and my "Who's Next" eight-track.

TWO

Early spring in my neck of the woods is a pleasure. "My neck of the woods" isn't just a saying, it's literal: I owned an A-frame cottage on Paradise Lake, a shimmering blue jewel nestled in a luxuriantly green setting. In a few weeks, Spring Break would fuck that up, sending college students swarming into nearby Lake Geneva. It's a harbinger of summer to come, only with a nasty frantic edge that wouldn't kick in again till late August. Girls in their late teens and early twenties in bikinis are fine by me, but not when they smell of beer puke.

This is not to say that I wouldn't be taking advantage of the impending (how shall I delicately put it?) influx of sweet young pussy. I still looked like a college student myself, and had learned enough from books and TV to pass for one. So if I could connect with some cupcake looking to make a memory, why not help her out? Assuming, of course, I could manage that before she got shit-faced. Hey, I'm just that kind of guy.

But really the kind of guy I am is one who prefers hardly any people around. My circle of friends was limited to a few employees and regulars of Wilma's Welcome Inn, a cheerfully ramshackle lodge with a tavern and convenience store, within walking distance; a handful of Lake Geneva residents—businessmen in my monthly poker game; regulars at the health club I frequented; and assorted waitresses from the Playboy Club.

Mine was a monastic existence, really, except for the balling Bunnies and college girls part; mostly I lived a solitary life in my A-frame, sitting on the deck out back, watching the lovely rippling lake, where I swam when the weather warmed. I even had a little motorboat and sometimes fished. During the fall and winter, I curled up by the fire reading paperback westerns or watching television—I had splurged on a very tall antenna that could pull in the Chicago stations.

With the generous advance I'd received before starting contract work, I'd been able to outright buy the cottage and my Opel GT—my two extravagances. No mortgage. No car payment. Who had a better life than mine? Particularly in the spring, when ski season was over and summer was just a threat. Superman had his Fortress of Solitude, and I had my A-frame on Paradise Lake.

So when the Broker showed up on my doorstep, it seemed like a violation. Worlds colliding. I hadn't even known he knew where exactly I lived. The routine so far was that I called once a week from a pay phone for instructions, which were usually just "call back next week." Same Bat Time, same Bat Channel.

Only now, here he stood, tall and morose, in a peach-colored sport shirt, lighter peach slacks, white shoes...and no jacket! Imagine that. More casual than I'd ever seen him, but also rumpled, with sweat stains under his arms like a regular human. It was like he walked off the golf course in the middle of a round that was going for shit.

"Sorry to drop by unannounced like this," he said. Barely audible, his manner distracted.

I was in a t-shirt and cut-off jeans and probably looked like a beachcomber to him. I hadn't even carried a gun to the door with me. Never again.

A silver Lincoln with a vinyl top sat in my gravel drive behind my Opel GT, like an opulent tank about to fire away on the indigent. Behind the wheel of the Lincoln was a shrimpy guy named Roger who I'd met a couple of times. He was ex-military, too, but not one of the contract workers. More a bodyguard/valet.

The Broker saw me looking. "Roger will stay put, I assure you. I know you dislike him."

"I don't anything him. But you're right I don't want him in my house. Come in. Come in."

He stepped inside and I shut the door behind him. He just stood there, looking a little dazed. It had been just under a week since the parking lot incident outside the Concort Inn. I had checked in once but got no answer. That happened sometimes, so I hadn't been overly concerned.

Still, the shooting had been hanging over things, a gray cloud threatening rain if not getting around to it.

Well, here was some rain. A whole Broker downpour. I stepped around him and curled a finger for him to follow and walked him down the hall past bedrooms and bathroom into the big open living room with its steel fireplace in the middle and kitchenette at left. The interior decoration was Early Dorm Room.

"Nice," he said, forcing a smile.

"It's nothing, but it's mine. Broker, what are you doing here?"

"…I need a word."

When did a conversation ever go well that started that way?

I gestured toward the fridge. "Can I get you a beer or a Coke or something?"

"Beer would be fine."

I pointed to the sliding glass doors onto the lake. "You go sit out on the deck. I'll join you in a minute."

"Fine. Uh, Quarry."

"Yeah?"

"Of course I know where you live. Why would you doubt that?"

Just like he'd known Boyd was gay.

"It's not that so much," I said. "It's just seeing you in…real life…that threw me."

He glanced around the space under the open-beamed A-ceiling. It was a landscape of throw pillows on the floor and one of the chairs was a bean bag. "Is that what this is? Real life?"

"Well, we don't generally socialize, you and me. Not on my turf. But I'll adjust." I gestured to the glass doors again. "Go on out. I'll get our drinks."

I got myself a Coke and a Coors for the Broker. He was sitting in one of the wooden deck chairs, looking out at the afternoon sun sparkling on the lake like a goddamn postcard.

"Really lovely," he said, as I settled in on a matching chair next to him. A little slatted wooden table between us took the drinks.

"I like it," I said with a shrug, slipping on sunglasses that had been on the table.

He turned the spooky gray eyes on me, enough glare off the pretty lake to make him squint at me like Clint Eastwood, if Clint Eastwood were much older. "We're not socializing, actually. Not that that would be unpleasant, but…this is business."

"Business like a contract."

His head angled to one side. "A contract, exactly. But not under the normal circumstances." He shook a professorly finger at me. "And I want it understood you have my blessing…or let's call it my 'okay'…to pass on this, this… opportunity."

"Opportunity, huh? How so?"

"It will pay fifty thousand dollars and all expenses."

That was an opportunity, all right.

I shrugged, as if unimpressed. "Well, you said it wasn't normal. So how else isn't it normal?"

An eyebrow raised. "You'll *know* who the client is."

That got a blink out of me. "We're breaking what-do-you-call-it, protocol, aren't we?"

"Indeed we are."

The Broker was one of the few people I ever knew who used that word in human speech. Not that there's any other kind.

I had a sip of Coke. "So who *is* this client?"

He looked out at the lake. "Who do you think I'm talking about, young man? Me."

That did make sense.

Somebody had tried to gun him down last week, and the Broker had been understandably shaken, and still was. I didn't know enough about the inter-workings of his business—hell, the workings period—to know whether being on the firing line himself was something that the Broker expected to occur, from time to time. As part of the price of doing business.

But I would have to say such an occurrence must have been rare, because six days later, the Broker appeared still to be reeling and, more than that, was right here smack in the middle of my world. The devil looking out at Paradise Lake.

"Obviously," I said, "this relates to last week's fun and games."

Slow single nod. "Obviously."

"And in the days since, you've determined who was behind that attempt."

Two nods, not so slow. "I have indeed. And I have your keen eyes to thank."

"Yeah?"

"That Mississippi license plate told the tale."

And then he told me one.

"For your own protection," he began, after two sips of Coors, "for the protection of all of those who work for me, I keep things on a need-to-know basis. Most of those we eliminate are from the world of business or perhaps politics, although never on a rarefied scale—we leave that to the CIA. Usually we remove fairly important people, because important people are involved in the kinds of affairs that can get a person removed."

"And not just business affairs," I said.

"No. Affairs of the heart, as well."

"Or the heart-on."

He didn't bother to wince at that, and simply went on: "You, *all* of you, are certainly aware that we do work for elements of organized crime—the so-called Mob. But your awareness is relatively vague. Again, you are provided intel on a need-to-know basis, while I protect you from interaction with those who have hired my...*our*...services."

"Okay," I said, trying not to sound impatient. I knew all this, but he was in a bad place, or anyway a strained one, and I wouldn't be needling him today. Much.

"One of the criminal organizations we do a fair share of work for is known as the Dixie Mafia." He looked from the lake to me. "Are you familiar with that term, Quarry?"

"No."

"It's not a phrase that indicates Italian or Sicilian ancestry. In fact, it's not a term that those involved in the group coined themselves—rather some newspaperman came up with it, to lend a little glamour to a rather slipshod enterprise, and this rabble embraced it. You will find in the so-called Dixie Mafia, for example, no 'don.' No 'boss of bosses.' Their roots are not Capone and Luciano, but Dillinger and Pretty Boy Floyd."

He explained that the Dixie Mafia comprised traveling criminals and roadhouse proprietors throughout the South—small-time thieves, bigger-time heist artists, car boosters, and con men; also, gambling- and whorehouse proprietors. Their only connection to the real Mafia was to pay a tax to the New Orleans mob, when on their turf.

"The Strip in Biloxi, Mississippi, has evolved into their base of operations," the Broker said. "It was a natural enough thing. Just as the Dixie Mafia is a ragtag coterie of criminals, the Strip is a squalid patchwork of striptease clubs, shabby motels and sleazy bars. These provide the perfect surroundings for these migratory miscreants to meet, to plan their 'capers.' "

"If there's no 'don,' " I asked, "who do we do contract work for?"

He held his palms up. "Well, in recent years, one of the club owners has risen to power—initially as a fence and a message service, later hiding men on the run, laundering their cash, even investing in their enterprises…underwriting more ambitious heists."

"This is the man you've done business with."

He squinted again, gazing out at the blue lake, his hands tented. He selected his words. Then: "Yes and no. I've dealt directly with him on just two occasions."

His hands were clenched. Was that fear? Jesus, that was fear.

"Jack Killian," he said, talking to the lake. "From a surprisingly upper-class background. Chose the Air Force over college. Became a car thief who graduated to bank robbery. Once just another of those traveling criminals, if a notably sadistic one, now the owner of every fleshpot on the Biloxi Strip. He is not the don, not in the traditional Mafia sense. More like a feudal lord."

"But you don't deal with him."

He shook his head, paused for a sip of Coors. "Killian's partner, Woodrow Colton—Mr. Woody, he is called—is the Dixie Mafia's number two. The banker. The money launderer, the fixer, co-owner of Killian's clubs." He smiled, as if recalling a pleasant afternoon with a friend. "An amiable sort, Mr. Woody—who navigates through the political world of Biloxi, spreading joy. And cash. *He* has been my contact. And a pleasure with whom to do business."

I was hearing things I was not supposed to know. That none of us who worked for the Broker were supposed to know.

"And it is through Mr. Colton," the Broker went on, glancing at me with a faint smile flickering on the thin lips under the well-trimmed mustache, "that we have our avenue for...well, revenge is such an unpleasant word, and a concept for lessers. Let us call it retaliation. Let us call it self-protection."

"Let us call it," I said, "who do I kill?"

He resumed his contemplation of the lake. The sun had slipped behind some gently moving clouds that were making shadows in an afternoon suddenly turned a cool blue.

"Mr. Killian has ambitions," he said. "Perhaps he does in fact see himself as the 'don' of the Dixie Mafia. He has been buying up roadhouses in the south, in particular the rather notorious State-line Strip between Tennessee and Mississippi. And, as I say, he owns virtually every striptease joint, shack-up motel and sleazy bar on the Biloxi Strip."

"What does that have to do with the services we perform for him?"

The Broker was facing the lake but his eyes were closed now. "He has decided, Mr. Colton informs me, that he will henceforth handle all necessary liquidations 'within house.' That is certainly his privilege. I hold no long-term contracts with anyone."

It seemed to me that every contract we handled was as about long-term as it got, but I let it go. Honestly, though, "henceforth"?

"I am viewed," the Broker said, his eyes open now and on me, "as a loose end. The expression, however trite, remains apt: '*I know too much.*'"

And now so did I.

"So it's Killian, then," I said. "Point me."

He shook his head, frowning. "It's not that simple, nothing

so straightforward. There's a need for this to seem like something other than a simple hit."

"I don't do accidents."

"No, I know, that requires special training, and gifts that are not among yours." He had a healthy swig of beer. "No, I have something in mind for how this might be handled, but first it requires that you go…well, I suppose the term is 'undercover.' "

"Come again?"

There was a twinkle in the gray eyes as he replied—a fucking twinkle, I swear. "Mr. Colton has agreed to help us remove Mr. Killian."

"Could we skip the 'misters'? We are talking about killing this prick. And what makes you think you can trust Colton?"

He batted that away. "I don't think it's a matter of the second-in-command wishing to stage a coup—more that Mr. Killian and his roughneck ways…no matter how well he may dress, and I understand he is quite the clotheshorse…is making enemies in certain Biloxi circles of power. His behavior is so outrageous and so damned grasping that the politicians would very much like to see him retire. Or I should say, 'retired.' "

"A gold watch with a bullet through it."

"Metaphorically correct." He twisted toward me in the wooden chair and his hands were folded, resting against an arm of it. "There is an opening on Mr. Killian's staff of bodyguards that Mr. Colton is in a position to arrange for you to fill. That will put you very close to Mr. Killian. Close enough for you to gain his trust, or at least his laxity."

"Close enough to put out his lights."

Short, quick nods. "But he is extremely well-insulated, and this must be accomplished in a manner that won't embarrass or, worse, implicate Mr. Colton. Are you willing?"

"Like the Pope said on his death bed, why me?"

The Broker gestured in a slow-motion manner. "As it happens, you've never done a job in that colorful region. Never done a job emanating from that client. You are, after all, fairly new to the business."

"Yeah, you can't beat a fresh face. But what about the guys in the green Caddy the other night? You know, the one with the Mississippi plates?"

Both eyebrows went up, the white caterpillars on their hind legs again. "Well, one of them is quite dead, and the other was occupied, and probably got little more than a glimpse of you, if that, in that under-lit lot. Additionally, you were firing that weapon of yours, and I'm sure the orange flames it was spitting were a distraction."

"They usually are. I don't have to use a Southern accent or anything, do I?"

"No! You'll be a damn Yankee, but one recommended by the Number Two in the organization. You'll use 'Quarry,' and is 'John' all right for a first name?"

"Sure. Why not."

He damn near beamed. Staying in the wooden deck chair, sticking his legs straight out, he dug in a pants pocket and withdrew a fat letter-sized envelope, folded over. "Here's expense money, and a Michigan driver's license."

I took it. Two grand in hundreds, and a license with a picture of me—Broker had plenty of those from various states for this exact purpose.

But I frowned at him. "If you already had this ready, why ask if I was okay with 'John'?"

"Why," he asked, frowning back, "aren't you all right with it?"

"No, that's not the point. It's just…skip it."

My saying yes had brightened his mood considerably. "You'll

need to buy some new clothes with some of that. As I said, Killian is a clotheshorse and he expects his people to dress professionally. That money should also be plenty to front a plane ticket. Fly into somewhere other than Biloxi, New Orleans perhaps, and rent a car. You can use any of your current identities for those operations."

There were many more details and we spoke into dusk. I invited him for a walleye dinner at Wilma's Welcome Inn, but he passed. He had a long drive home ahead of him.

We shook hands just outside my front door and he was smiling as he walked briskly to the Lincoln. Behind the wheel, Roger gave me a nod. I didn't return it.

I had a trip ahead of me, too.

I was fine with that—even if it was an unusual job that took me out of my element and meant I had to deal with people, which I didn't love. But fifty grand was fifty grand. So heading South was no big deal.

As long as the job didn't go south.

THREE

After getting in at New Orleans' Moisant Field around two, I rented a cobalt-blue Chevelle SS, signing on for a week but guessing I'd need it longer. The brunette Southern belle at the Avis counter wore a jaunty company cap and sported an accent thicker than a bowl of grits. She understood Yankee fluently, however, and helped me out with several maps.

The drive to Biloxi on U.S. Highway 90 should take maybe an hour and a half, I figured. I could go by way of the new Interstate 10, but the Broker had recommended "the parallel scenic view," which provided the benefit of taking me directly to the Biloxi Strip.

In a burgundy t-shirt and lightweight jeans, I'd braced myself for heat and humidity only to be greeted by a balmy seventy-five. I had a hunch this might be the last nice surprise of my trip. Barely out of the city, I stopped at a funky Cajun joint and chowed down on a plate of crawfish etouffee with a side of red beans and rice—I don't eat on airplanes. Not *that* damn reckless.

Heading east, I left the windows down, and not just because I was farting—a Gulf breeze was whipping up a heady concoction of magnolias, wild grass and brine. You just knew you were somewhere else. The Chevelle performed fine, or anyway it did after I found a rock station—every radio pre-set was country western. You'd at least think there'd be some fucking Zydeco.

The countryside was lush and green and kudzu-heavy, when I wasn't cruising through little towns where the major industry seemed to be poverty; new leaves reflected sunlight even as they provided a near tunnel of shade. Gulfport, of course, was no hamlet, offering up sandy-white beaches, fishing fleets, and white-columned antebellum mansions; and Biloxi itself had its share of the latter, too, with grounds arrayed with Spanish-moss-bearded oaks. But then I came upon a startling slice of surrealism: a dusty-looking Air Force jet on a pylon perched on the highway median like the discarded toy of a giant's spoiled child.

Military boosterism, and a dewy-eyed respect for the Old South—that seemed to be Biloxi all over.

That and a tourist attraction of a narrow strip of white sand separating the four-lane blacktop from the blue-steel vastness of the Gulf of Mexico. No tourists right now, though. Like back home at Paradise Lake, Biloxi's shore had that lovely lack of people—the smell of coconut butter had not yet impinged upon the salty air, the lawnmower churn of motorboats and jet skis nicely absent. And who needed girls in bikinis with what awaited along the highway?

On either side stood the shabby churches waiting to fleece their flock of sun worshipers—the Biloxi Strip. And so many denominations—bars, striptease clubs, Bonnie & Clyde motels, bars, fast-food franchise joints, striptease clubs, local crab shacks, bars, souvenir stands, and putt-putt golf. Also striptease clubs and bars. Or did I mention that?

On the north side of 90, Mr. Woody's sat on its own parking lot, looking more like a warehouse than a nightclub, which wasn't surprising because it had probably started out that way. A black sign on a rooftop pole said MR. WOODY'S in white letters with red polka dots in the OO's. I'll let you work out the symbolism of that. A white plastic marquee with black plastic letters above blacked-out double doors said:

TOPLESS
BOTTOMLESS
DRINKS

which struck me as ambiguous, and

PRIVATE DANCES
NO COVER

and that was ambiguous, too, don't you think?

I went inside and a big guy on the door looked me over, decided not to card me, and as my eyes adjusted to the smoky dusk of the place, I said, "Appointment with Mr. Colton. Never been here before. Point the way?"

He was maybe six three and pushing three hundred pounds in a black t-shirt and black jeans, which weren't all that slimming. Trimly brown-bearded with bored dark eyes that had seen everything twice, he had a couple of gold chains around the fat folds of his neck and his features had the blunt look of too much football.

"Stay put," he said, higher-pitched than you'd think. Behind him on the wall was a house phone and he used it, saying, "Guy here, Mr. Woody. Appointment, he says." He glanced at me. "Name?"

"Quarry," I said.

He repeated it into the phone, hung up and pointed a thick finger into the darkness, where way across the cavernous red-carpeted room a black door could be made out with white letters saying PRIVATE — NO ENTRY. Another big guy in black was standing next to it, arms folded like a bored genie.

It was 4:35 in the afternoon but not really—I'd entered into the Vegas-like endless midnight of the strip-club world. Big as it was, Mr. Woody's seemed bigger because of mirrored walls, which bounced around flashing blue and red lights from above, a pair of unblinking klieg lights at left and right crossing each other to hit the stage like a prison escape was in progress. The tables (black) were small but the chairs (red) were good-size with curving cushioned backs. A full bar at right sported several cute young female bartenders in tuxedo shirts and string ties and too much make-up, and weaving through the room were a couple of fetching waitresses in the same uniform, which included a black mini and black nylons.

Backed by a black curtain with the MR. WOODY'S logo, the main stage was just deep enough for a dancer to work the stripper pole, with a wide center runway into the audience, seating on either side, edged with flashing lights and a ledge for drinks. A smaller secondary stage, really just a platform with a stripper pole, was tucked away at left, not currently in use. The audience was entirely male, stopping off after work, both blue- and white-collar, and some young enlisted men from the Air Force base, still in uniform. The atmosphere could only have been smokier if the place was on fire. Gray and white tobacco-bred tendrils floated across the red and blue and white lighting like sleepy ghosts.

On stage was a small girl—and she was a girl, not a woman yet, possibly eighteen, though her hour-glass figure was time-less—with straight honey-blonde hair center-parted and cut off at her shoulders. Not really dancing, she was strutting around in clear plastic heels and moving her hands to "Fortunate Son" as it blared from high-mounted speakers. Out of the heels, she was probably five one or two at most, and her expression in-cluded a glazed smile and big glazed light-blue eyes as she gazed past her admirers into God knew what.

She was naked as the day she was born, but she hadn't been born with those perfect tip-tilted handfuls or that generous golden-brown tuft. She did not seem at all self-conscious, though it was still somehow surprising when she began to sit in front of each ringside-seater to smile and spread her legs like "make a wish" and use plenty of fingers to show off the pink place where life begins.

The little blonde had gathered some wadded-up green and moved on to the next lover of modern dance when I approached the big guy in black at the door marked PRIVATE, who was expecting me. He had a shaved head and Tony Orlando's mustache on loan.

"End of the hall," he said.

He opened the door for me. I wouldn't have expected less in such a classy place.

Several doors were on either side of the cream-color cement-block hallway. The one at the end said MR. WOODY. It also said: PLEASE KNOCK. Genteel way to put it.

So I knocked once, then said over the muffled sound of "Ramblin' Gamblin' Man" out in the club, "Quarry, Mr. Colton!"

"Come on in!" came a jovial, husky mid-range voice.

I went in and found myself in a surprisingly small office, no bigger than a supermarket manager's stuck on one side of his warehouse facilities. Maybe that's what it had been once.

Right now the modest space was dominated by a big steel desk bookended by set-back steel file cabinets, with comfy-looking black-leather chairs for visitors and a matching couch squeezed in along the wall to my right and a small refrigerator and well-stocked liquor cart to my left. The walls were home to framed MR. WOODY's posters featuring star strippers—Carol Doda, Candy Barr, Evelyn West, Chesty Morgan, Fanne Foxe— each warmly autographed to Mr. Woody ("You're the best!" "Wotta man!" "I'm yours any ole time!").

Speaking of Mr. Woody, he was rising behind that desk to offer me a hand to shake, grinning at me like I was an old war buddy suddenly dropped by. The effect of him was all eyes and teeth, the former magnified by the lenses of his big goggle-style tortoise-shell frames, the latter big and white and perfect, meaning he kept them in a glass at night. The eyes were hooded and hazel, his longish salt-and-pepper hair sprayed in place. A combover, I thought. He had sideburns, but nothing wacky.

Maybe fifty-five, he was around five-nine, darkly tan, stoop-shouldered with a paunch, in a pale pink short-sleeve shirt, a red-and-pink paisley tie, and red suspenders; his trousers were gray—had they been some other shade of red or pink, I might have bailed—and he looked like a used-car salesman or maybe a local politician.

"Mr. Quarry," he said. "You are kind to come, sir. At such short notice and all."

"Make it 'Quarry.' Or John if you like." I sat, shrugged. "Maybe Johnny, since we're past the Mason–Dixon line."

He winked and shot a forefinger at me. "Let's make it Quarry, then. John sounds like a crapper, and I already *got* a damn Jack in my life." He waved a hand heavy with gold-and-diamond rings toward the generous liquor cart. "May I offer you a libation?"

"No thanks." I jerked a thumb behind me. "I don't see much security here, Mr. Colton."

"Make it 'Mr. Woody.' Everybody and his mother calls me that. Might attract undue attention, otherwise. As for the scant security, I have never had no need. It's been my experience that if you deal with people in a straight-up manner, rarely does anyone kill your ass." He shook his head, his manner regretful. "The same, I'm afraid, can't be said to apply to Jack Killian."

I leaned back in the chair, crossed my arms and my legs. "I don't have any kind of cover story, Mr. Woody. Just a driver's license. Michigan."

His head was a little too small for the specs, so when he nodded, it was like the eyeglasses were doing it. "That should work handily. I have bidness contacts in Detroit, as our mutual friend the Broker well knows. That was probably his thinkin'."

"You didn't discuss this with him?"

His shrug was elaborate. "We've had minimal contact, Broker and me, since the attempt. After all, one never knows with phones. The FBI aren't the only ones use bugs these days. But if I tell Jack Killian you're from Detroit, we won't need any 'laborate cover story. He won't question the recommendation. All he'll likely say is, 'Fine. Long as he's not black.' "

This was the second time he'd referred to his first-in-command in that oddly formal both-names manner.

"Tell me about Killian," I said.

"Positive I can't get you a little somethin'?" he asked. He was on his feet, drifting to the liquor cabinet. A pink sportcoat was around the back of his swivel chair. He began pouring himself some Scotch in a tumbler.

"Any pop in that fridge?"

"Yessir. Root beer okay?"

"Sure."

He got a cold sweaty bottle of Barq's out. "Biloxi is strictly a root beer town. This is our home-brewed drink, y'know." He delivered the bottle, then he and his Scotch got behind the desk, which was free of work—just a phone and a notepad with pen.

His expression grew suddenly somber. "You must understand, Quarry, that I take no pleasure in bringin' you in for this necessary but most unfortunate task."

My head bobbed back, like I was ducking a punch. "Meaning no disrespect, sir, my contract is with the Broker. *He* sent me here. Although if you have an arrangement with him…if you're helping fund this…I'd just as soon *not* know. I view you as my contact, and a sort of…facilitator. Are you cool with that?"

He was nodding slowly, smiling, not big, but smiling. "I can see why the Broker sent you. You are obviously an intelligent young man. Vietnam, I assume."

"Yes, sir."

He gestured vaguely. "Some of the people on our staff—Jack

Killian's staff included—are likewise veterans, and you should know that I respect and admire your service. I was too young for World War Two, more's the pity, and too old for Vietnam."

That left Korea, but I let that go.

He sneered. "Some of these boys from the piney woods who think they're so goddamn tough got out of servin' one way or t'other. Political pull or medical reasons or 'cause of unstable mental health, which I guess is also medical, bein' crazy, when you come right down to it."

"Yes, sir."

"Now where was I?"

"Jack Killian. Necessary but most unfortunate task."

He nodded gravely. Sipped his Scotch. This might be a root beer town, but he wasn't having any. "Jackie is like a brother to me. That's why this pains me so."

From "Jack Killian" to "Jackie"—interesting.

He raised a palm and an eyebrow. "What you have to under-stand about Jack Killian is that he is highly unusual among the ranks of those that I, *we*, have done bidness with over the past thirty-some years. Most of those I done bidness with crawled out of a mire of poverty to scratch out a livin', maybe not an honest one, but a livin'. They come from backgrounds of utter despair and abject need. We're talkin' lowlife rabble, quite frankly, creatures that crawl."

"Then why do business with them?" I resisted the urge to say "bidness."

He raised his chin. "Because such men—and women—flawed though they may be, have overcome adversity. They are the dark underbelly of the American dream, true capitalists one and all. They value a dollar and there is little they won't do for one. My role in all of this is as a liaison between these hard-scrabble entrepreneurs and the upright world."

If they were so upright, why were they doing business with creatures that crawled?

Mr. Woody was saying, "Biloxi is a venerable, respectable, churchgoin' Southern community, Quarry. The Strip here is abided with only for two reasons: one of them is money. Can you guess the other?"

"You," I said.

The big teeth overtook the face again, very white against the dark tan. "You are sharp, son. Sharp indeed. But, uh, have I gotten off the road again?"

"Maybe you were headed back on. Jack Killian?"

He nodded and the smile faded. "Jackie is an unusual case. A unique case. He does not come from indigence. His background, in fact, is privileged. He's an Oklahoma boy whose father made a fortune as a criminal attorney and whose mother was from oil money. Jackie's pappy ran for governor and damn near made it—even today, he sits on the Oklahoma court of appeals."

"We're talking a silver-spoon hood."

"Absolutely. And a bad boy from birth. Grade school, gettin' in fights and beatin' other boys half to death. Knockin' up girls in junior high. Gettin' a Corvette in high school for his sixteenth birthday and celebratin' with a high-speed chase with the sheriff's patrol. Only stayed out of reform school by goin' to a military academy, not that any damn discipline got instilled there." He chuckled. "He was a wild one, ol' Jackie."

I frowned. "Why, did you know him as a kid? I thought you said he was from Oklahoma."

Another vague gesture. "His parents vacationed here. You see, his daddy—who served in both the House and Senate of the Sooner State, before becomin' a judge—had plenty of ties to folks right here on the Biloxi Strip. Like old Blackjack Boorman, who took me under his wing. Then, of course, Jackie at nineteen avoided a jail sentence by joinin' the Air National Guard, and got a year of active duty here in Biloxi. And that's when I took him under my wing, put him to work on his off-duty hours. Back then, I was just startin' out—four strip clubs and a bingo parlor."

"What did he do for you?" I didn't figure he sat at a mike calling out, "Bingo!"

"Jackie's a good man with a deck of cards, a regular mechanic, blackjack, poker, three-card monte, you name 'er. Big, dark-haired, good-lookin' charmer. Could make a friend out of a mark, usually promisin' to fix a fool up with a girl. Hell, he could clean damn near anybody out. I paid him a nice percentage of the take, too. But, of course, he got greedy, and back around '64? We come to a temporary partin' of the ways."

"Why was that?"

Another sip of Scotch. "He was gettin' the players drunk so's he could roll 'em in the parkin' lot. And he didn't just take their money, he would kick the holy ever-livin' shit out of them. To scare 'em, he said, from complainin' to the management or the cops."

"But you did get complaints."

"Sure. Shit, he was runnin' the badger game right out of this club for a while, settin' Air Force guys up with my girls and then robbin' them at one of my motels."

"This was not on your menu."

Fire flared in the magnified eyes. "Hell, no! We have always kept things on the straight and narrow, where the kids from Keesler is concerned."

He meant the Air Force base. Not the elves who make cookies.

He was saying, "It's unpatriotic, fuckin' them boys over, plus which it rubs the local powers-that-be very damn fuckin' wrong.

When it's off-season in Biloxi, we depend on them boys for their paychecks. They need to feel they're gettin' somethin' for their money."

"American way," I said. "So how did Killian come back into the fold?"

"Well, once he struck out on his own, he made a name for hisself as a heist artist. Fearless and smart if a little on the loco side. He ran a stolen car ring for a while, top chop shop racket in the South, and he put together a big bankroll. Over those years, we grew close again, because he became one of my best clients."

"Not sure I follow—a client how?"

That got a big smile out of Mr. Woody, but this time one showing no teeth; this one created a wealth of creases in the tanned flesh. "You must understand my role in all of this, Quarry—on one hand, I'm the post office. A communications source for all the freelancers out there in the world of, well, let's call it left-handed endeavor. Who's lookin' for a jug artist? Who needs a wheelman? Kind of thing. On the other hand, I am their banker. I hold cash. I launder cash. I sometimes invest for them. And I sometimes invest *in* them."

Bankrolling heists, drug deals, what-have-you.

"And that's all the Dixie Mafia is?" I asked. "A loose conglomeration of thieves and con men who depend on you here in Biloxi to help them deal with their proceeds?"

This assessment seemed to disappoint him, perhaps even hurt his feelings.

He said, "That's a major part, Quarry, surely…but there's more. Much more, really. Here on the Strip, these strip clubs are just the bait. But gamblin'—the rear of this buildin' is a casino, which is open right now. I'll give you a tour shortly. And there are a dozen more gamblin' dens of mine, ours, along this highway, although I take particular pride in *this* facility. Most of the girls workin' the stage are also trickin', high-end, hundred up. We help distribute bootleg liquor, tax-free stuff, a hangover from decades of Mississippi bein' dry. And most of the drugs in this and the adjacent states flow through our portals."

"Okay," I said.

This was definitely weird—I was hearing all the inside shit that the Broker usually protected me from. But to deal with Killian from the inside, I needed to know the inside of what.

I sat forward. "So what makes Jack Killian a problem?"

He tented his hands and rocked gently in the swivel chair. "I'll be frank with you, Quarry. Until he sent people to remove the Broker, I hadn't fully accepted that Jack Killian *was* a problem. I knew he was dangerous. A threat to the status quo. But just not how *serious*."

"Explain."

He nodded, the eyes behind the big lenses almost shut as he gathered his thoughts. Then: "Beyond our interests here on the Strip, the major functions of this organization remain those two I first mentioned: post office and bank. Part of what has allowed us to stay under the radar of both state and federal guv'ment is the fairly, uh…scattered nature of our clientele."

"I guess I follow that. You are not one central organization begging to be taken down."

He beamed. "That's well put, son. But in the past six months to a year, Jack Killian has been expandin'. He has been buyin' out clubs left and right—we now own every bar and club on this Strip, and that's dozens of 'em. He has moved into rural areas where similar strips of sin, shall we say, have been run by this one and that one. The strip in McNairy County on the Tennessee–Mississippi border is a prime example—a dozen clubs run by maybe six, seven individuals. Jack Killian has bought out all but a handful."

"And this attracts the wrong kind of attention."

"It does." He frowned. "But it goes beyond that. When somebody doesn't wanna sell, Jackie beats the shit out of 'em. He's had more than a few killed. This reflects badly on me."

"Can't have that."

"Which is why I am cooperatin' with you and my old buddy, the Broker. I reluctantly agree that Jack Killian has got to go. And I am in a position to put you next to him."

I took a last swig of Barq's. "What makes you so sure that it's Killian who sent that pair of shooters after the Broker?"

"Two things, really," he said, sitting forward, elbows on his desk. He ticked off a finger. "First, Jack told me a month ago that he was plannin' to cut off ties with outsiders."

"Like the Broker," I said.

A crisp nod.

"And second," he said, ticking off another finger, "one of Jackie's bodyguards drives a two-tone green Fleetwood. Which wouldn't be so tellin' if I didn't also know that Jackie's *short* a man on his staff right now. Asked if I knew of a top-notch replacement. Turns out I do."

FOUR

"You know, Quarry," Mr. Woody said with a chuckle and a gesture of a gold-ring-laden hand, "they call Biloxi the poor man's Riviera—only they ain't necessarily poor when they first get here."

The man in the pink sportscoat, gray slacks and white shoes was showing me around his casino, which took up the north half of the warehouse-like MR. WOODY's building. We'd entered from the strip club through an Employees Only door and were now at the rear of the Lucky Seven, as this part of the facility was called.

That this was nothing you'd confuse with the Riviera—whether you meant the French vacation spot or the Nevada hotel—seemed an understatement.

Starting with tacky gold-and-black brocade wallpaper and a wood-pattern linoleum tile floor, the surroundings were less than lavish. The casino, about the same square footage as the strip-club side, was doing a similarly modest off-season business; the main difference was an older crowd with some women mixed in, mostly blue-hair gals seated along the walls at old-fashioned slot machines, metal jobs that looked like Vegas cast-offs.

On either side of the room, seated in elevated chairs, middle-aged hardcases in white shirts with string ties and black trousers were watching everything, like shoeshine-stand customers wondering where the shine boy went.

A roulette wheel, where retirees stood staring into their limited futures, took center stage, with a craps table at one end and several blackjack tables spotted around. The sound level was subdued, with only the calls of the dealers, croupiers and stickmen discernible above the murmur of patrons.

Here at the rear of the room, under conical lamps, were four poker tables, only one of which had a game going. At left were cages for buying and cashing in chips, at right a fully stocked bar similar to the strip club's, though with a single bartender on duty, male, also in white shirt and string tie. A trio of waitresses in the same white shirt/black mini costumes as on the MR. WOODY'S side were threading through with complimentary drinks. A pair of floor men in suit and tie were on the prowl, while a few girls in skimpy halter tops and hot pants tight enough for a gynecological exam seemed to be shilling for the house, sidling up to unaccompanied men to help them make bad decisions.

Mr. Woody guided me to the far end of the bar. We were barely settled into our high-back stools when the bartender delivered a Scotch straight up to the boss.

I asked for a Coke. Not requesting Barq's root beer may have been a faux pas, but we would all just have to live with it.

Mr. Woody gave the bartender a glance that said give us plenty of space, and he did. No other stools were taken.

"Don't get the wrong idea, Quarry," Mr. Woody said, grinning as he glanced around at the underpopulated casino. "A month and a half from now, the ole Seven'll be packin' 'em in like the Kentucky Derby, minus the goddamn hats. And we got plenty more joints, all up and down the Strip, that'll be doin' likewise."

"*You* have plenty more joints," I asked, "or *Jack Killian* has plenty more?"

Barely audible above piped-in Sinatra, my host said, "Killian and me, we own 'em together. Monopolizin' the Strip ain't the problem, Quarry. Our group's held sway over this stretch of Highway 90 since 'fore you were born."

"Then what *is* the problem?"

Eyes narrowed behind the big lenses, and all those teeth got swallowed up in a close-mouthed scowl.

"It's that Jackie's gettin' out of hand," he said, upper lip twitching to let out the bitter words. "Reachin' too far. Tryin' to take over the whole damn South, one county at a time. Spreadin' like a goddamn cancer. You know, there's powerful people startin' to take notice, and not in a good way. Carlos Marcello and Santo Trafficante, for two."

Neither name meant shit to me, but I got his drift.

My Coke arrived in a tall glass with a lemon slice. I had a sip. The bartender had already evaporated.

"There was another man in that green Caddy," I said. "The driver? Possible he got a glimpse of me. I doubt it, but that's the biggest risk I face, being here."

"You don't face no risk," he said, shaking his head.

"You sound sure of yourself, Woody."

I couldn't quite bring myself to use the "Mister."

Very quietly he said, "That boy whose eyes you dotted last week, Quarry? Turned up dead in a ditch outside town. Jack has been tellin' all and sundry that one of his enemies done it, and that he was gonna find the guilty party, rip off his head, and fuck his skull in the eye holes."

The contents of my eye holes widened. "And *this* is why I don't face any risk?"

He patted the air reassuringly. "I'm told the late shooter enlisted a cousin of his from the moonshine bidness—as wheelman? And also that that self-same cousin shat hisself…whether this is a figurative expression, Quarry, or a literal one I cannot say… due to the violent nature by which his late relative passed."

"Do tell."

He showed me all those teeth again, and the magnified eyes

twinkled. "Seems the moonshiner cuz has gone into hidin', up in the hills near Hattiesburg, and is not currently on the local scene. So you are quite secure in your anonymity."

This struck me as thin: the spooked cousin wouldn't stay holed up forever. And any moonshiner I ever saw had a shotgun. Granted, that was in the movies and on TV....

I said, "Do I have to remind you that you're recommending as replacement the very guy who created the vacancy on Killian's staff? If 'Jackie' figures out who I am, where does that leave good ole Mr. Woody? Seems to me that shitting ourselves would be the least of it."

He waved that off. "I am well aware, Quarry, well aware. You must trust my judgment on this. We are within the margin of acceptable risk."

I shrugged. Let some air out. "Okay. I guess."

Mr. Woody sipped some Scotch and said, "Why, Quarry, you seem rather tense to me."

"No. Just by nature cautious. And this is...never mind."

"What, son?"

I let more air out. "This isn't a part of the country I've spent any time in. I feel like that fish out of water everybody talks about."

He frowned and the big glasses climbed his face a little. "Well, that's certainly not a good feelin'. Fishies out of water, they go belly up and can't breathe no more. And I *need* you *breathin'*, Quarry. I do indeed. Need you cool and calm and collected."

I batted all that away. "I'm fine. Just a little jetlagged. Thanks for your concern. When do I meet Killian?"

"Tonight." He glanced at his watch, a Rolex, or a damn good facsimile. "Nine o'clock sharp at his office at the Tropical Motel. Which is where you are stayin', by the way." He leaned across the bar a little. "Fred! Phone!"

Fred the bartender nodded and found a phone under the

counter and set it on the bar, half a dozen stools down from us. Mr. Woody went to use it while I watched the gambling action, such as it was. One of the halter-top hot-pants girls was leaving arm-in-arm with a man old enough to be her father, but presumably wasn't. He didn't seem to have any chips to cash in. After a losing afternoon, she was the consolation prize, though it would cost him even more at the adjacent motel.

Mr. Woody returned to his stool and was smiling, pleased with himself. "You are about to learn the meanin' of Southern hospitality, Quarry."

"That right?"

"I am determined to make you feel at home, son."

"Really, I'm fine."

He put his hand on my forearm. His touch was warm. "You are really gonna enjoy this. I'm gonna provide you with some company for the duration. A little tour guide to keep you feelin' like you know which way is up, and where it's at."

And maybe even what's happening.

"Woody, Mr. Woody, I don't need a tour guide. Just let me do the job I came to do."

"Well, of course. But have you ever been in Biloxi before?"

"No."

"Then trust me on this one, son. Take my word, you will thank me to your dyin' day."

Somehow it always came back around to death, didn't it?

He guided me back through the Employees Only door that connected us to the strip-club side. On stage, three strippers were doing some kind of all-nude finale, a lanky brunette with painfully fake tits, a short plump redhead with nicely real ones, and the little blonde I'd seen earlier, currently swinging around the center stage pole, her little pink pussy blowing everybody a sideways kiss. The song was "War" by Edwin Starr, and as anti-war demonstrations went, this was among the most convincing.

As a DJ in a booth stirred up some collective applause "for the vixenish Veronica, the gorgeous Ginger and the luscious Lolita," the girls collected their wadded-up dollars and gathered the wisps that were their discarded costumes. Then they exited down side steps, but not before they had taken time to swathe themselves in sheer negligee-style robes to preserve their modesty.

We took a little table well away from the stage, close to the unused secondary stage, in fact. Mr. Woody had brought his Scotch along.

Nodding toward my t-shirt and jeans ensemble, he said, "Before you meet with Jack Killian, do spruce yourself up some. Did you bring any suits along?"

"Yeah. Couple."

"What color?"

"Well, I guess one's tan and another is blue, navy blue."

"No black?"

"No. Should I have?"

"Wear the navy number. D'you bring some ties along?"

"Yeah."

"Patterned or solid color?"

"Well, one's kind of floral, the other's, what-you-call-it, paisley."

He thought that over, shrugged. "Well, that's okay. It'll make Jackie feel important."

"What will?"

"Sendin' you out to buy the right clothes. Makes him feel like a big shot.... Well, will you look at *this* little vision of loveliness!"

The little blonde stripper was walking over toward us. She had on a hot-pink halter top and matching hot pants, similar to the girls shilling in the Lucky Seven. Had a smile going but her eyes were cold.

"You wanted me, Mr. Woody?" She had a breathy little-girl

voice that didn't appear to be a put-on. Goldie Hawn without the irony.

"Yes, Lo. Sit, honey, sit yourself."

She sat herself. Glancing at me, she nodded but otherwise I didn't register with her any more than the dust motes floating in the stripper-stage lighting.

"This is my friend Mr. Quarry," he said to her. "John Quarry. He's in town to work for Mr. Killian for a while."

Her smile was sweet as she nodded to me. "Pleased," she said.

"Lo honey, Mr. Quarry needs some special attention. He's new to our fair city, doesn't know his way around at all, far from home. That can make a fella kinda lonely."

She nodded. "Okay. But I have three more sets."

"No, Lo, I've taken care of that. You're off the stage for a while."

"How long?"

"A while. Few days at least. You'll make double for this, even accountin' for tips."

She shrugged and nodded, her chin crinkling in *doesn't-sound-so-bad* acceptance.

Cute as she was, I was not liking the direction this was going.

"Uh, Mr. Woody," I said, "I appreciate the sentiment, but I can take care of myself."

He gave me a smile that had some smartass in it. "Do you know where the Tropical Motel is?"

"It's not that place next door is it?"

"Oh, my, *hell* no!" That gave him a good laugh. "Lo will show you."

Judging by what the DJ had said, "Lo" would seem to be short for Lolita. They had genuine (pronounced *gen-you-wine*) literary sensibilities down South, it would appear. Must have been the Faulkner influence.

"Now, honey," Mr. Woody said, putting a hand on a nearby knee of hers, "I will make the usual arrangements. Just be a good girl and be useful and never in the way."

She nodded, like a high school girl dutifully assuring daddy she'd be in before midnight.

"Quarry," he said, "they will be expectin' you at the front desk. All expenses taken care of, no credit card required, and they have a decent little restaurant there, too. Just sign every-thin' to your room. Enjoy yourself, son....Don't be late for Mr. Killian, now. Nine sharp!"

There was no getting around it. Little Lolita would be my Biloxi tour guide, for now anyway, and that was all there was to it. Somehow I'd handle this, but not with Mr. Woody around.

I shook hands with my host and he made his brisk way back toward his office, in a blur of eyes, teeth, gold rings, and hideous apparel.

I got up and so did she. I looked at her. She looked at me. I smiled. She smiled. I stopped smiling. She stopped smiling. I sighed (this, at least, she didn't echo) and took her gently by the arm and led her out into the parking lot, just as another stripper was coming on stage to "American Woman."

Outside I asked her, "Do you have a car here?"

A little pink purse was fig-leafed before her. She shook her head and the golden hair flicked bare shoulders, catching dying sunlight. "I don't have a car. I never learned to drive. Girlfriends I live with get me places. They work here, too."

I had the sense that I'd just heard about one-third of her life story.

"Okay, then," I said. "I'll drive and you navigate."

"What, you got a boat?"

"No. I mean, you'll point the way. To the Tropical?"

Her tone turned defensive: "I know."

We got into the Chevelle. The rock station came on and she seemed to like it, bobbing her head to "Bang a Gong." She told me to turn right out of the lot and we'd gone only half a block when I said, "You really don't need to do this."

She stopped bobbing and glanced at me with the slightest frown. "Do what?"

If her eyes had been any lighter blue, they would have been transparent.

"Show me around," I said. "I can take of myself. I'm a big boy."

"Are you really?"

"You bet. Took my training wheels off a long time ago."

"That's a silly thing to say."

"Is it?"

"Grown men don't need no training wheels. On their bikes. I bet you don't even have a bike. Less maybe a Harley."

I glanced at her to see if she was fucking with me. She didn't appear to be. She reminded me of that actress in *The Time Machine*—both her looks and her intellect.

I said, "It was just an expression."

We were at a light, a trashy row of bars and strip joints to our right, white beach and the blue expanse of the Gulf of Mexico to our left. The entire span of human existence seemed to take place between those two points.

"Keep goin'," she said, nodding at the intersection.

I did so.

After another block, I asked, "How old are you, Lo?"

"Twenty-one."

"No you aren't."

The blue eyes flashed at me. "Callin' me a liar?"

"I'm calling you…seventeen years old."

"Nineteen."

"If you're nineteen, why lie about it?"

"I don't lie. I fib sometimes."

"Why fib about it?"

"Got to be twenty-one to get a card in Biloxi."

"What kind of card?"

"Card that lets you work where they sell liquor."

"Oh."

"See it?"

"What?"

"The Tropical sign. See it?"

I saw it.

"Pull in there."

I did.

The motel wasn't something you'd encounter on the Riviera, either, nor was it much of a match for the Vegas version. But it was nicer than I'd figured, a pale pink brick eight-story with a vertical sign with a green neon palm tree at right and at left, in pink:

T

R

O

P

I

C

A

L

M

O

T

E

L

After I signed in at the desk in a pastel lobby with potted mini-palms and overstuffed wicker furniture, a guy about my age in a light-blue blazer and yellow tie gave me a smirky smile as he handed me two keys. He was blond, slender and weak-chinned, but the light-blue eyes probably got him laid.

He said, "You're on ground level with parking and entry from the outside. Drive around back of the building."

"I don't need two keys," I said.

"Two rooms, two keys," he said, smirking again.

I was just thinking about pasting him one when the girl tugged on my elbow and gave me a mildly impatient look, nodding toward the outside.

We went out and drove around to 117 and 118, parking in the space of the former.

As I got my suitcase from the Chevelle trunk, I said, "One of these rooms is yours, right?"

She gave me a pixie smile, the first real smile I'd seen from her. "Quicker than you look."

"And I suppose Mr. Woody is sending your things over."

"Uh-huh. I'm next door, kinda…on call. Only in your room when you want me in your room. Only around when you want me around. When you need me for somethin'."

I gestured to the world around us. "Like showing me around Biloxi. Maybe taking me to see where Jefferson Davis lived."

"I been there. It's nothin'. Don't bother."

I stared at her. She stared at me. We lived on the same planet. That was about the extent of what we had in common.

"You're in 117," she said.

"How do you know I'm not in 118?"

" 'Cause I been in these rooms before, and 117 is nicer. Bigger. Got a hot tub."

"Oh. Okay."

I carried my bag over to the door marked 117 and used the key. She was right behind me. Well, not right behind. Not crowding me or anything.

I held the door open for her and she went in. You couldn't find a speck of cellulite on the back of those legs if you used a high-power microscope. I closed the door behind us. She was already sitting on the double bed, on the foot, staring at the big 24-inch portable TV on the dresser opposite. Nothing was on, but she seemed to be contemplating watching something, sometime. She was rocking a little.

The room included a mirrored area with the hot tub. There was a full bathroom as well. A few touches said "tropical," like a framed Hawaiian landscape screwed onto the wall over the bed, and the pastel pink-and-green wallpaper, and the green padded bedspread with pink pillows. Otherwise this could be a room at a Holiday Inn.

I sat next to her on the edge of the bed. "What's your name?"

She was still looking at the blank TV screen. "You know what it is. Lolita."

"I'm not calling you Lolita."

"Nobody does. Everybody says Lo."

"But that's still not your name. What's your name?"

She looked at me as if for the first time, frowning just a little, noticing I was a human being. "You mean my real name?"

"No, the one you use on the Mickey Mouse Club."

"The what club?"

"Yes, your *real* name."

"Luann."

"Luann what?"

"Luann Lloyd."

"Okay, Luann Lloyd. I don't want to cause you any trouble. You just go next door and mind your business. Have yourself a little paid vacation. Maybe we'll go out and have a bite to eat now and then."

She was frowning at me like a slow student at a calculus problem on a blackboard. "I don't get you. Somethin' wrong with me?"

I thought for a moment. I put a hand on her shoulder, like a brother might. "I'm here on business. I understand, I think, that Mr. Woody wants you to…entertain me. Keep me company. But I don't…I don't mean to insult you. But I don't, uh…"

The little-girl voice mingled boredom with patience: "You don't never pay for it. You don't never go out with hookers. No sweat. This ain't costin' you anythin'."

She undid the halter top and let loose the breasts. I'd seen breasts before. I'd seen these breasts before, on stage back at the strip club. But they were right here and right now and they were perfect. Plump little handfuls, B cups crowding C, perfectly shaped and with slightly puffy aureoles and pert eraser-tip tips.

I didn't remember ever being erect and throbbing so fast. This vapid little hooker should have turned me off. She was obviously an ignorant dope. She had likely fucked hundreds of men in her young life and the inside of her was probably diseased like a decayed piece of fruit. The thought of her should sicken me, and maybe the thought did.

But the sight didn't.

She smiled and cocked her head, the light-blue eyes hooded. "Why, honey, don't tell me. You got to be in love a little before you can do it, that it? You just an old-fashion boy?"

"I don't have to be in love forever," I said. "But it helps to be in love at the moment."

She laughed a little. First time I heard her do that. "You should tell your pecker, pal."

She gave the tent pole in my pants a little spring action with a finger. This is where the *b-o-i-n-g* sound effect goes.

She bounced off the bed and grabbed a pink pillow and tossed it at my feet and knelt on it. Small deft hands wearing pink fingernail polish undid my pants and tugged them around my ankles.

"Stop," I said. Or maybe I just thought it.

She had me in her mouth and she was goddamn good at it, lots of saliva, sliding, gliding up and down the shaft, using mostly her mouth, but occasionally her hand when she was catching a breath. She suckled, she licked, she fucked with her mouth, rarely looking up at me. When she did, her expression wasn't bored exactly, more that of a skilled craftsmen using a lathe.

When I got very close, I put my hand on her shoulder, not like a brother (well, maybe like a brother—this *was* Mississippi) and then she paused, knowing I was seconds away, and said, "You want me to swallow, honey? I don't mind. Some guys like to see it all over my pretty little face. What's your pleasure?"

"Dealer's choice," I managed.

Just that much of a gentleman.

FIVE

Around seven, already in the navy leisure suit and lighter blue shirt for the Killian meeting, I took Luann to the Tropical's restaurant on the lobby floor. The Dockside, which despite its name served plenty of fare other than fish, had a pink-and-blue color scheme broken up by mounted shells and starfish and swordfish riding the walls, or maybe swimming them, plus a few framed photos of local shrimping boats. A dark-wood nautical-theme bar was at left with dining everywhere else, tables with white linen and plenty of wall- and window-hugging booths.

We took one of the latter, where the view was less dockside than highway-side, street lamps and headlights of the four-lane blacktop disrupting the dusk enough to make the Gulf's blue waters a barely discernible blur. We had the place almost to ourselves, the other off-season diners including an older couple and a foursome of businessmen.

My companion had changed into a shades-of-orange-and-yellow tie-dye sleeveless mini with a plunging neckline and a matching fabric belt, knotted at her little waist. With slightly more clothes on, how pretty she was somehow became more obvious. She looked young as hell, but then she *was* young as hell, and might have been taken for a college girl, unless you had a conversation with her.

She'd freshened her make-up, too, a little heavy-handed job of it—she was, after all, a stripper who hooked on the side—but her features nonetheless showed a surprising delicacy. Her red-lipsticked mouth was plump in the middle and thin on the sides, and the big blue eyes were accentuated by matching eye shadow.

The girl was gazing blankly out the window at the blur of highway and white beach and blue water beyond. She hadn't cracked open the menu. I guess she'd been here often enough to memorize it. After much study, I ordered fried green tomatoes with crab cakes—when in Rome.

I asked her what she was going to have.

"Salad."

"Just salad, Luann?"

"Little dressin'."

"Listen, I'm on expense account. Have whatever you like."

"I'm suppose to have salad."

"Why? Your boss trying to save money?"

"No. I got to stay under one-hundred-ten or I'm in trouble."

I frowned at her. "How much do you weigh now?"

"One-oh-one."

"Oh Jesus. Eat what you want. Go nuts."

"Shouldn't."

"I won't tell."

"Won't say nothin' to Mr. Woody?"

"Hell no. Screw Mr. Woody."

She made a face. "Not unless I have to." Then she studied me, taking a good look. "*Really* I can have what I want?"

"Go for it."

There was lobster on that menu and all kinds of pricey seafood and cuts of steak, but she had a cheeseburger and fries and gobbled them down like there was no tomorrow. It was amusing. Even cute. Also a little sad.

Wasn't it bad enough she had to fuck strangers? Couldn't she have the kind of meal she wanted once in a while? Did she have to take a guy's drawers down to get any fucking meat in her diet?

I was taking my time with the fried green tomatoes and crab

cakes. The latter I dug, the former I wasn't sure about. "Where do you live, Luann?"

She frowned just a tad. "I don't give out my address. No offense."

"I don't want your address. Just generally where. And who with."

"Why do you want to know?"

"I'm interested."

"Why?"

"Honey, I'm just making conversation. If we're going to spend time together, let's get to know each other a little bit."

She was chewing and thinking and that contorted her face. It kind of made her even prettier—less like a manikin and more like a female.

Still chewing, she said, "Apartment with some girls from work. Buildin' around the corner from the club. Comes with the job."

"That wasn't so hard, was it?" I sipped some iced tea—sickeningly sweet. I'd forgotten to ask for no sugar. You had to do that down South.

She shook her head, swallowed. "You don't have to be so nice."

She'd almost quoted the Lovin' Spoonful.

"Why," I said, "you like it some other way?"

"No. Nice is...nice. We can be friendly. Not good to get attached, though. I'm nobody you need to know. Just company when you're in the mood. That's how Mr. Woody wants it."

"Yeah, yeah. Do you like working for Mr. Woody?"

"It's okay." Her upper lip curled at one side, glistening wetly with the red lipstick, the world's smallest sneer. "I never worked for nobody else."

"What about Jack Killian?"

She paired up a couple of French fries, collected some ketchup off her plate. "What about him?"

"What kind of guy is he?"

She shook her head. "Don't ask."

"Then, not a nice man?"

She choked on her French fries for a few seconds, then got them down, and said, "No. Not a nice man."

"Anything I should know about him?"

She thought about that as she dragged two more French fries through a glob of Heinz as red as her lipstick. "Don't get on his bad side."

"And how do I avoid doing that?"

"Agree with him."

"Okay. I'll keep that in mind." I dipped a forkful of crab cake into remoulade.

"He talks a lot," she said with a shrug. "Just listen."

She was a cute kid for somebody whose life was shit.

"Luann, I might want your company later tonight. I have a meeting with Mr. Killian at nine and don't know exactly when I'll be back. Should I knock on your door, or…?"

"Could I wait in your room?" The light-blue eyes suddenly had life in them.

"Well, sure. I don't see why not."

"You have that really nice big TV. My room's TV is smaller than the piece of shit at the apartment. *Hawaii Five-O* is on tonight."

Of course. What else would you watch at the Tropical?

"Fine by me," I said.

So after some key lime pie, I walked her back to the room and when I left, she was on her tummy with her head toward the foot of the bed where I'd sat when she blew me. The famous Ventures theme song was coming on and she was smiling like Christmas. The mini was up over her bottom and her bikini pants were that same tie-dye. If her ass had looked any sweeter I'd have bust out crying.

I'd been told to report to the eighth floor but hadn't been given a room number. I stopped at the desk and asked the blue-blazer blond guy what number Mr. Killian's room was, and he said, "Just go up, Mr. Quarry." No smirks this time around. Apparently Mr. Killian was somebody you didn't smirk about even when he wasn't around.

When the elevator doors dinged open onto the eighth floor, I knew at once why a room number hadn't been required: Killian had this whole goddamn level.

I faced a wood-paneled vestibule where two big guys in black suits with white shirts and black ties were seated on either side of a dark-wood door that bore no numerals. They looked like greeters at a mortuary. Each had a small table next to him where they tossed magazines they'd been reading—*Penthouse* for the guy at left, *Sports Illustrated* for the guy at right.

By the time I stepped off, they were on their feet.

Those tables of theirs also had ashtrays with packs of cigarettes and lighters as well as a few more magazines and Styrofoam cups. Down at one end of the vestibule was a table with a coffee-maker and a few snacks. Cigarette smoke smell hung heavy. These fellas were on duty here for good long stretches.

"Quarry," I said, looking from one to the other. "I'm expected."

The one at left was maybe six-two with a dishwater butch and nearly invisible eyebrows. The one at right was a little shorter but broader in the shoulders with similarly short-cropped hair, jet black with matching unibrow.

Though bruisers, they were not the brawny bouncer types seen at Mr. Woody's; I made them ex-military, and not just because of their burr haircuts. The dark suits were high-end off-the-rack—had they been tailored, the bulges under their left arms wouldn't show, which they did even with their suit-coats unbuttoned. For easy access.

"You know the drill," the unibrow said.

I nodded, raised my hands, and the dishwater guy patted me down. I hadn't come armed. He finished his frisk and nodded to his buddy, who went to the door, knocked, and another short-haired ex-military type in a dark suit cracked it open. He had a wide face with close-set eyes.

"Mr. Killian's nine o'clock," the unibrow said, with a head bob toward me.

The close-set eyes narrowed at me; then the guy nodded to the unibrow and opened up.

The vestibule watchdogs both gestured toward the threshold, an Alphonse and Gaston move that would have been comical if I hadn't known they could kill my ass.

The door shut behind me, and I was led down a doorless hallway into a big high-ceilinged area that combined living room space with, at right, an up-to-date walk-in kitchen. Only a few lights were on, most of the illumination coming from a projection TV.

Nothing here indicated that this floor had once been a bunch of hotel rooms that got overhauled into living quarters for the current king of Biloxi, Mississippi.

The furnishings were contemporary, the colors not at all the standard Tropical pastel, more dark reds and dark blues and lots of masculine wood. Very bachelor pad, right down to the wide, vertical real-wood paneling, with framed abstractions in red and black and green and yellow. A big round captain's table with matching chairs near the kitchen was the only nod to the beachfront that the living room's wall of windows looked out upon.

Two more men in black suits were watching the big TV, one on a sofa, another in an easy chair—between them a leather Barcalounger had the best view of the screen but sat empty, apparently off-limits for anybody but the absent boss. The volume was down, but Jack Lord was barking at somebody. Not "Book 'em, Dano!"—too early in the show.

My black-suited guide with the eyes crowding his nose walked me down a hall off the living room to a closed door and raised a hand like a crossing guard to hold me back. Yeah, like I was surging forward.

"Your nine o'clock's here, Mr. Killian!"

"Send him in." The voice was deep and naturally loud enough not to require shouting through the closed door.

The door was opened for me, I went in, and the door closed behind me.

I was in an office.

Like Mr. Woody's, only about five times the size, if vaguely similar. Framed pictures of famous strippers, color eight-by-tens, were interspersed with photos of pro ball players and dinner-theater show biz types, all personally inscribed. A brown leather couch rode the wall at right and a liquor cart no bigger than a Dodge Dart was parked opposite.

Behind a big mahogany desk, and between dark-wood filing cabinets, the wall space was consumed by a vertical color photo of the Biloxi Strip at night, likely taken from a boat in the Gulf far enough out to turn that ribbon of sin into a sparkling abstraction.

Behind that desk sat the man who had to be Jack Killian. No military crew cut for him: glistening black hair was combed back revealing the widow's peak over the narrow oval of a face whose dark, lidded eyes had an almost Asian cast. He had a narrow, finely carved nose over a thin-lipped slash, as if he'd been born without a mouth and a doctor had to cut him one.

That suit was definitely not-off-the-rack: Italian, I'd guess, though I'm no expert. He wore gold-nugget cufflinks and a gold-nugget ring on his left hand.

Did he wear that suit every evening? I wondered. *Or just when he had a business meeting?*

Rising from his high-backed leather swivel chair, he didn't offer a hand to shake—tough to reach across that aircraft carrier of a desk—merely gestured to two brown-leather visitors' chairs. I picked one and gave him a tight smile and a nod.

"Mr. Quarry," he said. He had a smooth baritone, like a radio announcer or maybe the golf pro at the country club who was fucking your wife.

"Mr. Killian."

"Would you like a cigarette? Or maybe you prefer your own?" He indicated the smoke he had going in an ameba-shaped modern-art ashtray. Little else was on the glass-topped desk, just a multi-extension phone and a pencil/pen cup.

"I don't smoke, sir."

"Good to hear. Are you a drinking man?"

"Not really, sir."

" 'Sir' isn't necessary. 'Mr. Killian' will do fine."

"All right, Mr. Killian." I shifted in the chair. "May I ask a question?"

"Sure."

"Is this a job interview? I was under the impression I already had this position."

A black eyebrow arched. "Do you know what that position is, Mr. Quarry?"

"Other than I'll be working for you in some capacity, no."

The slash in his face turned upward on one side. "Then you don't already have the job, do you?"

I risked a small smile. "I guess I don't."

He had a drag on his cigarette. From the smell of the room, he didn't stint on them. "Woodrow sometimes oversteps. But he's a good man, our Mr. Woody, and I take his recommendation seriously. How much did he tell you?"

"Just that there'd been a fatality on your staff, and a slot needed filling."

He nodded twice. "What's your background, Mr. Quarry? Let's start with military."

"Marines. Vietnam. Three tours."

"What did you do there?"

"Sniper mostly. I was in some fire fights."

"Medals?"

"Yes."

That I'd not been specific sent the slash upward on the other side of his face; counting the last time, that made one whole smile. "And post-Vietnam, where did you work?"

"Detroit."

"Who did you work for and what did you do there?"

I shook my head. "With all due respect, sir...Mr. Killian... that's all I'm going to say on that subject."

His eyebrows tensed. "You think that's wise?"

"Very. Someday I may not be working for you. And when somebody asks me who I worked for last, and what did I do for him? I'm not going to say. Because I don't think your business is anybody else's."

The eyes were open almost all the way—he clearly liked that response. He took a few puffs from the cigarette, sent it back to the odd ashtray.

"How many people have you killed, Mr. Quarry?"

"Here or overseas?"

"Anywhere."

"Under a hundred."

He damn near blinked. "I would guess a sniper gets pretty cold-blooded about it."

"Killing from a distance can get easy. I've done up close and personal, too. It's messier. Mr. Killian, where is this going?"

He rocked a little in his swivel chair. He was looking past

me, then he gestured in that direction. "You've noticed I'm well-insulated."

"I picked up on that."

"Can you make an educated guess why?"

"You're a powerful man, and reading between the lines, I'd say you're getting more powerful all the time. That makes enemies."

"It does. It does."

He got up so suddenly, it startled me and I damn near showed it.

"Come with me," he said. "Let's take a little walk."

He moved swiftly past me and out the office door and I followed him, staying back some. He issued curt orders for the *Hawaii Five-O* watchers to spell the two watchdogs in the vestibule, who as he left his quarters he instructed to come with us.

That put all four of us in the elevator—me, Killian, the unibrow and the dishwater guy. Nobody said a word. There seemed to me a small chance that I might be in trouble. That the "walk" we were about to take might be the Biloxi equivalent of a Chicago ride.

I'd known I'd have to stand for a frisk, and so had left behind my nine millimeter and the knife I sometimes strapped to my leg, too. I was okay in hand-to-hand, but not exactly Bruce Lee.

And all three of these fuckers were armed. Anyway, the watchdogs were, and I assumed that tailored suit of Killian's allowed room for a weapon, on a hip or under a shoulder.

We walked briskly through the lobby. The blazer blond at the desk said, "Good evening, Mr. Killian!" This did not rate even a nod, much less a response.

Before I knew it we were outside in the parking lot. The night was breezy and cool, cooler than I'd imagined Biloxi might be—maybe forty degrees. Enough to give me goose pimples. Right. The weather was doing that. Sure.

Without a word, Killian—tall, broad-shouldered but slender in the sharp black suit—knifed through the night and across the four lanes of highway. Traffic was light, but somehow I had the impression he'd do the same if it were fucking streaming. I was between him and the two watchdogs, who were trailing, giving me more space than I expected.

Once we were across the street, Killian deposited the watchdogs on the sidewalk and took me by the arm and walked me onto the white beach. He planted himself, crossed his arms, and stared straight ahead. I did the same. A small-craft harbor was off to our left, and the vastness of the Gulf lay straight ahead. Salty air twitched at my nostrils.

How many bodies has this bastard dumped out there? I wondered.

"The man I lost," Killian said, lighting up a fresh cigarette with a gold JJK-initialed lighter, "wasn't just anybody."

"Yeah?"

The sound of water lapping joined with that of a boat engine somewhere out there to creep me the fuck out.

"He did special jobs for me," Killian said, exhaling smoke that the breeze carried away. "He took care of people. I don't know if Woodrow made that clear to you."

"Take care of people how?" Facetiously I added, "Like pick them up at the airport for you?"

Like shoot at the Broker and me in the Concort Inn parking lot?

He gave me a sideways grin. The teeth were wolfish and not as white as Mr. Woody's, but they didn't live in a glass at night. His black hair glistened in street- and moonlight.

"I'm going to guess you're educated, Mr. Quarry."

"Not really. Just high school." I shrugged. "I read some."

"Ah. Self-educated." Dragon smoke drifted out his nostrils. "I dropped out of college my freshman year. I could have aced that shit but I preferred booze, drugs and girls."

"Who doesn't?"

"Went into the service. I didn't go overseas, but…" He gave me a quick look, then returned his gaze to the Gulf. "…I've seen combat of a sort."

I said nothing.

He glanced behind him. "This Strip of mine has real potential, Mr. Quarry. We can rival Vegas. We can deserve that Riviera comparison some people make. The day will come when gambling is legal here, and until that time I will do business with those who are in a position to protect my present interests while paving the way for me to be a major part of that future. Politicians in Biloxi like their bread buttered on both sides, and my knife works both ways."

There wasn't a hint of Southern accent out of this guy. But then he was from Oklahoma. That was Midwest, sort of.

"Still, creating a cohesive whole out of this Strip is a challenge, and a difficult one. Expanding my reach beyond this backward state to our neighboring ones is an ongoing struggle. But I'm doing it. And I am up to it."

I said nothing.

He let out smoke in a disgusted sigh. "This Dixie Mafia you hear about is, or at least *has* been, just an inedible jambalaya of small-time crooks, scrambling for dollars, eking out individual petty existences, fighting among themselves. There needs to be organization and central leadership for what we have started here in Biloxi to flourish beyond state lines. To enjoy real success. *Enduring* success."

Killing this prick was going to be tricky. He was smooth and he was smart, and he had bodyguards hanging off the cypress trees like moss with guns.

If I'd had my nine millimeter on me, I could have taken him out here and now, and removed the unibrow and the dishwater dude as a lagniappe, as we say down South. But like I said, I wasn't armed, and now that I'd seen Killian in his castle, with all those guns between me and him, I knew a frontal assault wasn't going to make it. I had to get close to him and stay close to him and find my window.

"I need somebody like the man I lost," he said, and his eyes moved from the Gulf to me and back again. "I need somebody who would like to make some *real* money."

"I like real money."

He nodded back to the bodyguards on the sidewalk. They were well out of earshot. "You can be one of my army, Mr. Quarry, and pull down a grand a week. It'll be mostly tax free. You'll be on the books working in some negligible capacity for one of the many clubs I own, and pay taxes on ten thousand a year. We both benefit that way."

"Cool."

"Not as cool as two grand a week and a five-grand bonus any time I have something special for you to do." Now he looked right at me and gave me a smile turned up at both corners, even offering up a few wolf-like teeth. "Mr. Quarry, you are not from these parts."

"You noticed that."

"Understand that you are in a swamp. There are snakes and there are gators and there are inbred assholes who will fuck you and kill you and fuck you again. Can you handle yourself in such a place, among such creatures?"

"Give it a try."

He pitched the cig a good distance, though not quite to the

water or even its edge. "I have a job for you. It's the kind of job that requires someone new. Someone that the people I need to deal with have never seen before. A fresh face."

That was me all over. Everybody said so.

He settled a hand on my shoulder. "You pull this off, Mr. Quarry, and you will earn my thanks and a place at my side."

That would be a good position to pop him from.

"Sounds great," I said. "Details?"

He gave them to me, but not before asking me my size so he could arrange for some suits and ties for me.

But where he was sending me tomorrow would not require that kind of "professional attire."

Overalls maybe?

SIX

Early the following afternoon, we flew to Memphis, Luann and I, where I rented a dark blue Mustang. By late afternoon, under a sky full of sunshine, we were following the rambling thing that was U.S. Highway 45 along the Mississippi/Tennessee state line.

It had been my idea to take Luann along, and I'd asked no one's permission. She appeared to be in my temporary charge, and from what I understood about the job Jack Killian had assigned me, she might serve several useful purposes.

After my meeting with Killian, I'd sat with Luann in the hot tub, enjoying the Jacuzzi spray but having to talk up a little to get over the noise. I was at one end and she was at the other. With her hair damp, she had a baby bird look. A baby bird with nice tits bobbing in the water.

I asked, "You ever work any of the state-line clubs?"

"No."

"Not stripping *or* hooking?"

"No. One of my girlfriends did. One of my roommates."

"What does she say about it?"

"Plenty."

"Such as?"

"Don't work there."

I nodded. Those clear blue eyes were looking at me but with no discernible interest.

I said, "I have to do a job for Mr. Killian tomorrow at the Dixie Club."

"Oh." She closed her eyes and her face said the Jacuzzi spray felt good. Then she opened them. "Be careful."

"Okay. Any particular reason why?"

"There's a woman that runs it with her husband and she kills people with a hammer."

This may sound to you like a typically off-the-wall comment coming from a little blonde bimbo, but even if that's what she was, this specimen was neither flaky nor spacey. And anyway, this gibed with what Killian had told me.

Dixie and Dix Dixon—which was, let's face it, a lot of dicks —were a couple in their mid-forties who had been running roadhouses since the early '50s in McNairy County, Tennessee, and Alcorn County, Mississippi, along the state line, an area notorious for that kind of thing.

Currently they were running the Dixie Club, a restaurant with a gambling joint and a shady motel. Their specialty was rolling customers who complained about getting rooked or who flashed a big wad of dough without having the courtesy to lose it all at the Dixie. While locals were on occasion known to get this rough treatment, tourists almost always did, and drunks from anywhere.

"That kind of old-fashioned approach is small-picture thinking," Killian had said. "Big-picture thinking keeps the customers happy and coming back for more."

Which they didn't when they were killed and dumped in a river, swamp or along a highway's edge.

"Don't," Killian said, "let Dixie get behind you. She sometimes works as a bartender, so keep track of her whereabouts. Eyes peeled. She keeps a ball-peen in her apron."

"What," I said, "and she just pulls out Maxwell's silver hammer and bang bangs you in the head? Right in front of God and any other patrons?"

"Yes."

There was food for thought.

Seemed that Killian had bought out or into almost every

roadhouse on the Mississippi/Tennessee state line. The exceptions were the Dixie Club and three more such fleece-and-fuck joints owned by other members of the Dixon clan, who had turned down every offer and overture from the Biloxi boss these past six months. No matter how generous.

Now he needed something done about Dixie and Dix. And if you think he was sending me up there to reason with them, you aren't paying attention.

Late that same night, after fucking Luann in my bed and tucking her into hers, I had left the Tropical again to cross Highway 90 and walk to a beachfront phone booth. There I got the operator to make a collect call to a long-distance number I knew well.

I said, "I don't do jobs for just anybody."

"Job" was the over-the-phone euphemism for that other euphemism, "hit."

"I know," the Broker replied in that single-malt whiskey baritone. "You only do jobs for me. But this would seem an extension of that. And it does appear you are being paid. Which is, of course, an above-and-beyond benefit for you."

I sighed into the receiver. "This sounds dicey as hell, Broker, and it's well beyond anything you and I discussed. And I have to do the Biloxi job at my first reasonable opportunity, even if I haven't been paid yet for this side trip."

"If that proves to be the case," the Broker said smoothly, "you'll be taken care of on this end."

"Try that again, not so ambiguous."

"I will pay for the state-line trip if necessary."

"Thanks."

His sigh was weary but not irritated. "I well understand that you find yourself in a strange environment, undertaking an assignment of some delicacy. That the ground may be continually shifting under your feet…"

"There's sand under my feet, Broker."

"…but this is obviously a vital job not only for my future, but yours. I wish I had more encouraging words for you."

What was this, Home on the Fucking Range?

"Goodnight, Quarry. Get some rest. It would appear that you'll need it."

And he hung up.

This morning I had taken Luann to the Edgewater Mall, where there was a lot of construction. A famous adjacent hotel was getting torn down, and Sears and some other new stores were coming in. At a department store called Gayfers, I bought the girl some non-hookerish things in the teen department and picked up some collegiate things for myself.

At the same mall, we stopped at Godchaux's, which made Gayfers look like a Salvation Army shop. Three black suits and half a dozen silk ties were waiting, courtesy of Mr. Killian. I tried on the suits, which got marked up for alterations, and would be delivered to the Tropical tomorrow. That was fine, because I wouldn't need them where we were going today.

While Luann's participation was my idea, Killian had suggested I take the plane to Memphis, rather than make the nearly six-hour drive from Biloxi to the state-line strip. The girl's airfare came out of my pocket, but I figured the Broker would reimburse.

We were barely out of the rental car lot when Luann found a rock station. She liked it loud, but not blaring—she probably got enough of that on stage at Mr. Woody's—and I had a feeling she cranked it just to where conversation would be difficult. Conversation seemed to be something in life that she just put up with. Like fucking the occasional fat guy.

The idea was that she'd look like a nice girl, a coed or a newlywed, and the clothes I'd put her in did the trick: a red cotton short-sleeve top with a U-neck, a wide red belt with a big gold-and-red buckle, and striped jeans of red, white and pale blue. Her feet were in leather open-toed sandals with cork bottoms, or they were when she didn't have them off to paint her toenails red as we drove.

I had on dark brown jeans and a rust-color short-sleeved turtleneck, untucked, just a little big for me, enough to conceal the Browning nine millimeter stuck in my waistband. Since it got cool here at night, I'd have a brown windbreaker on, too, which would also help hide the weapon. I was wearing tan sneakers, anticipating I might need to move quickly.

Highway 45 alternated through tall piney woods and fertile farm country. Often roadsides were choked with thickets over-taken by kudzu, making odd shapes, like a topiary garden of extinct beasts. The land we were winding through had some roll to it, but was mostly flat, interrupted by the occasional small house and/or big barn. Country churches (where anti-state-line sermons surely flourished) sent their steeples skyward to greet the Lord and flee the overgrowth.

When the state-line strip kicked in, it wasn't a Vegas or even Biloxi kind of thing. The roadhouses—with names like the Shamrock, the Plantation, the Nitefall—popped up only now and then, like clusters of mushrooms, the kind you shouldn't swallow. Now and then one would be across the road from another. But mostly each joint ruled its own little roost.

The Dixie Club was no exception. The parking lot was big and gravel, the building itself a long, one-story white frame building with a green pitched roof, green-and-white striped awnings, and a central neon saying

DIXIE CLUB

in red with smaller neons along the right roof saying

DINE   DANCE   DRINK

while a metal Coca-Cola sign ran horizontally along the left roof adding

STEAK   CHICKEN   BURGERS   HOME-COOKING

although I doubted whoever was cooking actually lived there. The motel was a separate building off to the right, sitting at a forty-five degree angle with a red neon sign that said

DIXIE
COURT
TV   AIR-CONDITIONING   POOL

but the pool must have been in back.

Some roadhouses we passed had small fleets of campers where the hookers took their johns, the girls escorting their clients across parking lots while other fallen flowers leaned in camper doorways, in skimpy tops and hot pants or minis, casually displaying their wares. But the Dixie was much classier than that—the motel apparently served as its brothel.

The parking lot at 7:30 on a weeknight was maybe a third full, the motel's parking spaces about the same. I wondered if you could actually check in there, or was it strictly for working girls, and maybe cheaters paying by the hour.

But I gave it a try at a registration desk overseen by a hard-looking but not unattractive brunette in her late thirties who had apparently moved into management. She wore a sleeveless dress, white with cherries all over it; maybe that was irony. On the counter were dust-covered leaflets about the sites and attractions in the area and a tumbler of an amber liquid that was probably bourbon.

She frowned at me in confusion. "*All* night?"

"Yeah." I smiled over at Luann, who was staring blankly at nothing. Then I smiled back at the brunette in the cherry-strewn dress. "We're on our honeymoon. Kind of collecting out-of-the-way motels."

Her pretty face had more wrinkles than a slept-in suit.

"You kids have fun," she said. "That'll be thirty-five. No credit cards."

"No problem," I said, still smiling, but hoped not overdoing it. I handed over the cash, signed us in as Bob and Holly Johnson, and asked, "Is the food good over next door?"

"It's all one business," the brunette said, "so of course I'll say yes. Can't go wrong with the chicken. Meat's iffy by midweek."

"Thanks."

Our room was dingy but not dismal, with pea-soup color walls, a yellow nubby spread on the double bed (which for a quarter vibrated), and chairs covered in orange fake leather (not that any real leather came in orange). A darker green semi-sheer curtain covered a window onto the parking lot. A little hallway went past the john to a door to the pool area. The pool, which nobody was using, was small but serviceable, surrounded by sad-looking deck chairs, the kind that drifted up on a beach after a shipwreck.

Swimming was my chief mode of exercise, relaxation and reflection, but I didn't figure I'd be partaking of this particular perk of the Dixie Court.

Luann, not surprisingly, was trying out the TV, a futuristic mid-'60s portable on a stand.

"Shit reception," she said, sitting on the foot of the bed. She looked cute and young in the red top and the striped jeans.

I sat next to her. "Most people don't check in here to watch the tube."

She turned her eyes toward me. Such a light blue. Such a lack of interest. "If you want sex, I'm okay with it."

How could a man resist that kind of passion?

"No, Luann, we're not here for that, either."

I hadn't filled her in much, because my plan was still sketchy in my mind. Back at the Tropical, I did tell her that things might get dangerous and she could stay home if she wanted. She'd just shrugged and said that she knew any trip to the state-line strip could be hairy.

"We'll go over to the Dixie Club," I said, holding onto her right hand like she was a child I was reassuring, "and get something to eat. Your name is Holly and I'm Bob."

"Got it."

"I'm going over there to kind of…get the lay of the place."

"You said you didn't want sex."

"I mean just kind of…what would they say on *Hawaii Five-O*? Case the joint. Take a look at everything and everybody. That woman with the hammer is probably going to be there, and I want to get a handle on her."

"You better, because she's already got a handle. On her hammer."

This girl was not stupid. She just had lived in a kind of bubble. Of course, that bubble had been sleazy skin palaces like Mr. Woody's, so she should be able to take care of herself in a rough situation.

"After a while," I said, "I'll walk you back here. And I'll go back by myself."

"To do a job for Mr. Killian."

"That's right."

"Rob the place? I saw you put that gun in your suitcase."

"No. Something else. Something you don't need to think about. Don't need to know."

The downside of Luann's presence was that I was potentially bringing along a witness, and the last thing I wanted to do was have to snuff the little twat. But the upside was considerable.

With her next to me, the whores at the Dixie wouldn't swarm me. With her, I was a credible clean-cut young tourist just begging to be taken.

Whereas a guy alone could get rolled and killed.

And killing two young tourists, say a nice honeymooning couple, could get some real out-of-state interest stirred up in the side businesses at the Dixie Club.

So bringing Luann along seemed worth the risk.

Right now she was almost smiling at me. "Really, if you want to fuck before we go over there, it's no problem."

I had zero intention of fucking her or anybody else in this room. This was the kind of bed where you could catch twelve kinds of V.D. just jerking off.

"No, honey, this is business," I said.

She smirked as if to say, *And what I said* wasn't *business?*

Soon the clean-cut couple was walking across the gravel lot, where pick-up trucks mingled with sports cars and various stops between. We entered through red double doors into a big dining room with a high open-beam ceiling adding to a barn feel. Four waitresses in red-and-white checked uniforms with lacy aprons were taking orders and picking them up at a window. Nothing about the place, with its red-plastic tablecloths, folksy wooden chairs, and cement floor, conveyed anything fancy, much less sinister. What looked to be local couples aged twenties through fifties seemed comfortable dining here—not a lot of them tonight, half a dozen maybe.

A pleasant middle-aged waitress took our orders—two fried chicken baskets and Cokes—and, when I asked, said I was welcome to have a look around. But the dance hall (down to the right) was only open weekends. When our drinks came, Luann stayed behind as I did some reconnoitering.

At the far left I went through a push door into the bar, which was like entering into a different world. Country western from a jukebox, barely audible out in the dining room, blasted in here—Charley Pride singing "Kiss an Angel Good Morning." Charley was the only black person in here. The patrons appeared to be locals ranging from retail workers to lawyers to farmers to loggers to college kids. Beer neons glowed behind a long, well-stocked teakwood bar with ten stools and two bartenders, one of them female. The tables were rough varnished wood and so were the booths.

Here the hookers were hard at work, segregated from the respectable folk partaking of the dining room's countrified fare. This was a world of single men (well, men who'd come alone anyway) and decent-looking hookers no older than early thirties in bare-midriff blouses and minis or hot pants, doing the time-honored B-girl routine of getting watered-down drinks bought for them, with that motel next door just waiting to take it to the next rung of paradise.

On the far side of the room was a double-size doorway with a red drape hung from a curtain rod. Nobody stopped me when I pushed through into a casino that made Mr. Woody's look like Caesar's Palace. The walls were covered in cheap rec-room paneling, the floor cement again. More lighted beer signs rode the walls, many plastic, a few neon.

A roulette wheel, a craps table and two blackjack tables were well-attended by a mix of men similar to the bar's, which it was slightly bigger than. One side had four sectioned-off areas for poker, two tables in play. A couple of bouncers in black t-shirts and black slacks were walking the room—they looked like country boys, thick-armed, thick-thighed, and thick-browed, ex-farmhands who got fired for diddling the livestock.

Again, the hookers were working the room, bringing luck (of a sort) to various men, some of whom spurned them but many did not. The odd thing was the variant nature of the men—a frat boy in colored t-shirt and bellbottoms rated the same kind of twenty-something babe as the country-club type with a white vinyl belt in his plaid pants. A few waitresses in black hot pants and white halter tops were threading through, handing out complimentary drinks. When a hand landed on a shapely waitress behind, it just got lifted gently off, like a piece of lint.

I was heading through the bar to rejoin Luann when I heard somebody call to me. The voice was female, mid-range and as smoky as the room itself.

"Hey, honeymooner! Bring your cute buns over here."

The female behind the bar was in her mid-forties with a red beehive that had been in style when she dropped out of high school. Her features were formerly attractive, meaning booze and hard living had exploded them into caricature, with heavy make-up adding further cartoon touches—painted-on thick black eyebrows, big green bloodshot orbs under green eye shadow, pug nose with too-large nostrils, thin-lipped wide mouth with yellow teeth and vertical smoker's wrinkles.

She wore a waitress's uniform, black, cut low enough to expose as much of a shelf of bosom as possible without entering aureole territory. She also had on a white apron.

Her name tag said DIXIE.

I went over to her, leaning in between vacant bar stools. Down two from us, at the end of the counter, a deathly pale dark-haired sunken-cheeked guy—who had been handsome once in the way Dixie had been pretty once—was reading the sports section of a newspaper, smoking a cigarette, with a can of Miller's and a glass ashtray in front of him. This was Dixie's better half—Randolph "Dix" Dixon. Killian showed me pictures.

She said, "Fanny Rae snitched on you."

"She did?" Who the hell was Fanny Rae?

Reading my mind, she answered, "Your waitress, you silly goofus! She says you and the pretty little lady in there are on your honeymoon."

"Yeah, we are." I jerked a thumb in the general direction of the Dixie Court. "This'll make our seventh motel in as many nights."

Dixie chortled and all of that red hair moved as one, like Mickey Mouse's head at Disneyland. "Lucky seven!"

"Lucky seven," I said, grinning back at her.

She leaned in and rested her boobs on the bar. She smelled like face powder and too much perfume. Probably not cheap perfume, but too much. "Listen, handsome, I got a soft spot for kids just starting out. Can I buy you two a drink?"

"Sure. Just a Shirley Temple for Holly. She doesn't imbibe."

"Well, ain't that cute. How about you, good-lookin'? Do *you* 'imbibe'?"

"I wouldn't say no to a beer. Anything you have on tap is fine."

"We got Bud and Coors."

"Coors."

"You sure, kid? Drinkin' Coors is like makin' love in a boat, you know."

"Is that right?"

"Yeah—it's fuckin' close to water!"

I laughed, like I hadn't heard that a decade ago, and then pretended to read the name tag just under the exposed flesh of one vast breast. " 'Dixie'...are you *the* Dixie?"

"One and only. That's the hubby—Dix. Dix! Meet the honeymoon kid here....What's your name, good-lookin'?"

"Bob."

Dix managed a smile that was like a wrinkle in a hound dog's neck. He gave me a lazy glance from dark rheumy wide-set eyes, then stuck out a clammy hand that I shook, and he returned to his paper.

"You go in," Dixie said warmly, "and enjoy your dinner. That's the best chicken in either McNairy or Alcorn Counties. Shoo! I'll bring them drinks in myself."

I thanked her and returned to the table, wondering if Dixie's kindness was Act One of a melodrama that was destined to end with a good-lookin' honeymoon kid getting looted and beat to shit in the parking lot.

Back in the dining room, the chicken arrived about the same time Dixie did with the Shirley Temple and the pilsner of Coors. She was all smiles and shook Luann's hand, saying, "You done right good, honey. Your man's got some nice buns on him!"

Luann whipped up a smile that seemed to satisfy Dixie, who took her leave. In her business, Luann often had to whip up such smiles.

She was looking past me as Dixie hauled herself, big boobs and all, back into the bar. "Did you see that lump?" she asked.

"You mean in her throat, when she talked about us being honeymooners?"

"No. In her apron." '

"Yeah. Must be a tumor."

"What?"

"A tumor shaped remarkably like a ball-peen hammer."

The chicken was good enough that I understood how respectable people from nearby little towns might drive out here for it, even with prostitution and gambling running wide-open next door. Luann liked the well-battered stuff, too. She seemed at her happiest eating something that wasn't salad or some guy's johnson.

Using both hands to hold up a chicken breast, Luann said, "Don't let her fool you."

"She doesn't."

"She isn't nice."

I gestured with a chicken leg. "Well, she might be nice about some things, and not nice about others. People aren't just one thing, you know."

"They are mostly one thing."

"You mean nice or not nice."

She nodded and her tiny teeth tore off a bite of breast.

I ordered Luann a dish of ice cream with chocolate sauce and left her at the table again, so I could go back in the bar and thank Dixie for her generosity.

When I got there, she was dealing with an aggrieved customer. He was a small bald man about thirty-five in a brown off-the-rack suit and he was crying.

"My wife will kill me," he said. "My boss will *fire* me."

"You're a growed man, sir," Dixie said coldly. "You shouldn't ought to gamble more than you can afford."

He lowered his voice, and I had to edge up just a little closer to hear. "There's something you need to know. If I tell you, will you help me? I think it will help *you*."

Her mouth smiled but her eyes didn't. "Tell me and we'll see."

He swallowed. Pointing toward the red curtain onto the gambling hall, he said, "That man with the mustache and the glasses who deals poker for you? He's cheating both of us! I lost five hundred dollars to him. *All* my traveling money."

"Damn shame. I can stake you a twenty if that will help."

"I'm only halfway through my route! I sell watches. *Good* ones. Hundred up. My sample case is in my trunk." A thought jumped into his mind and his eyes. "I could give you a really fine watch, if you help me out!"

"That's right generous."

He was keeping his voice low. "I don't want to embarrass you. I know you and your husband run this place."

"We do," she said.

Dix, reading the funnies now, was glancing the salesman's way. He had the expression of somebody tasting an oyster for the first time.

Very quietly, the little guy said, "That mustached dealer of yours is cheating. Dealing off the bottom. I thought I saw him do it more than once. Then I saw him *for sure*. That's how I lost the big hand, and it's not right. He must be cheating *you*, too."

Her hand dropped to her apron's pouch, fingers slipping in there.

Maxwell's silver hammer?

But instead she brought out a fat wad of cash. She peeled off twenties to the tune of what must have been five hundred and said, "We'll just take care of this, sir. Thank you for callin' it to our 'tention, in such a gentlemanly fashion."

She handed him the cash.

He wasn't crying now. He was beaming. "Thank you! Oh, Dixie…may I call you Dixie?"

"Please do. And what's your name, hon?"

"Harold. Harold Reed."

"Mr. Reed, Harold," she said with a wide yellow smile, extending a hand and her big bosom over the bar, "don't you be a stranger now. Never let it be said the Dixie Club can't take a little 'structive criticism."

Grinning, Harold Reed was counting his money as he went out the bar exit.

I said, "That's damn decent of you, Dixie."

She looked distracted. "Uh, yeah. Price of doin' business."

"I just wanted to thank you for the free drinks for my wife and me."

She realized who I was suddenly (or anyway, thought she did).

"Well, it's my favorite honeymooner. You bet—my pleasure. You all come back."

"Oh we will."

I went quickly into the restaurant where Luann had just finished her ice cream. Without sitting, I took a look at the bill, which was under ten bucks, and left fifteen. Took my bride by the hand and went out.

They were fast. Dixie and her husband were already in motion, trailing the bouncer who was dragging the salesman from the parking lot to between the main building and the motel. A big air conditioner was making a lot of noise nearby.

I told Luann: "Get our bag out of the room and put it in the car. Here are the keys."

I handed them to her.

She nodded.

"You get in the car and wait for me. Keep your head down."

She nodded, and scurried off.

The slice of moon was painting the overgrown area behind the buildings a deceptively peaceful ivory. Forming a semi-circle, they were in the ankle-high grass, but a thicket of weeds and kudzu and God knew what else was waiting like an all too penetrable wall just a few yards away.

So pale he almost glowed, Dix was smoking, grinning, his mustache riding his sneer like a surfboard does a wave. He had a gun in one hand, a snubby .38. He stood near Dixie, who faced the bouncer and his prisoner. The captor had a roundish head, a stupid face, long brown stringy hair with sideburns, and was beefy verging on fat. His chin sat on another one and his little eyes peeked out from piggy pouches. For a big guy, he didn't look like much trouble to me.

But he was plenty of trouble for the salesman, whose arms he held pinned back...

…if not as much trouble as the big-boobed beehive redhead in the black waitress uniform and the white apron, which was already splashed with blood.

The three places where she had hit him in his bald skull with the hammer were easily visible, ribbons of red trailing from each. The little guy was woozy from pain but the mercy of unconsciousness hadn't come his way yet.

Chicken wasn't the only thing that got well-battered at the Dixie Club.

She snarled, "What do you think, Dix? Has our guest learned his lesson? Or does he go for a swim in the swamp?"

Dix had a laugh that was mostly cigarette cough, a harsh, terrible disruption in a night where insects and birds sang. "Put him out of his fuckin' misery. That sample case may not be no small change, ya know."

The little salesman said, "You can *have* the watches! Take them! Let me *go!*"

She raised the hammer and I said, "That's enough."

I stepped into view with the nine millimeter raised their way. No silencer, but that chugging air conditioner should do the trick.

Dix's gun was at his side, as limp as that jaw of his, which had just trapdoored open. The bosomy broad whirled toward me and blood flew off the hammer's head like scarlet spittle. Her lip was peeled back and her teeth looked feral and her big green bloodshot eyes looked fucking nuts.

"*You!*" she said.

"Drop the hammer," I said.

"Fuck you!"

I shot her husband.

She dropped the hammer.

And the bouncer dropped the little guy, and took off running, toward that wall of bushes. The nine millimeter slug entered his head in back and a clumpy stream of things that had been inside it projectile-vomited out his forehead.

Dix was slumped in the grass, awkwardly on his side, an uncomfortable position had he been alive; he was staring at us with a ragged hole just above one expressionless eye. Several yards away, the bouncer lay face down, dead as the Confederacy. Dixie just stood there with clawed hands trembling at her side, staring at me with hot hatred that might have got to me if I didn't have the gun.

The salesman was on his knees in the grass. He looked up at me, wondering if he had just been saved or was in the middle of something very bad about to get him killed.

"Have you ever seen me before?" I asked him.

"No."

"Could you recognize me again?"

"No!"

"Good. Why don't you take your five hundred dollars and go? *Go.* Don't look back."

"Thank you," he said, getting up unsteadily. "Thank you, thank you, thank you…."

And he scrambled to his feet and careened off toward the parking lot. It's hard getting your footing after somebody has hit you in the head with a hammer three times.

Dixie was wasting no time mourning her husband. All her energy was focused on hating me. Her hands were fists now.

"*Killian* sent you," she said.

"Well, it wasn't Kilroy."

A car engine started. Wheels spat gravel. The little salesman was on his way somewhere else.

Without taking my eyes off her, I picked up the hammer.

That gave her a start. She may not have known the term, but

she was clearly thinking poetic justice might be about to come her way.

"What are you going to do?" she spat. But there was fear in her bloodshot eyes. "*Kill* me with it?"

"What am I, a psychopath?"

And shot her in the head.

SEVEN

By eleven-thirty the next morning, I was back in Biloxi at the Tropical.

The three very sharp lightweight black suits and six silk ties had been delivered, the latter on the dresser, the former neatly hanging in the closet in a garment bag. After a shit and a shower, I was a new man, particularly once I'd tried on one of the suits. No shirts had been provided, but a light-blue one I'd brought with me worked well with a tie alternating two darker shades of blue.

The shoulder-holstered nine millimeter under my left arm did not bulge at all. I hadn't worn it for the fitting at Godchaux's, where apparently the tailor knew ahead to allow for it. Impressive a couple of ways.

In addition to the new threads, a message was waiting for me, indicated by the bedside phone's flashing light. The hotel switchboard operator read it to me: "Welcome home. Report in at one o'clock. JK."

At the connecting door between my room and Luann's, I knocked. She spoke through it: "Yes?"

"Need you for a second."

She opened the door and stood framed there. She'd been showering, too, and had a towel tied around her waist, leaving her bare-breasted like a native girl in a *National Geographic*.

"Well, look at you," she said, her hands on her hips, her perfect bare B cups staring at me as intently as the baby blues.

"Same back at you," I said. "You want lunch? I don't have to go to work till one."

"Sure. I should put somethin' on."

"Why not?"

We took the same booth at The Dockside, where business was a little better than the last time we'd been here, thanks to businessmen having multiple-martini lunches. Luann was wearing her back-up coed clothes from Gayfer's—a white shirt-style top with a floral explosion of colors, yellow short-shorts, plus the open-toed cork-heeled shoes again.

She ordered a pulled-pork sandwich and iced tea, and I had a fish sandwich basket. I was drinking Coke but she'd got a Tab, a nod toward the stripper's regimen I'd talked her into otherwise ignoring.

"I haven't seen you drink," I said, hunching over to make sure I didn't get tartar sauce on my fancy suit.

She sipped the Tab. She had barbecue sauce on her pretty face. "Sure you have."

"I mean, anything alcoholic. Or is that part of your diet?"

The sunlight from the window did nice things to her hair. "I never touch anythin' like that."

"Why?"

"That shit killed my mother."

"Oh. So how about drugs?"

"No thanks."

"No, I mean, do you smoke at all?"

"Cigarettes cause cancer."

"I mean the *other* smoke."

She shook her head and the blondeness shimmered. "My girlfriends, my roommates? They do grass all the time. I don't like the smell."

"I'm not a smoker or drinker either. I guess we're just a couple of health nuts."

She shrugged, spoke through a mouthful of pork. "I guess."

"What do you do for fun, Luann?"

"TV. Movies."

"You got a boyfriend?"

She made a face. "I get enough of that at work."

"So…do you and your girlfriends…?"

"Get it on? No. Well, *they* do. They're lezzies. Each his own."

"How long have you been working?"

She frowned in thought, finally cleaning barbecue sauce off her face with a cloth napkin. "Hookin' or strippin'?"

"Hooking."

"Since I was thirteen. No…twelve."

"Twelve." I had encountered my share of fucked-up shit, but this was right in there.

She shrugged. "My boobies come in early. Never got much *bigger*, but I got 'em."

Whoever had turned her out at that age could use a beating and a bullet. But that was a long time ago, and not my business.

Of course nothing about her life was my business, except that in a way it was. I was trying to size her up. To understand her. If she'd seen what I did last night, that would have made her a witness. Which really sucked. What had I been thinking?

I heard myself ask, "You a runaway?"

She shook her head and the blonde hair danced on her shoulders. "No."

"Then how did you come in contact with a pimp?"

"Didn't."

"How *did* you start?"

"You're awful curious today."

I had another bite of my sandwich. "Just interested, Luann. Who put you on the game?"

"I been with Mr. Woody for like…forever."

"*He* turned you out?"

She thought about that. Nibbled a French fry dipped in barbecue sauce. "Not really. See, my mom sold me to Mr. Woody."

"Sold you?"

"Yeah. She was running a house for him. He paid big money
for me." Then she did the damnedest thing: she grinned at me.
First time. "I guess they never heard of Abe Lincoln."

I put my half-eaten sandwich down. Takes something special
to get to me, but this one turned my stomach.

I pretended it hadn't, and sipped Coke. "What do you do
with your money? Mr. Woody *does* pay you...?"

"Sure he does. I'm not that big a slave. He's paid me all along."

"So what do you do with your money?"

"Save it."

"What for?"

"Tomorrow." She frowned in thought again. "Not *tomorrow*
tomorrow, but for...sometime."

I signed the check to my room, and as we walked back, she
did something even odder than grin at me: she slipped her
hand in mine.

"You're nice," she said. "Or am I over the line?"

"Not at all."

I guessed if blowing me within an hour of meeting me hadn't
been over the line, neither was this.

I said, "Well, I like you, too, Luann."

"I don't mean anythin' drippy."

She even *sounded* young.

She went on: "I just think you're nice. Because, what you did
last night? That was totally awesome."

I didn't know what she meant, or maybe I was afraid I did.
After what went down at the Dixie Club, I'd joined her in
the car, from which she shouldn't have been able to see anything. We had driven back to Memphis and she'd been very

quiet, sitting with her seat belt off and hugging her legs, heels of her feet on the Mustang's bucket seat. No radio, but also no conversation. The ninety-minute drive had been surreal, as we wove through a ghostly moon-swept night haunted by kudzu beasts. If that weren't frightening enough, we'd stayed at the airport Motel 6. There we'd shared a bed, but no conversation.

In the morning, I'd used a rubber (as was my habit with her) for some missionary sex, which proved fast, athletic and draining. She had a way of extracting a fuck out of a guy the way a dentist does a tooth.

Still, she'd seemed fine on the plane coming back. Or anyway she'd seemed that same painfully pretty shapely little thing with a hidden interior life.

We were at my motel room door. I had to ask. "What was so 'awesome' about it?"

She glanced to her right and her hair swung left. She glanced to her left and her hair swung right. Then she looked up at me and there was life in the eyes and she was smiling. "The way you saved that poor little man. *That* was awesome."

Then she got on her toes and kissed me lightly on the mouth. We'd had various kinds of sex any number of times, but this was the first kiss. She dropped back down on the soles of her feet, or anyway those cork heels, got her room key from a little leather purse, dangled it at me, and hustled to the next door down and went in, tossing me a little smile first.

Shit.

Once again, I was ushered into Jack Killian's office in his top-floor Tropical living quarters. This time he got up behind his aircraft-carrier desk and extended a hand for me to shake. I did so, and settled into one of two comfy waiting visitors' chairs as he returned to his swivel one.

His smile was an angular thing that emphasized the oddly Asian cast of the eyes in that pale handsome oblong oval. Black hair brushed back, in a fresh dark Italian suit with a pale yellow shirt and gold tie, he looked like something from a European issue of *GQ*.

Or maybe the Asp in *Little Orphan Annie*.

"The suit suits you," he said, nodding toward my new duds.

"Your other guys," I said, risking a smile, "seem to be in off-the-rack numbers. Why do I rate tailoring?"

The remark pleased him. He rocked gently, elbows close to his sides, fingers tented. "Because I have big things in mind for you, Mr. Quarry. One meeting with you and I *knew* I had found just the man I needed."

"Hope I don't disappoint."

He stopped rocking and his eyes met mine head-on. "You have already handily proven yourself. Since you've been in transit, you may not have seen or read any of the news."

"No. I don't suppose the war is over." Or maybe they'd finally cancelled *Gunsmoke*.

"If you mean Vietnam, no. But I think you may have averted a potential *other* war. Josie 'Dixie' Dixon and her husband Randolph, and one of their employees, whose name escapes me, were shot and killed last night outside their club near Selmer, Tennessee. Nothing much more has been made public thus far, other than a recap of their colorful history and the various charges and rumors that have swirled about their notorious enterprise."

"Did you want details of…?"

"No. I don't want to know."

"Okay."

"But I'm taking back-to-back meetings this afternoon, Mr. Quarry—the first will begin any moment now—and your presence may be helpful…to you and me both. These individuals are quite used to my having a bodyguard at such meetings, so you being here will raise no questions. Or hackles."

I shrugged a well-tailored shoulder. "Okay. Do you mind my asking what my usual duties will be?"

He nodded, and now his hands were folded on his desk, as if he were about to say grace. "I don't mind at all, but understand—you won't be joining my staff here in the suite."

"No?"

"No. Oh, you'll stay here at the Tropical, for now at least, and be on call for special instances that may, that *will*, come up."

"Fine."

"You see, whenever I leave this well-armed cocoon of mine to go out—whether for business or relaxation—I don't carry a large retinue. It sends the wrong signals."

"I get that."

He flipped a hand. "But I always travel with a driver and a bodyguard. Since you aren't familiar with this area, you are obviously not suited for chauffeur service. You'll act as my bodyguard. I need a deadly individual for that."

"Cool."

"My life, Mr. Quarry, will be in your capable hands."

"I'm up for that."

He twitched a smile. "There's a manila envelope waiting for you at the desk. Be sure to pick it up."

"I will." *What was that about?*

A knock came and Killian said, "Yes?"

The door cracked open and the watchdog with the close-set eyes stuck his head in, like a jack-in-the-box. "The sheriff is here."

That got my attention.

"Send him in," Killian said, almost cheerfully. He gestured

for me to move my chair and myself off to one side, which I did.

The man who entered was not in uniform, although he did have a big automatic on his hip and a Stetson-with-badge in his right hand. A tan heavyset six footer in a crisp brown suit with dark brown tie, he looked the part, uniform or no. His bucket head was home to short, neatly combed steel-gray hair, prominent ears, a broad flattened nose, and a wide, fleshy mouth.

"Jack," the sheriff said, in a raspy tenor that did not suit the rest of the picture, nodding, smiling, to his host.

"Jeff," Killian acknowledged, then gestured toward me. "This is my new man, John Quarry. Mr. Quarry, this is our good friend Sheriff Jefferson Davis Delmar."

I didn't know whether that "our" was editorial or if I was being included in this friendship.

Already on my feet, I said, "Sheriff," and offered my hand, which he shook and squeezed, trying too hard.

He took the remaining visitor's chair opposite Killian, then jerked a thumb my way. "Am I free to talk in front of Mr. Quarry here?"

"You are. He's a direct referral from Woodrow."

"Ah." The sheriff turned to give me a nod. Then back to Killian: "I suppose you've heard about the trouble up at the state line."

Killian's face registered nothing. "Yes. Tragic. But who was it said, 'Whatever one sows, so shall he reap?' "

"God or some shit," the sheriff said with a shrug. He was turning his Stetson in big blunt hands. "I have to ask you, Jack, in my official capacity—did you have anything to do with this thing?"

"I did not."

"And you don't know who did?"

"No idea."

The big head nodded twice. The Stetson kept turning like a wheel in the thick hands. "Now. I am gonna ask again, off the record, as a friend and business associate. Jack, did you have anything to do with this?"

"No."

"Any idea who did?"

"None." Killian's slash of a mouth did its imitation of a smile as he opened a palm in the direction of the liquor cart. "Could I interest you in a drink, Jeff? I think you could stand to relax some."

The sheriff gave the army of bottles a greedy look, then shook his head, saying, "Appreciate the offer, but I best keep the old noggin clear today. Lot of pressure comin' down, Jack, from press and citizenry…and do I have to tell you? The mayor's office."

Killian gazed at the sheriff with hooded eyes. "What concern is it of the mayor if some white-trash outlaws posing as restaurateurs get their due and just reward?"

The sheriff shifted his big rear end in the chair. "His Honor is concerned, Jack, that you are changin' the nature of the Biloxi Strip, particularly as to your expansion beyond our city limits."

"I've always had a good relationship," Killian said, "with His Honor. And with *you*, Jeff. We pay our tithe, don't we? Haven't we been more than generous?"

The sheriff raised a palm. "You have, you have…but in the past, you and Mr. Woody and your people, well, things have been…kind of spread around. Lot of small businesses, workin' to cooperate with each other, and with local government. Accordin'ly, realizin' the futility of tryin' to legislate morality, we in public service have made mutually beneficial arrangements with you and others. We put our focus more on protectin' the interests of the tourists who visit our little town, and of course our boys from the air base, and our own fine citizens. But when something happens like this mess at the Dixie Club, well…it sends up a kind of a…red flag."

Killian's eyebrows went up. "It does? And why is that?"

"You've gradually taken over nearly the whole strip yourself, Jack. But, all right, I understand that, that is after all the American way. However—expandin' around the state, and even *beyond* state lines, into Tennessee…with talk of Alabama and Kentucky and Louisiana…that kind of consolidation can attract attention, Jack. FBI attention."

Killian's shrug was barely perceptible. "They've never been a problem for us."

The sheriff sat forward. "They'll *start* to be. They ain't interested in a tithe from you fellas. They are interested in convictions, and million-dollar fuckin' fines, and with all the power you're gatherin', Jack, and all the enemies you're makin', you are stickin' your chin out beggin' for a RICO violation."

The Racketeer Influenced and Corrupt Organizations Act.

Even a small fry like me knew about that. And what the sheriff was saying made sense.

"Jeff," Killian said amiably, "I had nothing to do with what happened to the Dixons. Karma finally caught up with them, is all."

The sheriff's smile seemed a little sick. "That is a relief to hear, Jack. But there may be repercussions from the survivin' family members."

Though seated, Killian made a sort of half bow. "I will be reaching out to the Dixons to express my sympathy and give them my sincere assurance that I had nothing to do with their *tragic* loss.…Is there anything else, Jeff?"

The sheriff swallowed thickly. Many a wrongdoer must have sat across from Jefferson Davis Delmar and felt plenty intimidated.

But right now it was the sheriff who was sitting in the principal's office.

"Yes, Jack," he said, and his tone was almost conciliatory. "There's somethin' Mayor Clayton and I would very much like you to consider. This is an election year. We won't ask you to shut down, even temporarily, because everybody on both sides of the political fence knows what it takes to make a tourist town like Biloxi tick."

"Good to hear."

"But if you could help minimize the violence…as you say, you had nothing to do with what happened at the Dixie Club… but as for any other conflicts that might arise, here or elsewhere 'round the state? His Honor and I would very much appreciate you tampin' down the fireworks."

"You come in loud and clear."

The sheriff forced a big grin. "Let's keep the Strip a fun place for locals and out-of-towners alike to have a good ol' time. And let's keep the headlines free of any suggestion of…unpleasantness. Fair 'nuff?"

"Fair enough," Killian said, and smiled, and stood, extending his hand again. This was his way of saying the meeting was over.

The sheriff got to his feet, shook Killian's hand, nodded at me, and lumbered out, not looking very satisfied.

Killian's expression was similarly sour. "They stuff their pockets with my money and then tell me how to run my business. Can you imagine?"

"No." Actually, I could. Hypocritical politicians didn't exactly come as a shock to me.

Killian gave the air a karate chop. "Why don't they stick to what they're good for? Looking the other way!"

Another knock came, but before Killian could grant permission, Mr. Woody rushed in, looking put out. He was in a blue-plaid polyester sportcoat with a light-blue wing-collar shirt and darker blue trousers. No tie, which was probably a breach of protocol.

"I waited," Mr. Woody said, helping himself to the chair the sheriff vacated, "till Delmar was gone. He didn't see me."

"So what if he had?" Killian said. The meeting had barely begun and already he seemed bored.

Mr. Woody noticed me, nodded, and pressed on: "I didn't want our esteemed sheriff to think we were in some kinda crisis mode over this Dixon debacle. Jesus Jones, Jackie—did you do this thing?"

"No."

"Of course you didn't do it *yourself*. But did you *have* it done? Not that the world isn't a better place without them crazy assholes."

"I did not. The Dixons had plenty of enemies closer to home. Decades of outrageous misconduct finally caught up with them."

Mr. Woody was shaking his head, though his combover remained intact. "Maybe so, but it'll come back on us. Isn't that why Delmar was here?"

"Certainly."

"What did you tell him?"

"What I told you." Killian sat forward, his brow tense. "Now. Woodrow. Dix has a brother and some cousins who own clubs on both sides of the state line."

"Right. Those are the only ones you don't own along there, at this point."

"I want you to call the Dixon boys and express our condolences."

"Why don't you do it? You're the top of this here food chain."

Killian shrugged. "You've been friendlier with them than I. They might take it wrong, coming from me. Send our sympathy, blah blah blah, and make an offer on the Dixie Club."

"Oh, my God, how will they read *that*?"

"Make it a third again what we offered last time. They'll read it as money, and they'll read it as a way to get off the firing line."

"So you *did* do it."

"I didn't say that. But of course I know I'll be blamed. Fine. They won't in future fuck with Biloxi. We have too much power, and too much firepower. Just do it, Woodrow."

With a sigh, Mr. Woody got up and went over to the liquor cart and helped himself to some Scotch, filling a tumbler a third of the way, shaking a little as he did so.

Then he sat and sipped Scotch and mulled for a moment. "Well, hell, Jackie—we might as well make an offer on *their* clubs, too. A third more than last time?"

Killian shook his head once. "No. Same offer on theirs as we made before. Only up the ante on the Dixie. That should do the trick."

"Christ. All right." Mr. Woody emptied the tumbler down his gullet, rose, leaving the empty glass on the liquor cart.

He stopped at the door to add: "You mind if I borrow your boy Quarry for a moment, Jackie? I wanna see how the little gal I loaned him is workin' out."

Killian made a magnanimous open-handed gesture. "By all means. You know, I'm very satisfied with Mr. Quarry. That was a fine recommendation, Woodrow. He's a capable, discreet man."

I knew what "discreet" was code for: *don't tell Mr. Woody what you did at the state line last night.* He needn't have bothered.

As I was going out, Killian said, "Mr. Quarry, take the rest of the afternoon off. But stay handy. I may need you this evening."

I nodded.

Mr. Woody and I walked through the wood-paneled bachelor-pad suite with its several guards in black suits positioned here and there, and out where two more watched the elevator. He and I hadn't exchanged a word. We got on the elevator and went down.

Alone at last, Mr. Woody demanded, "Did you do that dirty work for Jackie at the Dixie?"

"No," I said. What business was it of his?

He kept pressing: "Did you overhear anythin'? Did he send somebody?"

"Not that I know of. But what if he did? It sounds like these were horrible people who could cause you a lot of trouble."

He let out a big sigh. "Well, they were. Fuckin' monsters, and good riddance. But this has to be another Killian takeover move, in which case he's courtin' disaster for all of us. If Marcello don't swat us like flies, the feds'll slam our asses in the slammer."

Which I believe is why they called it a slammer.

I said, "I'll let you know what I see and hear." Like hell.

We stepped off into the lobby, empty but for a young woman busy at the check-in desk. He walked me to one side, where we were well away from her.

"You seem to be nicely positioned on the inside," Mr. Woody said, speaking low.

Keeping my voice down as well, I said, "Inside a fortress. I don't relish shooting my way out."

Eyes flared behind the big lenses. "Well, you need to *act*, man. Jackie is obviously spinnin' out of control."

Actually, Killian seemed far more in control of himself than Mr. Woody here.

He was saying, "How are you gon' to do this thing?"

"I'm waiting for my window."

"Well, how—"

"You've heard the old saying. What you don't know can't etcetera?" Really, I was thinking what he didn't know couldn't hurt me.

He sighed, nodded, bowing to my wisdom. "You know, Jackie thinks he has these politicians by the short and curlies, and maybe he does, but nobody's immune from a bullet."

"How does he have them that way? Short and curlies, I mean. Just because he pays them off?"

Mr. Woody smirked and shook his head. "No, Quarry, it's more than pay-offs. Our Jackie's one smart cookie. He's got a fantasy hotel he uses. Down the Strip half a mile."

"What's a fantasy hotel?"

"It's got theme rooms—you know, Roman times, spacecrafts, jungles, caverns, all with beds in them. Whenever a politician comes into office, here in town or around the state—and I mean high-rankin'—U.S. Senator included—Jackie gives 'em an invitation for an all-expenses-paid fantasy night with one of our girls."

"So what?"

He grinned and raised a forefinger. "Them rooms are rigged with video cameras. He's got tapes on you-wouldn't-believe-how-many big shots. Startin' with our sheriff starring in a Candid Camera porno with that little gal I loaned you, for instance."

"No kidding."

"And of course it's been a real moneymaker for us, extendin' to well-off civilians, as well. Lots of married fellas who check into Fantasy Sweets without the missus go home with a keepsake that costs 'em plenty."

I grunted a laugh. "A keepsake they are not likely to share with 'the missus.' "

"Not hardly. It's not home movies of the Grand Canyon. Well, sometimes it is. Depends on which girl."

I walked him outside into sunshine and seventy-five degrees, the blue of the Gulf in our line of sight. Our talk of fantasy suites seemed to have cheered Mr. Woody up.

He put a hand on my shoulder, grinning at me. He smelled like Jade East. "Still enjoyin' Lo?"

He meant Luann.

"She's good company."

Mr. Woody's expression was reflective. "Nice girl. Sweet kid. I known her since she was knee-high to a grasshopper. Her mom was a great gal, too. Died way too young—drank herself into an early grave. Fuckin' tragic. Sometimes life ain't fair."

"Sometimes," I said.

He waved as he headed into the parking lot.

At the front desk a manila envelope was, as promised, waiting for me. I didn't look inside till I was back in my room.

Five grand in nice new hundreds.

So I didn't have to worry about not getting paid by Killian before I whacked him.

That was good.

EIGHT

When I signed on with the Broker, this kind of shit was not even in the fine print. Getting close to a target like Killian made me uncomfortable, as did coming into contact with so many people. Never mind the waitresses and patrons back at the Dixie Club—hell, they wouldn't connect me to anything or remember me at all.

But what about the small army of guys in black suits who worked for Killian? What about the hookers and bartenders and strippers who saw me getting shown around by Mr. Woody? What about the desk clerks at the Tropical, who knew I was connected to the man in the top-floor suite?

And Killian himself was a problem. I didn't *want* to get to know a target—their habits, their pattern, sure. But Killian had been decent to me, in his way, and seemed like one of the more admirable players in this foul game. He was trying to drag the Dixie Mafia screaming and kicking into the 1970s, enough so to make his number-two man eager to help remove him.

I had to keep in mind that Killian had ordered a hit on the Broker, a hit that had almost made collateral damage out of me, and that alone was enough to justify getting rid of him. Not that it needed justifying. He was just another contract, right? It wasn't that I liked him or anything. He was just another one of these Southern fried gangsters—granted, one with ambitions beyond anything that the bottom feeders around him could ever grasp.

Then there was Luann.

Should I have turned down Mr. Woody's gift of her services,

a gift apparently intended for the duration of my stay? Would that have seemed suspicious, or ungrateful? Why look a gift whore in the mouth? Having such a creature handy to provide creature comforts did not suck, even if *she* did, in a good way.

But things would be heating up and she might become an encumbrance. True, the little hooker would stay in her room if I told her to, and I had no reason to think she'd ever intrude. Only, goddamnit, she was becoming a person to me. Which was the same problem I was having with Killian, but worse. I felt sorry for this kid. Her own damn mother had sold her into the sex trade—even in a world as mean and meaningless as this one, that put a whole new spin on Mother of the Year. I did not have these thoughts while fucking the girl, I admit, but in my more reflective moments, like in the shower or on the can, I did.

Sending her back to Mr. Woody at this point wouldn't cut it. She was a witness now, and I had to keep an eye on her, keep track of her, in case I had to do something about it.

I couldn't face The Dockside a second time in one day, even though I could sign meals to my room there, so I drove Luann over to a touristy seafood restaurant on Rue Magnolia, just off Highway 90—Mary Mahoney's, an old French white-clapboard mansion right out of New Orleans.

The cute little Tonto to my Lone Ranger was in the red U-neck top and red-white-and-light-blue jeans again. Her hair was freshly washed and she smelled like Charlie perfume, very much maintaining that coed look she'd had at the Dixie Club. Under-dressed for the room, but what the hell.

"No cheeseburger tonight," I said. "Not allowed."

We were at a white-linen-covered table seated on white dining chairs in a room with pale yellow walls with framed pictures of pelicans on them. Business was slow, meaning nice privacy.

"Everythin's so expensive," she said.

"I came into some money."

"Let's share somethin'."

We did, a seafood platter. Her table manners were better than you'd think, but she put a lot of food away, including some bread pudding. I wasn't that hungry.

Back at the Tropical, as we approached our side-by-side rooms, she said, "You want me to come in?"

"Sure. You can watch TV if you want. I'm on call. I could use the company."

She followed me in and slipped into the bathroom. I went over and turned on the TV for her. Flip Wilson was on, doing his drag character, Geraldine. He said, "The devil made me do it!" and the audience roared.

The only light on was the bedside one. I took off my suitcoat and hung it over the back of a chair, got out of my tie, kicked off my shoes, and flopped onto the bed. She came out the bathroom, naked, and padded over to the TV and turned it off, her dimpled backside to me.

Then she came over and switched off the light and the only illumination was what bled in from the curtained windows onto the parking lot.

She began to unbutton my shirt and I said, "You don't have to do that."

She paid no heed. After she'd unbuttoned it, she took it off me, rested it gently on the chair where I'd left the suitcoat, and then began undoing my belt. She unzipped me and tugged the pants off, placed them carefully on the chair, then unceremoniously pulled down my jockey shorts. My dick bobbed at her, interested.

Now all I had on was black socks, like a guy in a stag film. If this had been the Fantasy Sweets, maybe I'd have been making an unwitting one.

Usually she got on top, my theory being that she had more

control that way and could squeeze the come out of you with that tight child's fist of a little snatch of hers, and sort of get it over with. This time she came around the bed and got beside me and was on her back, her legs spread wide, pink flower petals peeking out as they hid in the bush.

I reached for the bedside drawer where the Trojans were and she gripped my arm.

"No," she said.

"No?"

"No. I want to feel you in me."

"Honey, no offense, but…that's just not safe."

"I'm on the pill."

"But…it's not safe *other* ways…"

She shook her head and the blonde hair went a bunch of places, all nice ones. "No man's ever been in me without a rubber."

"*No* man?"

"Nope. It's not good business."

"You said you were on the pill."

"Keeps my periods short and regular. You gonna fuck me or what?"

But I didn't exactly fuck her. I'd done that three or four times over the past few days, but this was something else. This was sweet and tender and she was registering emotion, which was a first, her mouth open, her eyes rolled back, her cheeks red, her chest too, the aureoles wrinkled tight and their tips hard, blue veins pulsing in the pale whiteness of her breasts. She was tight, as always, but wet, too, and I plunged into her slowly and she ground her hips slowly, right with me, both of us building gradually to an explosion that wrenched loud, shuddering moans out of both of us.

I held her, trying not to put all of my weight on her, and she was hugging me, hugging me, hugging me.

Then she slipped out from under me and ran to the bathroom, like she'd seen a mouse.

I flopped back on the bed, feeling like I'd just fallen down the best flight of steps ever, and when my breath was normal, I noticed a sound from the bathroom. Well, I'd already heard water running and then a shower starting. But this was some other sound. I could use some washing off myself, so I got up and knocked at the almost-shut door.

"Luann?"

She was crying in there!

I went quickly in and she was sitting in the tub, at the back but with the shower on, the nozzle aimed away from her, hugging her legs to herself, her hair wet, her face wet, too, streaked with tears, mascara making a break for it.

"Are you all right, honey?"

She nodded, but she was still crying, her little chin all crinkled, her thin arms hugging her shapely legs to her.

I knelt beside the tub and put a hand on her head, got my fingers entwined in the wet hair. "What's wrong, kid?"

"Your…your name is John, right?"

Well, it was supposed to be, so I nodded.

"I never called you that," she said. "I never called you anythin'."

I shrugged. I hadn't noticed, but I guessed that was true.

"You know what a john is," she said.

"Sure."

"Well, I didn't want to call you that."

"Oh?"

"I…liked the way you look right away."

"You didn't show it."

"I try not to show things."

"Me, too. You don't want to call me 'John' because maybe I'm not just a john to you. Is that it?"

She nodded six times. Maybe seven.

She said, "Can I call you 'Johnny'?"

"Sure."

"I like the way you didn't want to call me 'Lolita.' "

It had just struck me as corny, but I said, "Luann's a pretty name."

Neither of us said anything for a while.

Then the light-blue eyes were on me and she said, "Johnny?"

I could barely hear her over the shower water drumming down nearby.

"Yes?" I said.

"I'm not cryin' 'cause I'm sad."

"No. Well, are you happy?"

And she laughed—I swear she did—and nodded four times. Maybe five.

She wiped tears, shower water and snot off her face, then asked, "You know why I'm cryin'?"

"Why?"

"I never did before."

"You never what before?"

"I never came before."

"You never…?"

She shook her head. Still squeezing her legs to her, water streaming from her damp hair like oversize tears. "I didn't think I could. I never liked sex. I just…did it."

"I get that."

"I liked it tonight, Johnny."

"Well…cool."

She nodded. "Cool. Really cool."

"You're crying. Didn't you like…coming?"

"Man! It was totally awesome."

So I helped her out of the shower, and started toweling her off, till she took over. Not crying anymore. Smiling. Happy.

And for all of you out there keeping track, add to my list of accomplishments the ability to make a girl of nineteen who'd been having sex since she was twelve finally experience an orgasm. I'll wait for the applause to die down before moving on.

The closet had a terry cloth robe with TROPICAL on the breast pocket—why a terry cloth robe needs a breast pocket is beyond me—but I bundled her in that, and we went back to the bed and cuddled there, on the bedspread, watching Flip Wilson and Bobby Darin sing, "It's Just One of Those Songs."

She was such a little thing, fitting snugly to me with my arm around her, that when a stray thought entered my mind, I tensed enough that she looked up at me.

I answered her look with, "Luann, I need to ask you something."

"Okay."

"Don't be upset."

"Okay."

"Did Mr. Woody ask you to keep tabs on me?"

I thought she might be hurt. That she might start to cry in a whole other way.

But instead she shook her head at the notion of being sent to my side as a spy, saying, "He wouldn't trust me with that. He thinks I'm just a dumb little cunt."

"Oh."

"You don't think that, do you?"

"No."

"You believe me? You trust me?"

"Sure."

"I'd never do anythin' bad to my knight in shiny armor."

"What?"

"That's what you are." She was beaming but looking past me. "The way you went to that little man's rescue last night…like a knight in shiny armor."

Christ, she *would* have to remind me that she'd witnessed that.

The nightstand phone rang.

I answered it.

"You're needed," Killian's voice said. "Now."

That the sprawling Keesler Air Force Base was located a mere three blocks north of much of the Biloxi Strip was no coincidence. The roughly three miles of sin palaces between Camelia Street and Rodenberg Avenue depended on the business of young airmen, particularly in off-season.

All I'd gathered was that a problem involving one of those airmen was bad enough to bring Jack Killian out of his (as he put it) well-armed cocoon. I was with Killian in back of a white Cadillac Coupe de Ville with red leather seats; a driver and one of the Tropical watchdogs, both in those trademark black suits, were up front.

The Caddy pulled into a mostly empty graveled parking lot on the south side of Highway 90. A one-and-a-half-story brown-brick building with darker-brown shingled roof squatted there, the white beach at its back. A small window in front could accommodate only a single beer neon, HAMM'S, which seemed fitting; the entrance was recessed, a windowless heavy-looking dark brown door, above which a plastic marquee said

BOTTOMS UP
GIRLS   GIRLS   GIRLS

NO COVER   NO MINIMUM

OPEN 7 DAYS A WEEK

HAPPY HOUR 4 PM.

Even among an array of joints with such elegant names as the Titty Ho, the Wits Inn, the Landing Strip and the Climax, this was one sleazy-looking dump.

The driver stayed with the car. The bodyguard, the unibrow guy from the vestibule, went in first. We were greeted by stale beer smell, cigarette fog, and Tom Jones blaring "She's a Lady," while—on a plywood stage with a stripper pole and green carpet (same stuff was on the walls)—a tall skinny brunette with fake tits did a topless/bottomless bump-and-grind that contradicted Mr. Jones. College boys, airmen and seamen (do your own joke) sat around the stage, contributing wadded-up dollars to the cause when the stripper came around to give them a closer look at the mystery of life. The small round tables on either side were empty. The hard-looking handful of waitresses, in halter tops and minis, looked bored, and the six feet of bar with a six-foot bartender behind it was otherwise unattended.

Seated on a stool just inside the door, a mustached bruiser in a black t-shirt and black jeans stood with his arms crossed in a way that made his biceps bulge even more. The scowl that was his reflex when anybody entered wiped itself off when Killian came in.

The bouncer said thickly, "Expectin' you, Mr. Killian. Boss is waitin' in back."

Killian nodded and took the lead. I fell in behind him with the unibrow bodyguard trailing; we cut past the backs of patrons seated at the stripper stage and the empty tables on the periphery.

Soon we were in a smallish storeroom where boxes of liquor and beer were piled up along several walls, leaving an open area where right now a slender red-headed ponytail stripper in a skimpy pink cotton robe was seated on a wooden chair, slumped, knees primly together, crying or anyway she had been crying.

Pacing behind her was a medium-sized, round-faced guy about forty with black-framed glasses, a lot of greasy black hair and too much sideburn, with a paunch that threatened to pop the lower buttons on his short-sleeve white shirt. His tie was wide and dark green. His pants were green plaid flared polyester.

Killian said, in a perfectly measured manner, "Morrie—I take it this is the young lady."

Morrie had frozen in his pacing upon noticing Killian's presence. Without joining us, he nervously pushed his glasses up on his nose and nodded, saying, "This is her. This is Kelly."

Killian walked to the girl. In his black suit and dark blue tie, this knife-blade of a man might have seemed threatening. But his voice was almost gentle.

"Kelly," he said. "You're not in trouble. Do you understand? You're not in trouble."

She swallowed and nodded, but did not look up at him.

He put his hand under her chin, forcing her gently to look up. "*Not* in trouble. Just tell me what happened."

She glanced back at Morrie, but Killian took her by the chin and, again not with any particular force, turned her narrow, almost pretty face his way. Big green eyes looked up at him, bloodshot and mascara smeary.

"His name is Tommy," she said. "He's been comin' in for... three weeks, I guess. Three or four times a week. He always wants to do coke."

Killian glanced past her at Morrie, who frowned and shrugged, in a what-are-you-gonna-do-with-these-kids manner.

"So I sold him some," she said, shrugging. "He always bought enough for me to have some, too."

"Did he come alone?"

She nodded. "Always."

"Did he drive over from the base?"

She shook her head. "Walked."

"Where did you get the coke, Kelly?"

She glanced back at Morrie, who gave her a look to kill.

Killian patted her on the head, like a dog who had piddled but still was loved, and walked to where Morrie was standing. As for me and the unibrow, we were near the door we'd come in, in front of some stacked boxes, watching this like a play.

"Morrie," Killian said, slipping an arm around the smaller man's shoulder, "you know how we operate. Our is a strictly wholesale business."

"I know that, Mr. Killian. She's lying her little cunt off! She never got that stuff from me."

"I don't recall her saying she did."

Kelly was crying again. Fear crying.

"You see, Morrie," Killian said, arm still around the trembling man's shoulder, "because we're moving quantities, and dealing with an established distribution system, we don't sell ourselves here at any of the clubs. That's strict policy."

"I know that, I really do, I know."

"We can look the other way when someone makes a transaction in a bathroom or out on the beach. That's commerce. That's capitalism. But if *we* do the selling, and something bad happens, like a bust...or like whatever happened to Tommy here...it can reflect badly on us."

"Absolutely," Morrie said, shaking his head, "it won't happen again."

"Where is the boy?"

Morrie swallowed and nodded. "Still in the Honeymoon Suite."

The Honeymoon Suite, it turned out, was a cubicle with a mattress and some dirty sheets behind the stripper's stage; the *thump thump thump* of the bass line of "Temptation Eyes" was bleeding through a plywood wall.

Killian, apparently wanting to instruct his new charge, had

taken me along for a look. There wasn't room for us in that cubicle, so we viewed it from the doorless doorway.

On that mattress, on his back with his mouth open and his eyes closed, was a kid a couple years younger than me, maybe five-ten with a fit-looking build and a blond butch haircut. His nose looked red around the nostrils. He wore a light yellow t-shirt and orange flared trousers and he was dead as shit.

Suddenly the little stripper was at Killian's side, clutching his arm, desperate. "Mr. Killian, I didn't give him that much. I swear! It *can't* be an overdose. He was on top of me dry humping and then he rolled off and was clutching his chest. Really hurting, trying to catch his breath and stuff."

He patted her shoulder. "Go sit down, Kelly. I'll be with you in a minute."

She nodded and went back to her chair. Behind her, Morrie was pacing again.

"Mr. Quarry," Killian said, "fetch Mr. Henderson, would you?"

That was the unibrow guy.

I brought him over and stepped away as Killian gave him some whispered, rather detailed instructions, eliciting nods. Then Henderson quickly went back out through the club.

Killian went over to Morrie and said, "Shut down for the night. Announce a gas leak. Get everybody out of here."

No discussion of that. Morrie just nodded and rushed off to fill the order.

That left Kelly on her chair. Killian walked casually over to her. I positioned myself near the door back into the club.

"Now, Kelly, you understand you can't speak of this to anyone."

"No, sir. I mean yes, sir."

"If you are questioned, you have to stay strong and just deny that you know anything about what happened to Tommy."

"I understand, sir."

"You could cause your family a lot of embarrassment and grief."

"I'm not local, sir. My family don't know where I am or care."

"I'm sorry. But you don't want to go to jail on a manslaughter charge, do you?"

"No!"

"Or for selling drugs?"

"No!"

"That's a good girl," he said.

I was impressed with the way Killian was handling this. I'd been told he was violent and a loose cannon, but what I'd observed the last few days was a self-controlled businessman who knew what he was doing.

He slipped behind her, withdrew something from his pocket that made a *snik* and grabbed her by the ponytail, yanking her head back, and slit her throat. A spray of blood painted the wall behind which Tommy's body lay on a dirty mattress.

She stayed slumped in the chair somehow, with her head tilted at a crazy angle, like it might break off and fall on the floor. Some blood had run down and soaked her pink robe, but not so much. Blood stops flowing when you're dead.

Well, then. That had been impressive, in a different way. Perhaps I'd misjudged Killian.

He wiped the blade off on a shoulder of the girl's pink robe, clicked the switchblade shut and slipped it in his pocket. He strolled over to me.

"Now Mr. Henderson and a couple of other comrades of ours will be rounding up a boat so we can dispose of the bodies."

"That kid is an airman…won't there be—?"

"Tommy is going AWOL tonight. And no one will look for him at the bottom of the Mississippi Sound."

"Ah. And Kelly's going with him?"

"Yes. Now, I need you to wait here until Mr. Henderson returns. There will be several others with him who will give this area a thorough cleansing. All I need from you is to keep watch here till they return. They'll come in through the rear...see there?"

I nodded.

"You don't need to participate further. Catch a cab. But in the meantime, I need *not* to be here. Mr. Phillips will take me back to the Tropical."

I gathered Mr. Phillips was his driver.

"Okay," I said.

"May I borrow your gun?"

I didn't love the sound of that.

"Certainly," I said, and got the nine millimeter out from under my arm and handed it to him. The safety was on, so that should give me time to react, if he was planning to make a dead witness out of me.

"Do you understand the concept of trust, Mr. Quarry?"

"I think I do."

"Perhaps you don't. Trust is based on secrets. Mutual secrets. Secrets that one individual could reveal to expose the other, but does not, because that individual could reveal similarly damaging secrets about the other."

"Makes sense."

The door from the club opened and Morrie came in. There was a jog around some boxes that kept him from immediately seeing Kelly in her chair, and he was talking as he came: "We're all clear. Gas leak sent everybody running. Two of my girls ran bare-ass out into the...*shit!*"

Morrie moved like the mummy through a swamp as he approached Kelly. "What the fuck happened here?" He turned to look at Killian, who shot him in the head.

Morrie's surprised expression was his reaction to Kelly, not to getting killed, because he didn't have time to process that before going down on his back and splashing in some of Kelly's blood.

Killian handed me the nine millimeter.

"Trust, Mr. Quarry," he said.

And he was gone before I realized that I'd just missed the perfect opportunity to ice his ass.

That left me with two corpses in the storeroom of the Bottoms Up, three counting Tommy on his grungy mattress beyond the plywood wall. I went out into the empty club, where the lights were down. Behind the bar, I got myself a glass of Coke and sat at one of the tables, as if I were waiting for a stripper to come out.

And not a clean-up crew with bleach and a boat.

NINE

Just before ten the next morning, Killian called me to come up to his office in his suite at the Tropical. I said I'd be there in ten minutes.

I was still in the shorts I'd slept in, but had been up for maybe an hour. Luann and I'd had a light room-service breakfast, and now she was in her room next door, watching television. She watched a lot of it when she wasn't working, I gathered—game shows and soap operas by day, various dramatic series and movies at night.

So I got into one of the goddamn suits, feeling like a working stiff and not crazy about it, and soon was making my way through the top-floor bachelor-pad digs without an escort now—one of the family—rating bored nods from others in the black-suit brigade, two of whom were reading newspapers and drinking coffee at the captain's table by the kitchen area.

I knocked once on the office door, said, "Quarry," and got a "*Come.*"

The slender, Asian-eyed man was in his own black suit and dark silk tie, if more expensive than mine, seated behind the massive desk with a ledger before him, which he marked with a built-in ribbon and closed before smiling at me and leaning back in the swivel chair.

"Good morning, Mr. Quarry."

I nodded. "Mr. Killian."

"You did well last night."

I shrugged. "Not much to it. Your other minions took care of the hard stuff."

He chuckled at my use of the word "minions." Probably not

a lot of his staff tossed that one around much. You pick up a lot reading paperback novels.

Then his smile dissolved into something serious—not grave, just businesslike. "You don't need to know the details…"

"I don't want to."

"…you don't need to know them, right, but you do need to know that everything's been taken care of."

I wanted to tell him to go fuck himself. That was *my* gun he used on his minion Morrie. I guessed it couldn't come back on me, if the late manager of the Bottoms Up was face down with the fishes, but I hadn't liked that at all.

"Airmen go AWOL all the time," he said, matter of fact. "Few servicemen have families who can hire investigators, and certainly the officials in our fair city won't put up much of a fuss."

"Because you'll tell them not to?"

He shook his head. "I don't have to. I depend on their general benign neglect and inherent incompetence. And they know that the occasional out-of-towner or airman or whomever is going to drop off the edge of the world."

"Ah."

"Speaking with Woodrow, who oversees all of our clubs, I've learned that the girl—what was her name?"

Kelly.

"Doesn't matter," he said, waving it away. "She was a runaway we took in half a dozen years ago, and a druggie, and she really won't be missed. As for the manager I fired, he has an ex-wife in another state who hasn't been able to squeeze an ounce of child support or alimony out of him, so he will not be missed, either."

"Okay," I said, not really caring. This was his mess, if it was a mess. "Mr. Woody is cool with all of this?"

That got half a smile out of the slash under his nose. "Of

course not. He's upset with me. He's always upset with me lately. He is one enormous pussy, these days. He thinks the other people running clubs for us up and down the Strip will hear the scuttlebutt that the manager of a certain establishment was let go in a…harsh manner."

I shrugged. "Well, any of us who were in on it last night won't make a peep."

"I agree wholeheartedly. But it's *Woodrow* who will spread the word."

I frowned at that. "Really?"

"Of course. He'll want our people to know that I'm someone not to be taken lightly, and that he doesn't approve, but can't do anything about it. Thus reinforcing the notion that he's a mensch and I'm a hardass."

"What's a mensch?" You can't learn everything from paperbacks.

"A good guy. Woodrow understands very well that a firm hand keeps everybody in line. But being loved himself makes his life's work go smoother."

"Makes sense." I shifted in my chair. "Anything in mind for me today?"

He nodded. "Something that won't take much of your time, but *is* important. To me, anyway."

"Okay."

He sat forward slightly, folded his hands in that prayerful manner. "I trust my people, but that only goes so far."

Trust again.

He was saying, "I'm spending the evening tonight with a female friend. Not *all* night—just a few hours. The circumstances are…delicate. Meaning, discretion is key." When I didn't say anything, he continued: "Mr. Quarry, this is a married woman, and she has a husband of…let's just say influence."

"Whatever you need." I had no idea why he felt the need to explain himself. So he and Mrs. Jones had a thang going on. Who gave a shit?

"As I say, I trust my staff, but I don't see any need for needless risk."

Said the guy who last night offhandedly slashed a hooker's throat and a shot a minion in the head.

"Yeah," I yes-manned. "Why take a needless risk?"

"So I'm taking no retinue along at all…except yourself."

That perked me up, but I didn't show it.

"You'll drive me," he said. "I realize you're not familiar with the area, but the Fantasy Sweets is only a few blocks from here."

"Do we need to pick up your friend?"

He shook his head. "No. She'll already be in the suite when I get there. I'll position you outside the door. You may want to bring something to read. You can commandeer a chair from the desk clerk."

"Sounds fine," I said. "What time?"

"Meet me downstairs at seven-forty-five. I told my friend I'd meet her at the suite at eight or shortly thereafter."

"Piece of cake."

"Piece of something," he said with a wicked smile.

That was about as witty as I heard him get.

I said, "Anything you need before then?"

"No. After last night, and the night before, you've gone above and beyond. Take this afternoon off. Relax. That little stripper that Mr. Woody provided—she showing you a good time?"

"I'm showing her a good time. Taught her how to achieve orgasm yesterday."

That made him chuckle again. "I never know when you're kidding, Mr. Quarry."

"That's my charm."

He dismissed me and I went back out, nodding at the various black suits between Killian's office and the elevator.

I collected Luann. I ditched the black suit for a blue t-shirt and jeans, and she got into her yellow halter top and hot pants. We had another lunch at The Dockside, then I drove her over to the nearby Saenger Theater on Reynoir Street for a movie. They had two screens—we had a choice between *The Godfather* and *What's Up Doc?* I opted for the latter, because it was a comedy. I'd heard the Mafia movie was good, but I didn't need a bunch of violent shit in my head right now.

In the car, on Beach Boulevard, I said to her, "Do you like to swim?"

"Sure."

"I do, too. It's driving me crazy being this close to all that blue water and not taking a dip."

"And our motel doesn't have a pool, Johnny. I know. Bummer."

Our motel. Something about her putting it that way was nice. And troubling.

"*I* know where we can swim," she said, sitting up with rare enthusiasm. "Gulf's too cold right now, but there's a hotel where they know me."

"Yeah?"

"We could stop at one of these souvenir stands and buy suits. If you want."

"Man, I'd like that, Luann."

She pointed to one of the tourist-trap stores on the south side of the four-lane blacktop and I pulled in. My trunks cost ten bucks, her bikini twenty. Highway robbery. Well, this *was* a highway....

When she pointed to the hotel where she wanted me to pull in, I froze for a second.

She caught it. "What's wrong, Johnny?"

"Nothing," I said.

The hotel was a Tudor affair of white stucco and dark wood trim, and the sign on the overhang where you pulled in for check-in said in fancy English lettering:

FANTASY SWEETS
YOUR WISH IS OUR COMMAND.

What the hell. Like they said on *Hawaii Five-O*, I could case the joint.

We went in a rear door close to the pool, which was in a big echoey area. Along one wall, the sliding glass of motel rooms opened onto this chlorine-scented chamber, with its giant twisty slide for kiddies and a ceiling that could be cranked back in warm weather, closed now. Apparently seventy degrees was arctic weather for Biloxi.

We hadn't cleared this with anybody, but nobody said a word as we headed into the changing rooms and got into our suits. My boxer-style trunks were blue polyester, her suit a modest two-piece with pink flowers on a royal blue that wouldn't impress the crowd at Mr. Woody's.

The water was warm, not too warm, but like Goldilocks said, just right. The best part was that we had it all to ourselves. She didn't really swim, just kind of walked around *ooohing* and *aaahing* in the shallow till she got to the edge of the deep, enjoying the feel of it on her pretty skin. She went down the slide a few times, laughing as she went, as happy as I'd ever seen her, looking distressingly young. Maybe she wasn't nineteen. Not that it mattered in Mississippi. I figured legal age here must be around fourteen, thirteen for cousins.

I took some nice long laps, though the layout of the pool was odd, sort of scalloped and accommodating that big slide. Still, it relaxed me, and I got used to it. Tonight held real promise for getting this job done. I was starting to feel an attachment for this blonde kid in the floral bikini, and what that meant was, I better wrap this thing the fuck up. I was approaching get-out-of-Dodge time.

She did a little dog-paddling and I swam on my back for a while, and after half an hour we went over to the hot tub and relaxed. Sure, we had one of those back at the Tropical, but this one really put out some heat. There was room to sit back and stretch out your legs and kick a little, too.

Having to work my voice up over the bubble action, I said, "Is this whole place those theme suites?"

She shook her head. Almost had to shout when she answered: "No. This is mostly just a hotel. There's one wing of those."

"How many?"

"Oh. Six, I think." She thought, then nodded. "Six."

"I hear some of them are pretty wild."

She nodded again, smiling, but just a little. "You want to fuck in one?"

"You must be in really solid with the management."

"They know me here. You wanna take a tour?"

"Sure."

We got dressed. She walked me to the front desk. The interior of the place was similar to the exterior—stucco off-white walls trimmed with very rough wood, cheap stuff painted dark brown, the carpet indoor/outdoor stuff. Not any fantasy of mine. The check-in area was surprisingly small, with a gas fireplace I doubted got lighted much in a wall that was otherwise a bookcase offering up *Reader's Digest* condensed-book volumes.

Nobody was behind the desk, and an office visible through an open doorway was similarly empty. I was about to ding the desk bell when Luann clutched my wrist.

"Don't bother," she said.

She got behind the counter and from a wall of keys plucked an unmarked one from the far left of the bottom row.

She held it up like a prize, grinning. "Master key. We'll put it back before it's missed."

I followed her up the open stairs, also made of that rough cheap dark-painted wood, and down a hallway. She opened a door and we went into a room with a castle motif—gray-silver textured walls with matching hard-foam pillars, a big canopy double bed with gold-trimmed scarlet velvet spread, several decent pieces of faux-period furniture, and a definitely not authentic suit of armor. In an area past a foam archway was that typical Medieval touch: a hot tub. But it was fun. Well-executed crap.

Next was a typical bridal suite centered on a heart-shaped bed with a heart-shaped mirror overhead, plus lots of red velvet and cupids and red faux-leather furniture and so on. We looked at a space capsule room, an igloo room, and a jungle room. In the latter, Luann pulled off her hot pants and leaned over the zebra-print bed under mosquito netting and presented me with a heart-shaped behind better suited to the bridal suite. Not wanting to hurt her feelings, I took her up on it. The roundness and tightness of her made for a quick one.

With her hot pants in hand, she padded on the green-shag jungle carpet into a bathroom with banana wallpaper and freshened up in a traditional tub—the big hot tub with the waterfall in the outer room seemed suited for less practical matters.

"You didn't come," I said.

She shrugged. "I will another time. This was just for some naughty fun."

If you were wondering what kind of fun might seem naughty to a nineteen-year-old stripper/hooker, now you know.

"One more room to show you," she said. "Caligula Suite."

I wondered if it came with a horse.

Turned out it didn't, but nonetheless was the most elaborate of the suites by far. We went in through an employees-only door (guests entered a floor down) onto a balcony that included a round canopy bed supported by faux-marble columns with a pinkish cast, the carpet a deeper pink. Those pink columns were everywhere, including the orgy-size hot tub below where rose petals floated. Several plump couches down there suggested the room could also be used for a swingers' party. Mirrors, artificial greenery, purple drapes and naked statues of both sexes added to the Ancient Rome effect, even if the projection TV and full bar didn't.

When we returned to the front desk, a clerk had materialized—a pimple-faced guy in glasses (repaired at the bridge by adhesive tape) and a white shirt and black bow tie and no chin. He apparently misplaced his pocket protector.

He broke out into a big smile, seeing Luann.

"Hiiiii, Lolita," he said breathlessly. When he stopped talking, he left his mouth open, apparently because you can't pant through your nose.

"I just gave my friend a tour, Henry." She smiled at him and held up the master key like a fish she'd just caught. "Hope you don't mind."

"Not at all, not at all." He grinned stupidly and took the key from her and placed it back on its bottom-row hook, in its unlabeled position. "Anytime, anything, Lo-li-ta."

Brother, did that trip off his tongue repulsively.

I took her back to the Tropical and deposited her in her room.

"Mr. Killian has a date tonight," I said. "And I'm the chaperone."

"Probably where we just were."

"Why do you say that?"

She shrugged. "That's where he always takes 'em."

I had the uncomfortable feeling she'd been in that Caligula Suite with Killian herself. Why it made me uncomfortable, I couldn't tell you.

She was saying, "You want me when you get back, Johnny, just knock on the connectin' door."

"I probably will, unless I'm really tired. Don't take it as an insult if I don't."

"I won't."

"If you get hungry, use room service and charge it to me."

"Okay. There's movies on NBC and CBS I can watch."

"No series tonight?"

"No. *Partridge Family*?" She made a "yuck" face.

Who needed *TV Guide* with Luann in your life?

She gave me a little girl riffle of her fingers that was her wave and closed herself away.

I needed to get ready for tonight. I had an extra nine-millimeter barrel in my suitcase that I replaced on the weapon, having disposed of the previous barrel down a sewer opening last night. Even in a corrupt town like Biloxi, forensics can bite you in the ass.

Also in my suitcase was a silencer for the Browning, but it was a tubular eight-inch affair that would have to be kept in a pocket. That was one thing the tailor at Godchaux's hadn't allowed for. My thinking was that I probably wouldn't need it. A pillow or a shot with the barrel pressed against the flesh should suffice. So in the suitcase it stayed.

I cleaned the weapon, field-stripping it and wiping down the components, even the new barrel, which obviously didn't need it, applied solvent, scrubbed everything with a toothbrush (not *that* toothbrush, smart-ass), wiped everything down, oiled and greased the parts, then reassembled it.

I also used a slightly damp washcloth on the inside and out-side of the shoulder holster, then with the dry part of the cloth worked in a few drops of leather balm. I hadn't done this for a while, because I don't usually wear a shoulder holster.

As promised, Killian was alone that evening when we met in the Tropical lobby at 7:45. For once he was not in a dark tailored suit—this was a casual night out for the boss, after all. He wore a kelly-green long-sleeve shirt with pointed collars, a white-orange-and-green Italian silk scarf knotted to one side of his throat, and flared jeans with a green-and-yellow tapestry pattern, like a really ugly Navajo blanket.

Suddenly those black suits seemed just fine. If Godchaux's had sent threads like that to my room, I'd have gone AWOL quicker than Tommy at the Bottoms Up.

The desk clerk, the smirky blond again, did not appear to notice us pass, busy checking in a guest. I liked the way this was going. None of the black-suit boys upstairs had seen me this evening, and probably Killian hadn't mentioned me to them, soul of discretion that he was in the adultery department.

At the Fantasy Sweets, we went in the same back way Luann and I had earlier. But Killian did not lead me toward the front of the building and the check-in desk, instead turning down a hallway. Quickly we reached a door with no number on its dark rough surface, just a bronze plaque that said "Caligula Suite."

Killian turned to me with a sly smile. I was having trouble getting used to him in anything but black. If he poked me in the eye with one of those collars, I would strangle him with that dumb scarf.

"I'm going to be a while," he said. "Probably a good two hours. There are chairs in the lobby. Get yourself one—but stay alert. With your help, Mr. Quarry, I've made new enemies this week."

"And pissed off old ones," I reminded him.

He gave me a patronizing pat on the shoulder, used his room key and went in.

I waited about half an hour before heading to the small lobby. No one had wandered down the surprisingly narrow corridor in all that time—place seemed very dead. Off-season rearing its head again.

The nerdy desk clerk (or any desk clerk for that matter) was not behind the counter, a small sign that said "RING FOR SER-VICE" leaning against the dinger. The clerk's office door was closed. Napping or whacking off or something. No other guests in the mini-lobby, either.

I had a look out a narrow vertical window beside the entrance, to see if anybody was about to check in.

Nobody.

I slipped behind the counter and plucked the master key off its unmarked hook. I also helped myself to a straight-back chair from the wall adjacent to the Reader's Digest Book Club shelves.

For another forty minutes or so, I sat with my back to the wall near the door to the Caligula Suite, and tried not to be nervous. Usually my nerves are very steady, and they really weren't that bad tonight. Just not as good as usual.

Normally I would be in control of a situation. Tonight I had control of certain elements, but no control over others.

There are always unexpected possibilities in the contract business, even when you have first-rate intel on the patterns of a target. I would give the average hit about 90% reliability based upon what the passive half of the team has learned and provided.

But that other 10% was impossible to get rid of—human beings being fucked-up creatures means you never know what curves might be thrown your way. And here in Biloxi I was improvising and bobbing and weaving, and the curves were coming at me from left and right and front and back, like rounds in a firefight.

Speaking of curves, at about the hour-and-a-half point, the door opened and a woman came out, her manner crisp yet casual.

In her well-preserved forties, she was tall and curvy in a top-heavy way, her dark blonde hair up, her narrow face with the high cheekbones of a model and the heavy blue eye shadow of a porn star. She sported a stylish white pants suit with a black-and-white checked vest under a blazer-style jacket, flared trousers, and open-toe white sandals. Like Killian, she had a scarf knotted at her neck, but hers was a solid yellow.

Mrs. Somebody swung her head in my direction, and her gold hoop earrings took the trip. I'd gotten to my feet and she was giving me a Mona Lisa smile and an even smaller nod before walking briskly off toward the rear exit. Not a lot of sex in her gait, just efficiency. Yet she oozed sex just the same—sex and money.

The wife of somebody with bucks, well worth the bang.

She'd seen me. But then I'd seen her. And who was it that said trust was when you have something on the other guy?

I gave it fifteen minutes. All through the nearly two hours I'd been seated here in the corridor, not a single guest or hotel employee had made an appearance. I got up, ditched the chair around a corner, and took the rear stairs up a flight. At the employee's entrance to the Caligula Suite, I got the master key out, used it as quietly as possible, edged open the door, dropped the key in my suitcoat pocket, withdrew my nine millimeter from under my left arm, and went slowly in.

The smell of chlorine and the bubbling of the Jacuzzi told me where I'd find Killian. The rumpled, unmade bed and his ugly casual clothes on a white pseudo-Roman chair said the same. Edging to the white railing, I peered down at the hot tub in the room's center.

His back to me, his dark hair a damp skullcap, Killian was naked in the faux-marble tub, sitting on one of the steps down into the frothing water, his shoulders and the upper half of his chest exposed. His arms were spread, like a king on his throne, or maybe Caesar on whatever the hell he sat on. Anyway, Jack Killian looked relaxed and his head was tilted down, just a little. A glass of red wine was near his right hand.

He appeared to be sleeping, though he might be awake and merely very relaxed. Somebody else's wife, and a hell of a one, had recently helped him rumple those sheets in the balcony bed. He had a right to be tired. And in that steamy, churning Jacuzzi, a right to be relaxed.

But I couldn't see his damn eyes, so whether he was slumbering or just unwinding, I couldn't tell for sure.

The stairs down had a bit of a curve to them, but they were carpeted and absorbed my footsteps, so I was able to keep the gun aimed at him all the way down. Not seeing his eyes was unsettling, but both his hands were showing and no weapon seemed at reach.

I approached him from behind with the nine millimeter raised. Probably should have brought a pillow down with me, but I didn't relish the awkwardness of that. If I put the nose of the nine millimeter to back of his skull, the effect would be ideal though noisy. I could press the nose into his back, opposite his heart, flush with his flesh, and the sound would be muffled. This whirlpool would help.

But I didn't do either. I moved quietly around to his left and saw that he was indeed asleep, his chest heaving, his breath heavy. He was just short of sawing logs. His hair, appropriately enough, made Caesar-like ringlets on his forehead.

I put the gun away.

I slipped out of the black suit coat and tossed it on a nearby chair. Fortunately I was in a short-sleeve shirt. I tossed the tie over my shoulder as my right hand took him by the wet hair atop his head and my left gripped a shoulder and shoved him under.

I held him there a long time and when he began to struggle, it was half-hearted, sluggish. That was good. I wasn't holding onto him in a way that would leave bruises.

An unsettling thing happened, though, as the automatic turn-off stopped the Jacuzzi, and now the only bubbling was coming from Killian.

But soon it stopped, too.

TEN

Somebody said once that it's better to be lucky than smart. But the truth is, it's best to be lucky *and* smart.

Last night I'd certainly been lucky. The hotel had been under-populated and even the desk clerk had been a ghost. But I'd been at least a little smart, too. When we arrived at the Fantasy Sweets last night, I left the Caddy unlocked, so that I could leave the car keys with Killian in the Caligula Suite and still be able to wipe my fingerprints off the steering wheel before hoofing it the three blocks to the Tropical.

From the phone booth across the highway, I'd called Mr. Woody at his club and said, "Just so you know, Jack Killian drove himself to the Fantasy Sweets around eight this evening. I had the night off."

"So then…"

"So then you might want to have somebody at the hotel check on him. Like maybe you expected him to stop by Mr. Woody's at ten or so but you haven't heard from him."

"It isn't ten."

Was he slow on the uptake or what?

Patiently, I said, "Wait till eleven and call the desk at the hotel. To check on Jackie boy. You know, if you haven't heard from him."

"All right. Sorry. I follow."

"Good. Good night."

"Quarry!"

"Yeah?"

"Listen, come around tomorrow mornin'. We should talk about the future."

"What future?"

"Well, the comin' days."

"I'm out of here by noon."

"No. Come see me first."

"Where? Your club?"

"My home. Got a pad and somethin' to write with?"

I wrote down the directions and said I'd see him at ten.

"Uh, Quarry…?"

"Yeah?"

"Just in case? You might talk to the girl."

He meant Luann, getting her to cover for me. Talking murder on a possibly tapped phone was always a pain in the ass.

So this morning around eight I knocked on the connecting door between our rooms. I had to do it a couple of times before Luann opened it and stood there yawning, raising her hands over her head. She'd been sleeping in a Led Zeppelin t-shirt and the yawn pulled it up to reveal her triangular muff like a curtain rising at the start of a show.

I wasn't in the mood for a show or anything else. I had no desire to hang around Biloxi for even a morning, and needed a clean break with my little companion here. But Mr. Woody had thrown a wrench in my works, maybe just a morning's worth, but a wrench.

"Let's get some breakfast," I said.

"Okay. Give me fifteen."

"Take twenty."

We both showered and got dressed. She emerged through the connecting door in the red top and striped jeans from the Dixie Club trip. Out of habit, and as not to raise any suspicion if the wrong somebody noticed me, I got into my last clean black suit, a pale blue shirt and a red-and-navy tie. Mr. Conservative Businessman, that's me.

I drove us to a nearby Waffle House where, just to be rebels, we had pancakes. Silver-dollar ones. This time I remembered to ask for unsweetened iced tea. Luann looked a little tired to me, puffy around the eyes.

"Rough night?" I asked.

"Watched TV too late. You?"

"That's what I want to talk to you about."

"Oh?"

"I don't think it'll come up, but if anybody asks, we watched TV together last night."

"Oh. Okay. Like who would ask?"

"Cops maybe. Probably won't happen."

She frowned just a touch. "Should I tell you what I…what we watched?"

"Wouldn't hurt."

She told me what the movies were—*The Impossible Years* with David Niven and *In the Cool of the Day* with Hanoi Jane—and it turned out I'd seen them both first-run, so no synopses were required. Both terrible.

"You need to forget what I told you," I said, "about where I was going and what I was doing last night."

"You were watchin' movies with me."

"Good girl. Thanks."

She shrugged and ate a forkful of pancakes. I had taken her so far off her diet there was no going back. Before she knew it, she'd be a big fat sloppy hundred-and-five.

"I have to work at Mr. Woody's tonight," she said. "A dancer called in sick."

"Oh. Well, I guess you can't loaf around with me forever."

She smiled and licked maple syrup of her fork. "I'd like to, Johnny. I'm done at eleven. Out by eleven-fifteen."

"Like me to pick you up?"

"If you want."

"That'd be swell."

She drank some orange juice. "You gonna stay around town a while?"

"I honestly don't know."

"If you do, you can't live in a motel forever."

Killian had. Of course, forever hadn't taken that long.

I said, "Neither can you, Luann."

"Well...if you got an apartment, I wouldn't mind movin' out of mine. Be cool to live somewhere with no pot smoke and girls makin' noise. When they're making it. You know."

"Luann...I don't think I'll be in Biloxi that long."

She nodded. "Guess I gotta face up to it."

"To what, honey?"

"That it's back to Mr. Woody's for me." She shrugged. "Oh well. A couple three years, I can cash out and go somewhere's else. Do somethin' else."

"Yeah? Like what?"

She shrugged. "Buy my own strip bar maybe."

That was the problem, living in a particular bubble: you only saw the possibilities that were inside that bubble.

Judging by the upscale neighborhood Woodrow Colton lived in, running sleazy joints on Biloxi's Strip paid very goddamn well. The rambling shades-of-brown-brick ranch-style, with its wide drive and double carport, perched on a tree-shaded, shrub-hugged, gently sloping lawn on Country Club Lane, which said it all.

I pulled my rental Chevelle in behind the two-tone brown Cadillac in the carport—the Dixie Mafia boys did love their Caddies. The vehicle looked like its colors had been selected to go with the house. Or maybe it was vice versa.

I felt like a Mormon or Jehovah's Witness in my black suit,

going up the walk to the deeply recessed front door—all I lacked was Good Books. I rang the bell and Mr. Woody answered almost immediately, all magnified eyes and grinning teeth as usual. He was in khaki pants, an untucked cream-color cotton shirt, and sandals, a glass of Scotch in hand, though it was only late morning. He looked like a gardener who was sneaking a drink while the wealthy homeowner was away.

"Come in, come in," he said, waving me to do so, and I did. He gave me a used-car salesman's smile. "Let's talk by the pool."

The house we moved through was really something—rich wood floors, pastel plaster walls, open-beamed ceilings, modern kitchen, elaborate bar, all very open, giving a glimpse of a dining room here, living room with fieldstone fireplace there, taste-fully selected Southern-landscape artwork on walls, and plush contemporary furnishings.

He led me into a pool area almost as expansive as the one at the Fantasy Sweets, only nicer. This screened-in cathedral overlooked a landscaped backyard that fell to a stream or a river or something—anyway, water enough to rate a dock and a motorboat. This was the kind of Olympic-sized pool I wished I owned.

He realized he had a drink in hand, and as he gestured me to a black wrought-iron chair at a black wrought-iron table, he asked, "Somethin' to drink? Barq's maybe?"

I sat. "Coke would be nice."

He had a smaller bar out here, so that was no problem. He delivered a glass of the pop with ice and then settled next to me in his own black wrought-iron chair.

"Very safe to talk here," he said, though the pool area made his words reverberate some. "I have it debugged now and then."

"For microphones or cockroaches?"

He smiled a little as he sipped his Scotch. "Both. The mikes are small these days, Quarry, and the cockroaches are big."

Enough small talk.

I said, "Why shouldn't I leave town, Woody?"

"All sorts of reasons, son." A hand brushed his silver comb-over, as if it needed help under that hairspray. "Startin' with, you *owe* me that much."

"Owe you? What do you have to do with it?"

"I recommended you. That's known by more than just us and the late Jackie. If the new man, who I recommended, up and disappears, right after Jackie's demise, how does that look?"

"What does it matter how it looks? Killian died accidentally. Drank too much red wine, fell asleep, and drowned in his own decadence."

That was a line Killian might have appreciated. Possibly it was lost on Mr. Woody.

"Quarry, accidental drownin' will no doubt be the official determination. As you might guess, I've spent considerable time, startin' in the wee hours of last night and the early mornin', in discussion with Sheriff Delmar. He will do everythin' in his considerable power to see that this death goes down as a tragic mishap. Why, there won't even be an autopsy."

"I don't think an autopsy would show anything. He really was asleep. I just helped him a little."

He waved his free hand. "Be that as it may, among Jackie's people are a number of loyal souls who simply must not suspect that I played a role, however minor, in the passin' of the torch to my own self. So I would appreciate it very much if you would stick around for a while."

"What's 'a while?' "

"Maybe a week. Shade more, shade less." He leaned over and the magnified hazel eyes narrowed while his toothy smile expanded. "I can arrange for that little Lolita gal to keep you company as long as you're here. Or if you're bored with her, we can line up somebody else to tickle your fancy and wet your wick."

"The girl is fine. She's no trouble."

He gave a *heh-heh* laugh. "Doesn't surprise me. She's a sweet young thing. I've known her a long time, Quarry. Long time."

"Yeah. Since she was knee-high to a grasshopper. I remember."

He frowned, seemingly in concern, not irritation. "Are you cross with me, son? Have I done somethin' to offend? After all, I thought I'd been of considerable help to you."

"You were. You are. I'm just…after a job, what I normally do? Is get the hell out. That's the way it's usually done, anyway. I really should already be gone."

"But what is there about this job that's been 'usual?' "

He had a point.

"You just hang around the Tropical for a few days," he said with a flip of the hand. "I'll be movin' my office into Jackie's in that upstairs suite of his. I don't really require the livin' quarters, but it'll be nice to have a little hideaway, 'way from home." He leaned in conspiratorially, licking his lips, leaving them wet. "Never know when you might desire a night away from the little woman."

"Yeah. Sure. You're keeping Killian's staff on?"

He nodded. "But I may loosen up the dress code. Let me give it some thought, over the next day or so, as to what exact role you'll play durin' this…transitional period."

"Will I have to talk to cops? That sheriff or any deputies?"

He shook his head. "No one knows that you were at the Fantasy Sweets last night."

"You know. I know." Luann knew.

He half-smiled. "Well, it's a funny thing. Jackie used to always talk about the basis of trust. He said—"

"I heard it."

My host shrugged, had a last sip of Scotch. "Tell you what, Quarry. Agree to stay another week, and you'll find ten grand in your stockin', and you won't even have to wait till Christmas."

"Woody, that's generous, more than generous…but I need to clear all this with the Broker. Like I said, he'll be expecting me to be gone already."

But Mr. Woody had begun shaking his head halfway through that. "Quarry, I've *already* discussed this with the Broker."

"What? When?"

"This mornin'."

"By phone?"

"Not by semaphore, son. You should call him yourself. See what his instructions are. I think you'll find they mirror my own."

A female voice behind us said, "Woody! Do you have a minute? Sorry to interrupt…."

He turned to look at her, poised in the opening of glass doors, and so did I.

Woody had scored himself a fine-looking wife. Or at least I didn't figure his housekeeper was a tall dark-blonde with the features of a model and the bosom of a centerfold. She was in a kind of half-sarong with a halter top, a tropical print of green and yellow and white. Her sandals were open-toed, with red nails. Her fingernails were red, too.

"You're not interruptin' anythin' much, sweetheart," he said, and rose, and presented her with a loving smile that held no indication of a desire for a getaway pad minus the "little woman." Who was easily two inches taller than him.

She came hesitantly over and Mr. Woody said, "This is John Quarry, dear. He was workin' for Jackie but he's with me now."

Her smile was quick. "I guess everyone is now." She nodded. "Mr. Quarry. Pleasure."

I was on my feet and took the hand she offered, not shaking it, just sort of holding and squeezing it a little. "Mrs. Colton."

"Call me Wanda, please." Then her attention went to her husband. "I'm goin' out golfin' this afternoon with my gal pals. Do you mind catchin' dinner on your way to the club?"

"Not at all, darlin'," he said, and beamed at her.

She nodded, smiled politely to me, and was gone.

But her eyes had confirmed that she'd recognized me just as I had recognized her…

…as the married woman I'd seen leaving the Caligula Suite last night.

Luann and I had lunch at The Dockside. Nothing of import occurred, although she was happy to hear I would be staying in Biloxi for a while.

I said, "Mr. Woody says you can stay on as my tour guide, if you like."

"Is that what I am?"

"No. Much more, honey."

But I really didn't know what she was. I knew I liked her, and wasn't having a fuck bunny on call the dream of every road-company Hefner? Only on some level, she was just one more aspect of this job that was off-kilter.

She had to go in to the club at two-thirty that afternoon. I dropped her off at the front door of Mr. Woody's and promised to return at eleven-fifteen.

I parked the Chevelle in the space next to the outer door of my Tropical room but did not go in. Instead, I hiked across the highway to the phone booth that was becoming my home away from home.

I got the Broker right away.

I told him, in the necessarily elliptical fashion, that the Killian job was done but that Woody Colton expected me to hang around for a while, apparently to help cover his ass with the troops.

"He says," I said, "that he talked to you about this."

"He did," the Broker said. "His reasoning is sound. But I would stay no longer than a week. I don't want Woodrow getting used to you."

"What do you mean?"

"A young man of your skills, your aptitude, would come in handy. Can't have you stolen away from me."

"Sweet talker."

The conversation with the Broker went on a while after that, but covered nothing new. Oh, he promised me an extra five grand for staying another week. Nothing else of significance.

In the hotel room, I considered climbing into the hot tub to relax, but thought better of it, even though I hadn't had any red wine. But at least I could get out of the tailored suit and tie and into something comfortable. I put on a blue t-shirt and jeans and flopped on the bed.

I'm not sure how long I'd been sleeping when the knock came. Oddly, it was from the door to the outside, by the parked Chevelle, not the hall one. I got the nine millimeter from the nightstand and went to the door, which had no night-latch, and cracked it.

A beautiful high-cheekboned female face looked at me plaintively, the dark blue eyes going surprisingly well with the lighter blue eye shadow.

"Please," Mrs. Woodrow Colton said. Her hair was up, like it had been last night. "Might we talk?"

"Sure," I said, and let her in, keeping the pistol behind my back.

She was in a light-blue pullover skirt that looked like a Polo shirt with a long tail, though in this case it made a short mini. A metallic belt was at her narrow waist. Too young an outfit for her, but I'm not a stickler about stuff like that.

She touched my shoulder, standing very near to me. She was as tall as me in her sandals with heels. Her narrow face was almost horsey, but the features were too finely carved for that to be a problem. She smelled great. My Sin, I think. Somebody's sin.

In a breathy contralto, she said, "You were kind not to say anything in front of Woody."

"You're welcome."

Her eyes popped. "No one can know I was there last night."

"I get that."

She nodded, then walked to the bed and sat on the foot, her knees together primly. Those legs were a little slender for my taste, but my God they went on and on.

"There's nothing I can give you for your silence," she stated.

"I don't want anything."

"Woody and me, all our money is in a joint account. If I withdrew somethin', he'd know. Woody would know."

"Not necessary."

She shook her head and a few dark-blonde tendrils fled the pinned-up hair. "You don't know him."

"Sure I do."

"You think he's nice. You think he's sweet."

"I wouldn't say sweet."

"He can be brutal. He can be violent. He might…would you think I exaggerate if I said he might kill me?"

"No. People have been known to do that."

"I wouldn't be surprised if…if *he* had Jack killed. If somebody came in after I left, somebody he hired, and drowned him or something."

"Pretty far-fetched." Was she fucking with me?

"Mr. Quarry...should I call you 'Mr. Quarry?' "

"Just Quarry is fine. Most people call me that."

"Your last name?"

"Yeah. Unless you want to call me 'Jack.' "

"No! No."

Didn't think so.

She patted the bed next to her. I came over and sat, bringing the nine millimeter with me, draping it in my lap.

"What's that for?" she asked, wide-eyed.

"Surprises. What do you want, Mrs. Colton?"

"Call me Wanda."

"Okay. What do you want, Wanda?"

But she didn't answer, at least not directly.

"Quarry...I'll try to get used to that...Quarry, have you talked to the police?"

"No. As far as they're concerned, I wasn't there last night."

"But you were."

"No. Mr. Killian drove himself."

She thought about that. "So you can't say a word about seein' me there without..."

"That's right. So you don't really have anything to worry about."

"That's wonderful. Oh...I mean, nothing's wonderful about it, but...thank you. Thank you so much."

"It's mutually beneficial, that's all. Somebody once told me that trust is when two people each have something on the other."

"I heard that somewhere, too."

"So then we're cool."

"We're…we're cool. But I would *still* like to thank you."

She stood. She undid the belt, tossed it with a clunk on the nearby bureau by where the TV squatted. "Put that gun somewhere."

I got up and placed it on the nightstand, then turned to her and said, "I don't need any thanks."

"Do you have any protection?"

"Besides the gun?"

"Yes. Besides the gun."

"You mean, like Trojans?"

"Yes. I mean like Trojans."

I shook my head. "Not necessary."

"Maybe my thanks aren't. But a Trojan is."

She pulled the Polo dress over her head and tossed it like a spent paper cup. Then the only thing she was wearing was a wicked smile. She was olive-complected and those legs didn't stop till her neatly trimmed pubic triangle demanded it. The flare of her hips was emphasized by the narrowness of her waist, and the large full breasts drooped some, due to age and gravity, but were astonishing nonetheless, their areolae the size of silver-dollar pancakes at the Waffle House.

She shoved me onto the bed. I really didn't need this. I'd been having so much sex with Luann lately I was raw.

She demanded, "The Trojans—where are they?"

It was like the demand of a Greek goddess.

I pointed to the opposite nightstand, the one without the gun. She found the rubbers, tossed one little package on the bed. There was an unsettling confidence about her—she moved like a man. Nothing mannish about her ass, though, which was beautifully shaped and dimpled. She came over, undid my belt and yanked my jeans and shorts down around my ankles. She snugged the Trojan onto the part of me currently doing my thinking. She piled two pillows against the headboard and said, "Get comfy."

I got comfy.

She crawled up between my legs like a panther on the prowl and the eyes were cold as she said, "Just so you know—I don't suck dick."

"Nobody's perfect," I said.

She climbed onboard and fucked me like I was a steer she was trying to break, and she never got tossed. Her eyes and nostrils flared and her upper lip curled back over feral teeth and the long tips of the huge breasts shook at me like scolding fingers. I was breathing so hard I was wheezing, and then with me still in her, she rolled us over and wrapped the endless legs around me and squeezed and squeezed and churned her hips in rhythmic abandon. It was savage and it was intense and it was lustful as hell, without an ounce of tenderness. It was like fucking Hitler, if Hitler had great tits and a nice ass.

She got off me and went in the bathroom and washed up and came back and gave me a businesslike look, her head tilted. "So do we have an understandin'?"

"Sure."

"I wasn't there last night. You weren't there last night."

"Where?"

"Good," she said. She gathered her purse and was about to go out the door, then turned and came over and gave me a little kiss on the forehead. I was still on my back with my dick wilting into the damp rubber.

"Bye, Quarry," she said.

And was gone.

I went in and pitched the rubber in the crapper, making sure it flushed—couldn't have my little hooker knowing I had cheated on her with Mrs. Caligula—and took a long, hot shower. I felt dirty. I never felt this way after killing somebody, but this was different. I'd come hard and long and I knew that over the years there would be nights when I would reflect on this wild, sudden, bizarre fuck and remember just how hard and long I'd come and how little I'd felt.

Christ, I wanted out of Biloxi. There was just too much killing and fucking going on in this goddamn town.

Even for me.

ELEVEN

I pulled off Highway 90 on the beach side, into the under-illuminated lot of the warehouse-like strip club, its painted MR. WOODY'S sign lit up by low-mounted white floods. The place looked to be doing okay off-season business, a good dozen cars worth, anyway. For the hell of it, I drove around to the mini-casino, which announced itself modestly in a window with a small LUCKY SEVEN neon sharing space with glowing beer signs. Nine or ten vehicles back here—respectable but nothing to brag about on a Friday night. Two months from now it would be packed.

When I swung the Chevelle back around to the front of the building, Luann was just coming out, a canvas tote bag in hand. Wearing no make-up, she was in a loose gray t-shirt with cut-off sleeves and baggy jeans and sandals, her long hair ponytailed back. A stripper leaving a club after her last set did not go out into the world—much less the parking lot—all dolled-up. Not unless she was looking for a john.

And Luann already had a john, right?

I leaned across and opened the door for her and she got in and gave me a tiny smile, shutting herself in. The sweatshirt, I noticed, said OLE MISS in red letters. Somehow I didn't figure Luann had ever attended.

"Thanks," she said.

"Back to the old bump-and-grind, huh?"

My levity didn't register on her. "Just fillin' in. You're still my…you know."

"Assignment?"

She shrugged, flicked me another smile.

My God, in the dashboard glow, without make-up, hair off her shoulders and up in a girlish ponytail, boobs lost in that oversize tee, she looked about thirteen. The age her mother sold her.

She was staring straight ahead. It was only five minutes down the Strip to the Tropical, but her silence made it seem longer.

Halfway there, I asked, "Something wrong, Luann?"

"No. Tired is all."

"Sure that's it?"

She nodded a couple times.

Since I'd already been laid today, I generously said, "Take the night off, why don't you? You can go to your room."

That last came off funny—like I was a daddy sending his daughter upstairs for punishment.

She swallowed and, very quietly, said, "Thanks. Maybe I should. I'm pretty beat."

Something *was* wrong. Had something happened tonight at the club? That had to be it. But I didn't press it.

At the Tropical, I pulled the Chevelle into its slot and we stepped into the motel room using that outer entrance.

I hadn't even switched on the light when she looked up at me and said, "We have to talk."

Never in the history of mankind, when a female spoke those words to a male, did that phrase precede anything positive. Not in your bunk bed at eight years, not in junior high after a sock hop, not in your first year of marriage, not in your last year of marriage, and certainly not in a motel room with a little hooker you'd been banging for half a week.

This couldn't be about me knocking her up or anything. I hadn't been in town that long.

The door to the outside was still ajar. Standing there in the near dark, I asked, "Honey, is something wrong?"

She glanced into the barely visible motel room and said, "Not here. You never know about these rooms. Let's go somewhere."

"How about across the street?"

"There's nothin' across the street."

"Right."

She tossed her canvas tote inside and we went back out. I closed the motel room door and took her hand and we made our way through four light lanes of traffic and across the sidewalk to the beach. In one direction was that small-boat harbor, in the other could be seen the white shaft of a historic lighthouse. From here the sleazy clubs lining much of this stretch of Highway 90 weren't visible.

Like her, I was in jeans and a short-sleeve t-shirt. We were both young enough to seem like a couple of sweethearts out for a beachfront stroll. Maybe we went to Ole Miss.

The evening was pleasantly warm and slightly breezy. I sat on the slope of white sand about three feet from where water lazily lapped. Behind us were the lights of the city. Ahead was the Mississippi Sound and a handful of islands and all the Gulf beyond. Not much moon, but clear. Few clouds. Plenty of stars.

She was not sitting next to me. She had taken off her sandals and was wading along the water's edge. Not in a playful way. Just kind of walking, pacing really, going a few yards, turning, then walking back, making tiny splashes. Turning and starting over.

"This white beach is fake," she said, still pacing wetly.

"Seems real enough to me."

"It's not. They dredge it up from the bottom of the sea and these trucks spray it. Like stucco on a house."

"That's weird."

"Brings in tourists. Like the Strip." She glanced around the beach as she paced. "Before too long, when the season kicks in? Won't be so peaceful along here."

"No?"

She nodded, watched her feet lightly splash in the water. "They's a lot of drug deals go down on the sand. Girls sell sex or trade for a few lines. No cops around unless they need some arrests to look better." She sighed. "Pretty here by day, though."

"What's on your mind, Luann?"

She stopped pacing. Her stillness was stark against the easy lapping of the water. She was not quite a silhouette.

"I don't want to hurt you," she said.

"Well, I don't want you to. Come sit by me."

She thought about that and did, though she kept a little distance between us. She hugged her knees to herself. It was like Sandra Dee in *Gidget*, dreaming about surfing. But somehow I didn't think that was it.

"I know you're not evil," she said.

"That's good to hear."

"But I saw what you did the other night."

So that was what was bugging her. She'd probably been having trouble getting to sleep, thinking about that nightmare at the Dixie Club.

"You said it yourself, Luann," I said offhandedly. "That awful woman would have killed that little man with her hammer, and—"

"No," she said sharply, with a glance just as sharp, before looking back out into the surreal shimmer of Gulf water. "I mean *last* night."

"Last night...?"

"When you drowned that man."

That hit me low in the belly.

"What are you talking about, Luann?"

She swallowed, but her chin came up. She may have looked like a little bird but her face was full of large determination.

"Johnny, I followed you last night."

"What? Why…?"

"Just listen. You said Mr. Killian had a date at the Fantasy Sweets. I walked over there. It's only a few blocks. I guess you know I know my way around the place. One thing I didn't show you, when I give you that tour? Was the booth."

"Booth?" My stomach was tight. "What are you talking about?"

She shrugged. "There's this booth built in behind the balcony in that suite."

"Caligula Suite."

She nodded. "That's the one that Mr. Killian uses to get the goods on people."

And I understood her.

I got the whole goddamn picture in a fucking flash—the Caligula Suite was rigged for video recording. It was the most lavish of the theme rooms and the logical one for Killian to provide to politicians—and anyone else he wanted a hold over— for a fun Roman orgy-type evening with a fuck bunny or two. With everything on the house.

But in Biloxi, the house always won.

She was saying, "I been in that room plenty of times. Not the booth, I mean the bed and the hot tub. But I was in it before, too, the booth." She made a little grunt. "I must be on a dozen of them tapes."

Trying to keep my voice steady and unthreatening, I said, "Tell me about the booth, Luann."

"Small. Six by six maybe? A chair and two TVs side-by-side facin' you, and two big heavy machines on steel racks down below. Videotape machines. They're not that complicated. You just press 'record' and 'play,' at the same time. Won't work with just 'record.' "

"I see."

"I wish they made them to have at home. I could watch my shows any time I wanted."

"The booth, Luann."

She nodded. "There are two cameras out there in the room, tucked away, you know, hidden, like Allen Funt? One sees you on the bed. The other points down at the hot tub." She turned to me, reached for my hand, then thought better of it. "Johnny, I didn't go there to catch you, last night. You have to understand. You have to believe me."

"I believe you. Why *were* you there?"

She swallowed again. Gazed out at the Gulf, even as the gulf between us widened. "Some girls at work have been whisperin'."

"About what?"

"About how Mr. Killian is fuckin' Mr. Woody's wife. *Was* fuckin' Mrs. Woody's wife. I mean, he's dead now, right? Anyway, that suite was Mr. Killian's favorite. It's the nicest one. He must not have thought about how it was rigged to catch people. You know, that he could get caught in his own trap."

Keeping my voice nice and calm, I said, "Bet he never did. Why did you want to trap him, Luann?"

Her eyes were on the water. "I thought maybe if I had a tape of him fuckin' Mrs. Woody, then I could use it to get out of here. Biloxi sucks in case you didn't notice, and my life sucks worse than that. I could use that tape to make Mr. Woody let me go."

"Why not just *go*? You have money saved."

She shook her head and the ponytail swung. For a moment I was reminded of Kelly in the back room of the Bottoms Up. "I *do* have money saved, but it goes into an account with Mr. Woody's name on it. *And* mine, but I can't get at it unless he signs off."

Working at not showing anything, I said, "Okay. So you were going to sell him the tape? All right. But why not just *tell* him what you knew?"

"He wouldn't believe it. Not without that tape. He thinks his wife is a damn saint."

"He's wrong."

"Seems like. But I don't know her that well. She don't come around to the club much. But also I thought about maybe goin' to Mr. Killian instead. I hadn't made my mind up, which one. I just knew if I had that tape…I mean, tapes…one of the bed, one of the hot tub? I would have somethin' to hold over people."

"Something to use to blackmail Killian."

"That's an ugly word."

The sound of a small-craft motor echoed across the water. But you couldn't see anything moving out there.

"Yeah, it is," I said. "But that's the word for it, Luann— blackmail. And it would've been risky. Killian was a dangerous guy."

"So is Mr. Woody! You have no idea." She hugged herself, as if it had gotten suddenly chilly. I was feeling a kind of a chill myself. "Either way was risky. But I saw an opportunity and I took it. I'm…I'm sorry, Johnny."

I made myself smile a little. "You got nothing to be sorry about. You want out of this life. I understand that. You were, uh…in that booth last night when…?"

She nodded and the ponytail bobbed. "I saw what you did."

Five more words that never boded well.

She added, "On the TV."

That was so much of her life, wasn't it? What she saw on the

TV. Had *Hawaii Five-O* and fucking *Ironside* taught her about blackmail? Hadn't she noticed how those shows turned out for the blackmailers?

She was saying, "I wasn't there to get you on tape. I didn't mean to. You *know* that's true—I didn't know you was goin' there to do...what you did."

I said, "I guess I'm not your knight in shiny armor anymore."

She gave me a smile with some warmth in it. Actual warmth, and this time she did touch my hand. She was so damn small, I could have taken her by the waist and walked her into the water and very quickly she'd be as dead as Killian.

But that wouldn't solve the problem of the tapes.

Because she surely had them, and they weren't in her motel room. She'd gone to work this afternoon. She could have given them to a girlfriend or hidden them there or slipped home to her nearby apartment and stowed them somewhere and...shit. Maybe I could find them.

Maybe.

"That man was evil," she said. "That Mr. Killian. I'm *glad* he's dead. He done terrible things."

I wondered if some of those terrible things had been done to her. Maybe in that goddamn Caligula Suite. Ancient Rome had nothing on modern-day Biloxi.

Now she squeezed my hand, and those light-blue eyes were large with urgency. "Johnny, I want out. Of here, of my life, of this town. You may *think* Mr. Woody is a nice man..."

"I don't."

"...but he's just as bad as Mr. Killian. Maybe worse." She looked away, eyes on the water again. "When I was thirteen, he took me home with him and...broke me in. That's what he called it. Broke me in. For a month he fucked me every way there is to be fucked. I was bleedin' out my backside for weeks."

She shook her head, the pendulum of the ponytail swinging.

"Johnny, I've had girlfriends at the club just…disappear. Last year, one had a bad habit, you know, heroin? And she started lookin' bad, real skinny, and she fell down a couple times on stage, dancin', and then one night Mr. Woody, he walked her out into the parking lot and after that, she was just gone. I asked the other girls and they said don't ask. I asked Mr. Woody and he smiled with those big teeth and said, 'You really want to know, Sugar Tits?' "

This outburst, this outpouring of words and emotion, was not accompanied by tears. On the contrary, her pretty face was tight with anger. Some tremor in her voice, but contained. Controlled.

She was saying, "When I turned eighteen, I told Mr. Woody I wanted my money and wanted to go out on my own. It was after hours and he took me and threw me down on the stage and he had all the bouncers come over and they fuckin' *gangbanged* me, Johnny. It was just awful! I was on my back with come on my face and used rubbers all around. And when it was over, and I was cryin' my heart out, Mr. Woody himself come over and beat me till I was black and blue all over. I couldn't dance for two weeks. You may *think* he's nice…"

"I *don't*."

"…but he *is* evil. That's what I mean when I say, even knowin' that you *do* bad things, Johnny, that…that you aren't evil."

Gently, touching her hand, I said, "Luann. I need those tapes. You know I need those tapes."

"I know." She nodded reassuringly. "I do know. And I'll give them to you."

Relief flooded through me.

"Thank you, Luann. That means a lot to me."

"Oh I know. They got the gas chamber in Mississippi."

Another sucker punch to the belly.

She clutched my arm. "Johnny, I'm gonna give you them tapes. I *am*. But I have to ask you to do me a favor. It's kind of a big favor, but it's what I need."

"What favor?"

"And don't you *dare* use that word."

"What word?"

"Blackmail. This is a *favor* you'll do me, and then I'll give them to you as a gift, those tapes. You don't have to worry about copies, 'cause I don't know how to make them. If there's a way to hook up them two clunky tape machines, I don't know what it is."

She could have been fucking with me. She was smart enough to know that making copies was an issue. But I didn't think she was lying. I think she'd spent all day rationalizing how she was going to approach me about this, and the favor/gift thing was what she came up with.

I asked, "What's the favor?"

"I need you to kill somebody for me."

"Jesus, Luann…"

She held up a "stop" hand. "I *know* you do that. I think maybe you was brought here to do that to Mr. Killian. Maybe by Mr. Woody. I think that's why we went to the Dixie Club, too. For you to kill those people."

Said the little witness who I had thought it a good idea to bring along on the outing.

"So," she said, "I know you're a killer."

"Luann…"

"I don't think you *like* it. You kill like I fuck. It's a job, right? And maybe you only kill bad people. That would be nice. I mean, the four people I seen you kill all kind of deserved it."

"Listen to me now," I began, though I had no idea what I would say next.

"I know what you are. What you do." She frowned as she thought, and then she found the *Hawaii Five-O* word: "You're a hitman."

"Luann, please…"

She clenched both fists, steadied herself to say the last of the things she'd wanted to get me off alone to say.

"Johnny, I want you to do a hit for me. And then you can have those tapes. You can throw 'em out in the Gulf or you can break 'em up with a hammer, I don't care. They're yours. For doin' me a favor."

"What favor, Luann?"

"Johnny, you know what I need. Don't you already know?"

I did.

She said, "I need you to kill Mr. Woody for me."

TWELVE

Just after ten the next morning, I knocked on the door of what had been Killian's suite. No vestibule watchdogs on duty today, and the guy who answered—the one with the wide face, close-set eyes and butch haircut—was not in one of his late employer's standard-issue black suits. Instead he wore a red plaid sportcoat, dark red shirt with pointy collar, no tie and white slacks-socks-shoes. Was he going fucking golfing?

I wasn't in my black suit, either, with a dark brown sportcoat over the rust-color turtleneck and dark brown jeans I'd worn to the Dixie Club. The sportcoat, which I'd picked up at Gayfers before that same trip, was a little big and did a decent job of concealing the nine millimeter in its shoulder holster.

I was greeted with none of the formality of the previous administration's approach. The guy with the close-set eyes just nodded, said, "Quarry," and went off to do something else as I wandered into the suite. No other staff around. I headed toward what had been Killian's office and found the door open.

Mr. Woody, who fifteen minutes ago had summoned me up, was seated behind the aircraft-carrier desk, which was piled with file folders. A file cabinet nearby had its top drawer open with those below slightly ajar.

In a cream-color cotton shirt, a tan leisure-suit jacket draped over a leather-couch arm, Mr. Woody said, "Well, good mornin', Quarry. Isn't this just a lovely day?"

"Beauty."

"Sit down, son, sit down. Oh, there's orange juice and soft

drinks in the kitchen—go out and help yourself, if you like. I know you're no drinker."

He already had a glass of Scotch going.

"I'm fine," I said, sitting.

The previous tenant's personal framed autographed photos were carelessly tossed in cardboard boxes lining walls wearing nothing now but their nails. Everything in here looked a little off-kilter, except the liquor cart.

All those teeth grinned at me and the hazel eyes narrowed behind the magnifying lenses. "Pardon the mess. Hell, know how movin' day can be."

"Sure. You don't seem to have many helpers."

He waved that off. "I give most of the boys the day off. Jackie has his loyalists, you know. Best I handle 'em with kid gloves. Tough transition for some."

I just nodded.

A hand absentmindedly brushed the frozen silver combover. "Have you had a chance to mull what we spoke about?"

"You mean me staying on for a week? For ten grand? Hard to say no to that kind of money for so little time."

He slapped a hand on the desk; actually, on some folders. "Then you'll stay?"

"For a week."

"Capital."

Behind me a female voice, a breathy alto, said, "And what shall we do with *these* hideous things?"

I glanced back and Mrs. Woodrow Colter, her dark blonde hair up with a few tendrils loose, her tall slender top-heavy figure in a patchwork denim pants suit with a red bandana blouse and knotted scarf, stood poised in the open doorway. She had a framed abstract-art painting in either hand.

"Darlin'," Mr. Woody said, "just lean all that junk against the wall in the spare room. I know the gallery where Jackie got 'em from. Believe it or not, they're worth money." He glanced at me. "Quarry, you remember my wife—Wanda. Wanda, you remember Mr. Quarry."

I gave her a polite smile. "Mrs. Colton."

She gave me a nod. "Mr. Quarry."

Her eyes tightened, for a fraction of a second, then she turned and was gone.

Mr. Woody was looking after her fondly. "That is one handsome woman, Quarry. And *smaaaaart*." Confidentially, he said, "But let me tell you—she's mean as snake when you cross her. Do not fuck with *that* one."

"I'll keep that in mind."

He sat back, rocking in the swivel chair. "Quarry, I want to explore the possibility of a longer-term employment opportunity. You impress me as the kind of person I need about now. A young man with skills and abilities and a whole lot of potential."

I gave him half a grin. "I don't know about that, Woody. I'm a Northern boy. This part of the country and me don't mix."

"For the right amount of money, son, even a Yankee can adjust." He sat forward. "I got an important bidness meetin' this mornin'—why don't you come along? Be educational for you to sit in on it."

"Okay."

He checked his Rolex. "Hell, we should go *now*. You can drive me over."

"Woody, I don't have a handle on this town yet."

He was up and fetching his leisure-suit jacket. "Just over to the Krispy Kreme. It's right there on the boulevard."

I knew where that was.

I got up. "Just the two of us?"

"You're all the bodyguard I need. I ain't some paranoid lunatic like Jackie, always thinkin' somebody's out to get him."

I let that slide.

Then I was driving him over there, him in the passenger seat of his big two-tone brown Caddy, and pulling in past a free-standing metal-and-neon sign big enough for a Vegas casino. I pondered what kind of important "bidness" meeting might be taking place at the Krispy Kreme, which—like the Waffle House—appeared to be a common Southern chain. So much sugar down here. Did it help banish the sour taste of losing a certain war? I parked and followed the energetic strip club impresario into a sterile-looking white building with a green-tile roof.

We passed through a cafeteria-style set-up where Mr. Woody collected two glazed doughnuts and a cup of coffee with cream and sugar. I don't like coffee and had already eaten breakfast, so I opted for iced tea. Absentmindedly I forgot to ask for un-sweetened. Shit.

Seemed slow here for mid-morning on a Saturday. Of course, everything was slow in Biloxi in the quiet before the tourist storm. You could see doughnuts being made through a window, the results parading along in an oil-filled trench. The ventilation appeared purposely poor, to force the aroma of baking doughnuts into your nostrils.

Mr. Woody selected a table in the corner away from where everybody else was sitting and we'd barely plopped down when Sheriff Delmar, in plainclothes but for his hat with its badge, strolled in. He touched the hat brim to us, then went through the cafeteria line, joining us with a cup of black coffee and three glazed doughnuts on a paper plate. Well, that paunch had to come from somewhere.

The big man settled in opposite Mr. Woody, nodded to me (ten to one he didn't remember my name), and tossed his hat on the empty one of our four chairs. "His Honor sends his regrets."

Mr. Woody frowned. "Sorry to hear that. I hoped to *talk* to His Honor personal about matters of vital interest to Biloxi in general and us in partic'lar."

His expression neutral, the sheriff shook his head. "I don't think Mayor Clayton wants to be seen in public with anyone directly associated with the Strip right now. Not with his re-election campaign about to swing into gear."

Mr. Woody cocked his head. "Well, though I see where he's comin' from, I have to say I *do* take umbrage."

"Now, there's no reason to—"

"Sheriff Delmar, I am a respected businessman in this community. I did not suggest we meet in a dark alley or a back room or in a saloon. What can be more respectable than an informal meetin' at the Krispy Kreme?"

"Well, now…"

Mr. Woody pointed a doughnut at the sheriff. "You tell His Honor that in future I expect to be treated with respect. And he can expect the same treatment from yours truly."

The sheriff was nodding. "I understand, Mr. Woody. I surely do. And let me convey not only my appreciation, but His Honor's, for the way you've conducted yourself where the, uh, tragic loss of Mr. Jack Killian is concerned."

Mr. Woody smiled as he bit into the glazed doughnut. Sugar bits clung to his lips. "Well, of course I had nothin' to do with Jackie's unfortunate passin'. Such a bizarre mishap. So damn tragic. Jack Killian was a close friend and a trusted bidness associate."

"Oh, I'm very aware of that." Now the sheriff bit into a glazed doughnut; his fleshy, wet lips latched onto even more sugary residue than Mr. Woody's.

Chewing, Delmar went on: "Still, that Mr. Killian's death was an accidental one has had a calmin' effect in certain quarters here in our city and county and even around our great state."

"Good to hear."

"Had one of Mr. Killian's, uh, business rivals caught up with him, and dispatched him in a violent manner, that would almost certainly have painted Biloxi in a most unfavorable light."

Mr. Woody smiled as if to say, *You're welcome*, and had a healthy sip of coffee. "Well, Sheriff…Jeff…it's funny, ain't it? Not funny ha ha, funny odd? How sometimes things just work themselves out for the better?"

Nodding, the sheriff finished one glazed doughnut and started another; by now his right hand was also glazed. Didn't these people know what fucking napkins were for?

Licking his lips, not very successfully, the sheriff said, "What can you tell me about a young airman, a Thomas Huffman, who has gone AWOL? Some of his buddies at the base say he had a thing for a little gal at the Bottoms Up."

"That, Jeff, is somethin' you would have to discuss with Jack Killian. Which is, of course, impossible." Mr. Woody chewed and swallowed a bite of doughnut before adding, "And if you were to go sniffin' around? You might turn up more than you care to."

"You mean regardin' rumors of an exotic dancer who's also gone AWOL, and a longtime club manager who up and quit and run off to parts unknown?"

Mr. Woody shrugged. "You tell me, Jeff—you're the trained investigator. But I do know that if you don't want to know somethin', best not go around askin' about it."

The sheriff now had enough glaze on his face to rival any doughnut on the premises. Mr. Woody was in marginally better shape. I got up, excused myself, and went through the line and came back with two doughnuts. Not glazed—chocolate-frosted.

As disgusting as my companions were in their dining habits, the smell of fresh doughnuts trumped all.

"You need to convey to His Honor," Mr. Woody was saying, "that under my leadership, the Biloxi Strip will no longer be run in the reckless fashion of recent months. You won't have airmen and out-of-towners and even wayward employees sufferin' mysterious misfortunes, left and right."

"Good to hear," the sheriff said again, getting started on doughnut number three. I was still on number one, being civilized. Using a napkin slows things down.

"But what," the sheriff was saying, "about these expansion efforts of Killian's? That land grab of his at the state line?"

"Well, first off," Mr. Woody said, "you should know that I have already made peace with the Dixon clan. They have been assured we won't be encroachin' on their territory no more. And I am in the process of divestin' myself of all our holdings up that way, and elsewhere 'round the state and beyond. Oh, we'll hold onto a little piece of the action here and there— that's just good bidness. But the Biloxi Strip will once again be strictly the Biloxi Strip. With plenty of home-grown commerce to support me and my people."

"That is *very* good to hear," the sheriff said, the doughnuts gone. Finally he reached for a napkin. "We need to get things back to normal in these parts."

Did he really say that? These parts?

"And we will," Mr. Woody said. "We *are*. Now, Jeff, I intend to make a gesture of good faith to His Honor, but first he needs to know that I will expect to work out the details in a *face-to-face* meetin'. At the location of his choice, but I will not be disrespected."

"What do you have in mind, Mr. Woody?"

"We all know Mayor Clayton is likely to be up against a

reform candidate. So, for several weeks prior to the election, we will coordinate a kind of cosmetic clean-up of the Strip. We'll shut some places down, and the few that we do keep up and runnin', the Mayor can send his troops in on raids and make some arrests."

The sheriff frowned in surprise. "Includin' yourself, Mr. Woody?"

"Oh, hell no. But we have people on the payroll who we can afford to have sit in the county jail for a few days, even weeks, till election's passed and we can get 'em up in front of a friendly judge."

The sheriff was nodding now, smiling, damn near grinning. "That all sounds highly possible. Let me bring this to His Honor and get back to you."

Some small talk followed, meaningless to me, and then the sheriff and Mr. Woody stood and shook their sugary hands. I stood and nodded at Delmar, but didn't shake hands with anybody.

With the county's top law enforcer gone, I sat and sipped my sickeningly sweet ice tea as Mr. Woody finished his coffee.

"*Now* we can get things back on an even keel," Mr. Woody said, with a satisfaction approached only by when the sheriff finished his third doughnut. "And this is where *you* come in, Quarry."

"It is?"

"Damn straight, son. You have brains, not to mention more balls than a Brahma fuckin' bull."

"Thank you. I guess."

He leaned forward, the eyes behind the lenses narrowing again, the teeth lurking behind the straight line his mouth made. "I want you to stay on in Biloxi as my second in command. My number-one advisor and bodyguard and the key man to do my occasional…I believe the term in the military is *'wet work.'* "

So much for Killian's death making things less violent.

"I don't think so, Woody. But I do appreciate the offer."

He raised both hands as if in surrender. "You don't have to say yes right this second. You already said you'd stay on here for a week. See how you like it. I know what kinda money you make with the Broker. And I realize with him that you don't have to report in for work every mornin' like the rest of us poor workaday slobs. But I'm prepared to triple what he pays you, with bonuses for those…*special* jobs."

"Why me?"

He sighed, shook his head. "I just don't feel like I can trust anybody that Jackie hired."

"Well, I can see that."

He gave me a lascivious grin. "You know, son, you can hang onto that little whore long as you like. We'll set you up in a nice pad and she's yours, long as you want her. I'll take her off the schedule at the club, no more dancin', no more trickin'—she'll be a one-man woman. But you? You can have all the pussy on the side you want."

Around us, well out of earshot, were the everyday folks of Biloxi—moms, dads, kids, having a wholesome snack of dough-nuts and coffee or milk or too-sweet iced tea. The avuncular middle-aged man with the combover and the big glasses and big teeth must have seemed as harmless as that nice man next door. Of course, sometimes that nice man next door had bodies buried in his cellar.

"Okay," I said. "It's a tempting offer. I'll give it serious con-sideration."

"You made my day, son!" he blurted, and stuck out his hand.

It wasn't as sticky as I expected.

But it was sticky enough.

❋

That evening Luann and I ate at The Dockside in a rerun of our first meal there—cheeseburger for her and crab cakes for me—and smiled at each other and were pleasant enough, but said very little. There was a strain between us, no question. That can happen with a couple when the girl asks the guy to kill somebody, and the guy says let me get back to you.

But at least everybody was giving me a little time to chew things over. Mr. Woody said I had a week to decide about this new employment opportunity. And Luann wasn't pressing me at all about whether I was willing to do her that "favor" for the "gift" of the videotape she had of me drowning a guy.

Luann knew I had a lot on my mind, and said she'd watch a movie in her room while I "thought things over." Which was as close to pressing me about it as she came. I suggested she could stay in my room and watch, since the TV was bigger and better, but she politely declined.

"Just knock if you want me," she said, and slipped into her room.

So I lay back on the bed and I thought about my options.

And I did have them, options. But they were all messier than Sheriff Jefferson Davis Delmar eating a glazed doughnut.

For example.

If I took Mr. Woody up on his offer—and the money was goddamn good—where did that leave me with Luann? I'd have to somehow finesse those videotapes out of her, and then, *goddamnit*, get rid of her.

Or maybe, in negotiating the terms of my employment, I could ask Mr. Woody to let me have the girl—after all, he'd once upon a time bought her, so in his view she belonged to him. And, as part of the transaction, I could secure the release of her banked money as well as the severing of any ties between him and her.

That might be enough to get the girl to cough up those tapes. She was not really a blackmailer at heart and maybe, under those circumstances, I could even risk letting her walk around.

Maybe.

Another option was to come clean with Mr. Woody about Luann having Killian's murder on tape, and let *him* handle her. He was in a better position to find the tapes and could dispose of her without me having to get my hands dirty. Of course, if he looked at the tapes, he'd see his wife fucking Killian, and who knew what kind of shit would hit the fan then?

Shit that would almost certainly include Wicked Wanda telling Mr. Woody that I'd fucked her. Which was bullshit. She fucked *me*!

And in that scenario, *Mr. Woody* would wind up with the tapes...and was I *really* any better off with him having the things than little Luann? Christ, leading Mr. Woody to those recordings was like handing your soul to the devil without bothering to get anything out of the deal.

Then there was the option that got me the hell out of Biloxi. Kill Mr. Woody and return to my life in the Broker's world... after getting those tapes from the girl.

You remember the girl—the one who saw me commit three murders at the Dixie Club, and another at the Fantasy Sweets?

So...once I'd collected the tapes from her, I'd have to dispose of her. What, suffocate her in her sleep so she didn't suffer much? I didn't know jack shit about poison or setting up drug overdoses or anything. It's not like anybody had ever asked me to do a humane hit. And now, ironically, I was asking it of myself.

I liked the kid. She deserved better than getting dumped on

a roadside or in the Gulf. But survival was my only religion, and I kept the faith.

So where did all this leave me?

Kill Mr. Woody?

Kill the girl?

Kill them both?

Decisions, decisions.

Around eleven, I knocked on the connecting door.

A few seconds passed and she opened it halfway.

"Want me?" she asked.

She was in that large Led Zeppelin t-shirt again. No make-up and her hair tousled. She looked like a girl of thirteen, but a girl of thirteen who was blossoming nicely.

"Come in," I said.

She did.

I shut the door. The only light on was the nightstand lamp on the side of the mirrored area with the hot tub.

"Sit," I said.

She hopped up on the bed and sat like an Indian. I perched on the edge of the bed and twisted toward her, making eye contact. Her eyes were like pools of water you could jump into. If they were bigger or you were smaller.

"Look," I said, "there might be ways around this. What if I could talk Mr. Woody into turning your savings over to you? And to essentially...turn *you* over to me."

"You mean you'd buy me off him?" Very flat, nothing negative in it.

"No. He'd 'give' you to me. Not that one human being can do that with another, but...that seems to be his fucked-up thinking."

She just nodded.

I went on: "Then I wouldn't have to…deal with him, and you wouldn't be an…accessory to anything."

She raised a "hold on" finger.

I paused, and she got off the bed and turned the hot-tub faucets noisily on.

She held up the "wait" finger again.

When the hot tub was filled enough, she shut off the faucets, pulled off her t-shirt, tossed it, and crawled over into the steamy water, then curled a finger for me to join her.

I nodded. I understood. She'd expressed fear last night that the room might be bugged, and that wasn't unreasonable. I got out of my t-shirt and jeans and shorts and shoes and crawled in with her. She started the Jacuzzi spray going, and then came over to me and I slipped an arm around her and we leaned back against the curve of the tub. Drowning her in this thing would be a cinch, but I didn't want to make a habit out of that kind of thing.

The flesh of our naked sides kissed, though nothing terribly sexual was going on. She leaned her face up alongside mine and whispered in my ear: "Please kill him."

Then I whispered in her ear: "You're not a killer."

The whispering continued, as she said, "*You* are."

"But you aren't. This makes you one."

"I don't care. He's an evil man."

"You could leave with me."

"Where to?"

"Somewhere not here."

"That sounds nice. But I know things about him."

"What kind of things?"

"I already told you some. He'd come after me."

Or send somebody, I thought. *Somebody like me.*

She was whispering in my ear, voice barely audible above

the bubbling: "I saw things. If he thought I was…runnin' free? He'd make me dead."

"I could protect you."

"You might not always be there."

"…You really want him dead."

"He has to be. You have to kill him."

"Okay."

She forgot about the whispering and squealed: "You *will*?"

It was like Daddy had just told her she could borrow the T-Bird. Fun fun fun.

"Yeah," I said.

We got out of the tub, let it drain as we dried off with big fluffy towels and then got onto the bed, on the spread. She crawled between my legs like a cat sneaking up on a mouse and took me into her mouth with a whole new enthusiasm. This wasn't a plumber cleaning your pipes. This was a young woman who wanted you to feel really, really good, and having a good time doing it.

I hadn't been lying to her. But I hadn't exactly been telling the truth, either. Really, I hadn't made my mind up yet. But I did know the likelihood of me doing anything bad to this sweet child was nil. I did like her. I didn't like that I liked her, because there are parts of me I don't like having touched. This did not include my dick, obviously.

She got me good and hard, and then she stopped and said, "I'm gon' to give you something better than a blow job."

"This should be good."

She scampered off the bed, bending over in a way that made both me and my hard-on drool at her, down there unzipping the canvas tote bag. She dug in it for a while, then came back with first one, then a second, thick rectangle of plastic. It actually took me a second to figure out that these were the tapes—

video cassettes like TV stations used, with me doing murder on one.

She hadn't really hidden the things at all.

"My gift," she said. "For your favor."

"But…"

"You'll come through."

"How can you—"

"I trust you, Johnny."

Trust again.

I said, "Put them back for now."

She stuffed them back in the bag and zipped it up and hopped on the bed again, very kid-like. As if a pillow fight might ensue.

"I wanna see if I can come on top," she said.

"Be my guest."

"So far I only came when I was on the bottom."

"Well, give it a try."

She climbed on top of me and inserted me into herself like a key and she moved herself while I moved in her, as if trying to unlock something inside her. Once again, we did not use a rubber, and the feel of it was wonderful, wet but with some nice friction, warm as the warmest kiss, and those pert breasts were in my face, begging to be nuzzled, and I wasn't about to deny them. That she had learned some moves as a stripper became apparent when she did a bump and grind, forward, back, sideways, pumping, churning, and the door from outside burst open and slammed shut and I was trying to get out from under her when somebody came over in a blur and latched onto Luann and tossed her off of me like a Frisbee, flinging her into the porcelain side of the hot tub. She hit hard, hitting her head, sliding to the floor in an ungainly sitting position, head slumped, feet sticking out.

Somebody slapped the nightstand lamp and it crashed to the floor and before I'd got any kind of look at them, we were in darkness. Still, I sensed two of them on me. I shoved the guy nearest me away and dove for the other nightstand, where the nine millimeter rested, but somebody had me by the legs and pulled me onto the floor, and I landed hard next to the bed, near that canvas bag with the tapes in it. I was flailing, but it did no good. They dragged me out past the bed, the carpet burn making my skin scream, and then it began.

A guy hovering over me, I could not see a damn thing about him except that there was a lot of size, was battering me with his fists. My face took a lot of it, my eyes, my mouth, my ears, and there was blood all over my face but I couldn't tell where it was coming from. He worked over my chest and belly, too, while the other guy was kicking me and the only saving grace was my bare dick and balls took none of the kicks, just my legs and my side. This went on forever or maybe a minute, and then the door opened and somebody said, "That's enough! Come on."

One guy was on one side of me hauling me under my arm and the other guy was doing the same with my other arm, dragging me face down, and this time my dick and balls did get some rough treatment as they hauled me bare-ass out of my motel room across the narrow strip of cement sidewalk to a vehicle, its trunk lid up, in the parking slot by Luann's room. The guy who'd spoken seemed to just be sort of directing things, making sure that trunk lid was all the way up, while all sorts of hands were on me, lifting me up as I was pulled toward the open trunk.

I never got a good look at them, though there was limited light outside, but before somebody hit me on the back of the head with a lead pipe or something, I realized I knew what car this was. What car my unconscious body was about to be dumped into the trunk of.

A two-tone green Fleetwood, last seen roaring through the parking lot of the Concort Inn in Davenport, Iowa, with a rider firing shots at the Broker and me shooting back.

THIRTEEN

Consciousness returned to me in fits and starts, the way you awaken in the middle of the night to the sounds of a storm that builds and builds, wind momentarily rousing you, then rain intruding, finally hail opening your eyes wide.

My storm was the jostling of the vehicle on a bumpy road, and when I was fully awake within the metallic womb, I knew at once where I was with a clarity that belied the pain of my throbbing head and the aches all over me where fists and boots had taken a toll.

I knew, for example, that this road must be fairly rough, because I'd been stuffed into a Fleetwood Caddy, and a Fleetwood Caddy was normally a smooth ride. Of course I'd never ridden in the trunk of one before.

I didn't try to move at first. The fetal position I was in was oddly comforting if not comfortable, the Cadillac floor carpeted and my head resting on a spare tire with a carpet cover snugged over it. Very muffled country western music was playing on the car stereo and some intermittent unintelligible conversation was bleeding back to me.

Tire rumble and engine noise seemed very loud back here.

How long I'd been out was a mystery. A clue was that I was stiff in a way that suggested I'd been on my side with my legs tucked up for some time—the Caddy had a roomy trunk but not *that* roomy. Even motionless and prone like this, I could tell a few things about my condition. One eye was swollen shut and my lips felt puffy, the coppery taste of blood lingering. My tongue checked for missing teeth and came back with a full inventory. My nose hadn't been broken. Despite the pervasive aches, I didn't sense that *anything* had been broken—ribs the obvious possibility. This seemed to be bruises and contusions.

I spent maybe five minutes just breathing and getting used to being alive. My nakedness was disconcerting. I really was like a big baby who'd suffered a tough delivery. I was breathing heavily and some of that seemed to be anxiety, so I slowed it down. I hurt too much to allow myself to get worked up.

I started exploring my carpeted metal coffin. The jack in these vehicles was normally tucked toward the back, near a small ledge. The ledge was there, but not the jack. My chauffeurs must have prepared my travel quarters by removing the thing. A jack, of course, carried the most obvious potential for a makeshift weapon. But no.

The spare tire that was my pillow was the next best possibility—not the tire itself in any way, but there would be a wing nut as part of the hardware keeping the spare in place. That wing nut might be sharp enough to slash with, or maybe it could be rubbed on other metal into sharpness.

But with the trunk lid down, I couldn't get that cloth cover off the tire to get at it. I worked my fingers around the bottom of the covered tire, all around its roundness, tugging, pulling, and got nowhere. Standing at the rear of the vehicle, with the trunk lid up, you could just lean in and remove that cover. With the lid shut, the only thing I could accomplish was the amplification of every pain in my body. And I had plenty of those.

Tire rumble and engine noise.

I lay my head back on my spare-tire pillow and wept for a while. I wasn't feeling sorry for myself and falling into despair or some such shit. I was fucking hurting. Never once did I wish I was dead. Never once did I stop wishing to make the fuckers dead who were taking me on this ride. In fact, I wanted them to suffer. I am not by nature a sadistic person. I take no relish in the suffering of others.

Normally.

But I had been pulled out of bed mid-fuck to get the shit kicked out of me and tossed naked into a car trunk and driven off in the night, God knew where. This earned some people a very nasty goddamn death, if I didn't suffer one first.

I twisted around onto my back, though that required turning my knees toward the rear of the trunk. This hurt no more than pulling your eyelids back over the top of your head and making a knot. My fingers explored the underside of the trunk lid. The metal had some curves and nooks and crannies that seemed promising but gave up nothing helpful.

But then I remembered: *there would be a trunk light*.

I searched over toward the center left of the lid, where it curved down, near the latching mechanism. Living there, within a metallic hood, like a little glass nun, was a small light bulb.

Holding onto the outer metallic protective piece with my left hand, I tried to unscrew the precious little thing. It didn't give, and I quickly realized it must not be threaded—had to be a pop-in, pop-out kind of item.

It popped out.

I held it tight, but not too tight, in my right hand. I never smiled wider or probably more grotesquely either, if anybody could have seen me. I opened my hand slowly and carefully, as if I'd caught a butterfly and wanted a peek before it flew away. Of course I couldn't see a goddamn thing, but the fingers of my left hand could, in the sense that they explored the tiny object with a respectful delicacy. The rounded metal shaft was maybe an inch long, the glass bulb maybe an inch tall, and slightly plumper than the base.

Tire rumble, engine noise.

I held this prize in my palm, in a loose fist, and I knew that this little metal-and-glass baby dick was all that stood between me and nothingness. I thought about what to do with it. Would my captors open the trunk, notice the light was off and know what I'd done?

No. Not likely.

Was it best that I break the glass now, turn it into a tiny weapon, and wait till we'd stopped and then leap out of the trunk at whoever opened it, weapon in hand? I considered this seriously for maybe five minutes, practicing holding the thing by the short metal shaft in my fist.

At first I was liking it, then I considered that the idea of me leaping out of this trunk in my condition was laughable—in an it-only-hurts-when-I-laugh kind of way. And while I might do damage to the guy closest to me, there were two other men in this thing, and I was in no condition to emerge from my Cadillac womb and immediately deal with all three.

Somebody would surely shoot me.

It's what *I* would do. Although I would never do to anybody what had been done to me tonight. Mid-fuck, kicked to shit, stuffed in a trunk, driven to nowhere. That kind of sick shit just did not go down with me.

Tire rumble, engine noise.

How long had I been out? I wondered.

My stiffness indicated quite a while. Hours, maybe. Though I was operating from a whole new perspective, I judged we weren't speeding—doing fifty? And the road was fairly rough but not torn up or anything. Not interstate. Poor condition highway or secondary road. Air was coming in from somewhere, thankfully not carbon monoxide-flavored, so this was a less stuffy ride than you might expect. Like the little light bulb, a small blessing.

I moved my head toward the rear of the trunk, toward the back seat, not to get closer to that God-awful country western but to try to pick up on the occasional conversation by the driver and rider. And it did seem to be just two people—if the third man was in the vehicle, he was either sleeping or staying quiet. Or maybe he didn't make the trip. Or possibly he was in another car. If this weren't a Caddy, I'd think they might dump it and me in a river, and drive off in another vehicle.

Tire rumble, engine noise.

For maybe an hour—or ten minutes or half an hour, who the hell knows?—I went over various scenarios in which I took down two men, maybe three, with my little tiny trunk light. I will not bore you with these pathetic plans of action. But it did finally come to me that my best chance would be to palm my tiny potential weapon and allow my captors to remove me from the car trunk and transport me to wherever they might have in mind. Probably inside somewhere, but not necessarily. Maybe to a stream in the piney woods where they could kill me and dump me.

If I played dead, or that is unconscious, I might find a moment to act. But I would have to do that before anybody tied my hands, because I didn't think being bound and then somehow breaking the bulb would provide me with anything sufficient to cut rope or even duct tape, at least not with any efficiency or haste. This might mean acting as soon as they got me up and out, and again my physical state would be less than ideal.

So I breathed evenly and I began to utilize my limited space to move my limbs, lifting my knees up and then back, working my arms, stretching muscles that wanted to be left the hell alone, flexing joints, rotating my shoulders, my neck, even working my feet and toes. I might be on my side with my head on a spare tire, but goddamnit, I needed to limber up.

Tire rumble, engine noise.

Now and then the vehicle would decelerate and my breath would accelerate and I would do my best to control and slow my breathing, readying myself for the car to stop and that lid to come up. But apparently we were only cutting speed as we moved through towns, small ones I'd judge, and then we would be back on rough road, going fifty.

After many false alarms, however, came something that immediately seemed real. The turn signal came on and a red glow filled the trunk. The vehicle slowed way down and I felt it make its turn and heard the tires crunching on gravel, then roll across what might be a parking lot and finally come to a stop.

Inside myself, I braced for what lay ahead, but I made my body go limp. If they knew I was awake, I might be dead so fast a semi-load of little light bulbs wouldn't help.

Throughout my ride, I hadn't been able to make out any words in the muffled conversations drowned out by the country-western radio that added insult to my injury. Now I heard doors open on either side and feet hit gravel, and somebody said, "*You* haul 'im out, Buck. I'll keep you covered. He's a tricky fucker."

"Hell, he's probably already a dead fucker. We worked him over good, Chuck."

So these two were Buck and Chuck.

In other circumstances, that might have struck me as amusing or maybe pitiful. Right now all it meant to me was that Buck was probably bigger and that Chuck had a gun.

A key worked in the trunk lock—there was no doubt an automatic release up front, but they probably wanted to prevent me from leaping out and running away like a jackrabbit, which showed how little they knew. The lid raised and fresh air came in and hovering over me was a big guy in blue-jean coveralls and no shirt with a bushy beard and a bald head and a grizzly build and a grisly face. There was hair on his shoulders and he was shod in clodhoppers. My eyes were almost shut, just slitted enough to barely see, since I was supposed to be out cold, but I got that much of a look at Buck, anyway.

Nothing of Chuck yet, because Buck blotted most everything else out. Or the third man, either, if he was anywhere around.

Buck leaned in, said, "Come to daddy, baby boy," and took me and all my bruised and battered nakedness in his arms like I really was a baby or maybe a bride on her way to a threshold. I stayed limp, my head hanging to one side, arms dangling, the little glass bulb curled in the fingers of a hand that wasn't quite making a fist.

My slitted eyes finally showed me Chuck. He was big, too, just not a bear like Buck. He was in a short-sleeve white shirt with blue stripes and blue denim flares and tooled cowboy boots. His hair was long and greased back and up in an Elvis pompadour with the requisite sideburns. He had a .38, a snubnose, in his fist and he apparently didn't trust babies or brides, either, because he was pointing it right at me. He followed alongside Buck as the bigger man lumbered like the Frankenstein monster with a victim toward some double doors.

Until we were inside, I didn't realize where we were. Now my slitted eyes told me: this was the Dixie Club. We were on the gambling-den side, and the lights were mostly off, but a few neon beer signs provided scant illumination. I was beginning to suspect who Buck and Chuck were, or anyway who they represented.

Buck carried me between and past green-felt-covered tables through a door into a cement-floored storeroom. Boxes of beer and liquor were stacked along the walls. It reminded me of the Bottoms Up storeroom, but smaller. A chair borrowed from the restaurant side waited for me more or less in the middle of the open space.

In my line of slitted vision was an ancient-looking work-bench—against the only wall that lacked boxes of booze and beer—loomed over by a pegboard display of pliers, hand saws, screwdrivers, chisels, wrenches, hand drills and other do-it-yourself implements. A few items were scattered on the work-bench itself, notably a very old-fashioned-looking brass-based blowtorch, a coil of clothesline, and a big ball-peen hammer that I may have seen before.

After carrying me so gently to this destination, Buck dropped me hard onto the dining-hall chair. Maybe he meant to wake me up. I didn't. I sat there slumped to one side, arms dangling, the bulb still tucked in my curled fingers.

Buck and Chuck went over to the workbench. My slit-eyed view of them gave me more details. Bald, thicket-bearded Buck had a pie-pan face with big dumb half-lidded eyes, a button nose, and a tiny round mouth that formed a permanent "Oh." Despite the greasy pompadour and sideburns, Chuck resembled Margaret Hamilton more than Elvis, with his narrow face with its sharp features and prominent chin.

Chuck said, "Tie him up."

"What for? Fucker's out."

"Jesus! What if he's fakin'?"

"I *hope* he is. I hope he comes flyin' out of that chair and mixes it up, all fucked-up and naked, I would *love* that shit. After what he done to cousin Dixie? Fuck."

Suspicions confirmed.

Chuck set his .38 snubnose on the workbench and picked up the ball-peen hammer. "Who you tryin' to impress, shit-for-brains? She was *my* sister. Tie him up."

Double confirmation.

"Ah come on, now!" Buck blurted, and he turned the spigot on the blowtorch, sending a tongue of orange and blue licking at the air. "You afraid of this half-dead Yankee sumbitch? What are you, a little girl? I say if he's got some fight left him in, more power to his sorry ass."

Buck started toward me, taking his time, the blowtorch breathing flame like a lazy dragon.

Chuck frowned and took a step in my direction, but lagging behind his bear-like kin. "What you gon' do with that thing?"

"I'd gon' roast him like a marshmallow. I'm gonna smores his dick and balls."

"Me first." Chuck hefted the hammer. "This is the fucker that killed Dixie! I wanna get my licks in, Dixie-style."

"No, maaan! You'll kill him with that thing. Let me have *my* fun first."

Chuck scowled. "Okay, fine, but let's tie him up first. I'm tellin' you, bastard killed Dixie and Dix and Bubbah, bing bang boom, so you never fuckin' *know*."

Buck, about four feet away from me, turned toward Chuck, who was just a step back from him, and said, "Okay, okay, you pussy. But *you* get the rope."

I broke the bulb on the side of the chair and lurched forward and with my right raised fist jammed the jagged glass into Buck's left eye, then reached down and gripped his hand on the handle of the flamethrower, turning its flame toward Chuck. Buck was screaming, the metal shaft of the bulb sticking out of his mangled socket, blood streaming like tears, his hands coming up to cover his face, and I had the blowtorch now, turning the spigot higher and shooting a wide hissing tongue of flame that licked Chuck's narrow face from chin to hairline, turning the flesh red then orange then black. The hammer tumbled from his fingers and clunked on the cement as the whites of his eyes bulged against the crackling blackened flesh and he was already shrieking when the oily hair ignited. I tossed the still-fire-belching blow-torch like a spent match and scooped up the hammer just as Buck was recovering enough to come charging at me, howling in rage and pain, and I sunk the head of the ball-peen into his forehead and he froze there. When I pulled it out, the hammer made a sound like a boot freeing itself from mud, and when he dropped to his knees as if to beg or maybe pray, I swung three more hits onto the top of his bald head. Those didn't sink in as far but they made impressive dents. Chuck, his screaming as shrill now as a fire-engine siren, was running from one wall to another like an Indian in a burning headdress, waving his hands over his head as if they were what was on fire. Keeping the fallen Buck between me and the careening Chuck, I knelt over the bigger man and gave the back of his head enough blows to prove there actually was a brain in there. Just as I was finishing up, Chuck fell on his face, almost certainly dead, though the fire the oily hair had started was still alive, dancing orange-blue devils having a party.

I considered using the snubnose to put a bullet in the back of Chuck's head, but I figured maybe that was overkill. Anyway, there was a third man who might still be around and the sound of a gunshot might summon him, even if the screaming hadn't.

The frustrating thing was that I could salvage no clothes off either of these pricks. Chuck's shirt was scorched down past the shoulders and he'd pissed his pants. Despite the nasty moisture, I checked his pockets for car keys, but there weren't any. The keys weren't in Buck's coveralls, either, and as for harvesting those denims to wear, the things were bloody and anyway far too fucking big for me. And I wouldn't be caught dead in coveralls.

Taking the snubnose along, I left the storeroom and the crackle of burning hair and stench of charred flesh behind, walking bareass through the mini-casino, followed by my own bloody footprints. Outside, the air felt good, surprisingly cool. Must have been around forty-five degrees. I stepped carefully out into the parking lot and looked around, every which way.

In a few seconds, I took in quite a bit.

First, the Dixie Club in its entirety was closed, which considering the commotion I'd just caused was not surprising. Signs on every entry said boldly:

RE-OPENING SOON
UNDER NEW MANAGEMENT

The second thing I noticed was a pick-up truck, a nice new red Ford F-100, unlocked and with the keys in it. Probably Buck's or Chuck's, who were apparently trusting souls. Well, hell, this was the South where everybody was good neighbors.

The third thing I saw was the most interesting. The Dixie Court seemed to have one customer, even though it, too, was closed for business. On the far end, well away from the main Dixie Club buildings, the two-tone green Fleetwood filled the parking slot for Room 14.

So the third man was still here.

Why?

And what the hell was he doing in Room 14?

I tried to free my mind of car-trunk rides and screaming men with gouged-out eyes and their hair on fire. Just clear the cobwebs and think.

And right away I had it.

Assuming he started in Biloxi, the third man had driven here to pick up Buck and Chuck, many hours ago. Leaving the red pick-up behind, the three had driven the Caddy up to Biloxi, where my ass got grabbed. That made twelve hours in a car for the third man.

And now they had made another six-hour trip *back* up to the

Dixie Club, with either Buck or Chuck driving, the third man possibly resting, sleeping, maybe in the back seat. Once they returned to the Dixie Club, the third man had stood silently and apart as they hauled me out of the Fleetwood trunk and inside the Dixie Club to have their Dixon family fun with me…

…while he crashed in a room at the motel to catch a few z's before making yet another six-hour drive. After all, it was probably approaching four in the morning by now.

So he was in that cabin, snoozing, at this very moment. And though I had no idea what his name might be, I figured I knew who he was—the driver of the Fleetwood that night when those shots were taken at the Broker and me. I hadn't ever seen him, really, so I couldn't recognize him; but this all made sense to me. Maybe if I hadn't been naked and bloody and beaten-up, I might not have been quite so sure.

But in that parking lot, in my bare feet, with a snubnose in my hand and my dick hanging out, I was dead certain.

The third man was in Room 14.

I made it over to the check-in office, a CLOSED sign on its door, which proved unlocked. At some point, probably many hours ago, Buck or Chuck or some asshole had let the third man in here to collect a key to Room 14, so he could grab a nap before heading back to Biloxi on the last leg of this back-and-forth journey.

And one of the two keys to that room was still hanging on the wall behind the check-in desk.

Glad for a sidewalk, after my barefoot trip across a gravel parking lot, I walked quietly along the row of rooms with the gun in one hand and the room key in the other, stopping at the door near where the Fleetwood was parked. Because of the truncated evening Luann and I had spent in a Dixie Court room, I knew the layout. I worked the key slowly, gently, in the door numbered 14, pushed it open quick, and pointed the .38 at the bed.

But the covers were back in a rumpled pile, a .45 and a pint bottle of bourbon with a water glass on the nightstand; down the hallway that led to the swimming pool, the open door to the bathroom bled light. Sink water was running. Brushing his teeth or something. Washing his hands maybe.

I stood there waiting on his doorstep, and when he stepped out in his boxers and nothing else, unarmed, he sensed something, turned my way, and grimaced, recognizing me.

He even said, "Quarry!"

Like I said, I'd never seen him before, except in blurs—the blur that night in the Concort Inn parking lot, the blurs of him and Buck and Chuck grabbing me from my Tropical room and stuffing me in the trunk. He was about my size and was another of these ex-military guys, judging by his butch haircut and solid build, and that's all I can tell you about what he looked like.

Because he was a blur again, running down the hall toward that door onto the pool.

I didn't run. I moved fast, as fast as I was capable in my condition, but I didn't run, I just followed him, through the cabin, down that hallway, and when he pushed open the door and was halfway out, I fired the snubnose four times. They all hit him in a nice tight cluster, the dark spots where they went in standing out starkly in the moon- and starlight, ribbons of scarlet flying from him as if in celebration. He stumbled forward and he landed in the scummy pool with a belly-flop splash, his arms outstretched, like he was starting a lap.

But he wasn't going anywhere.

Back in the motel room, I caught a real break. First, the Fleetwood keys were on the nightstand. Second, the guy's clothes were my size.

I washed up a little and put some of them on.

When I went outside, I thought for a moment that dawn had come. But then it became clear that the light was generated by a conflagration—the Dixie Club was burning, that blowtorch igniting some of the booze, apparently. The wooden-frame building was going up fast, the gambling side already almost gone, the blaze working on the restaurant now, generating billowing black smoke but mostly orange-and-blue flames that were making glowing heat. Funny how the sound of a big fire is so similar to that of a rainstorm, but when I turned my back to it, that was exactly what the death of the Dixie Club sounded like.

I got in the Fleetwood, glad not to be in its trunk, and started it up and drove off, leaving all that hell behind.

With more awaiting me back in Biloxi.

FOURTEEN

In no shape to make the six-hour drive down to Biloxi, I considered checking in somewhere to sleep and recuperate a little—somewhere other than the Dixie Motel, that is. The trousers I'd appropriated in Room 14 had a wallet with $152 in its left back pocket, so I felt pretty flush for a guy who'd begun this outing naked, battered and stuffed in a car trunk.

But I needed to get back to Biloxi as soon as possible—I had things to deal with there, including little Luann, last seen flung against the side of a hot tub, knocked silly. I thought about calling her, but going through the Tropical switchboard might not be wise. Nor was I sure what ultimately to do about her.

Getting back to Biloxi by car meant dealing with various roads and highways and maps, and the thought of that made my head hurt even worse. But I knew how to get to Memphis and found myself heading there. A plane was out this time, as I didn't have the I.D. or the money.

At a gas station on the outskirts, I got directions to the bus depot, in whose lot I left the Fleetwood, after wiping it down for prints, trunk included. I left the keys in the ignition. A nice surprise for somebody.

A bus ticket to Biloxi cost me $22.50—the guy in the window goggled at my beat-to-shit countenance—and at a magazine stand I picked up two little tins of aspirin. A vending machine gave me stuff they claimed was Coke with floating shards they claimed was ice, and I washed down six tablets with the swill, then found a bench and waited for the 7:10 A.M. bus to Biloxi.

At the rear of the bus, I claimed the double seat, stretching

out on my back, putting my knees up a little, tucking a complimentary pillow behind my head, which was aching less, thanks
to the Bayer Company. A pleasant older woman in a floral dress
approached me, holding a hand out tentatively, as if to a dog
that needed help but might bite.

"Are you all right, young man?"

I knew I looked a horror, having washed up again in the bus
station john, where I'd applied a cold compress of wet paper
towels to my swollen eye. But I had on a dead man's brown
sportcoat, tan sportshirt and dark brown slacks, and the .38 was
in a pocket, so I looked fairly respectable.

"I'm fine, ma'am, thanks. Are you going all the way to Biloxi?"

"I am. My daughter and her little ones are there."

I nodded as if that mattered. "When we hit the city limits,
could you wake me?"

"Certainly. Were you in an accident?"

"You should see the other guys."

That made her smile a little. Good thing she couldn't really
see them.

She was true to her word and gently shook me awake when
we hit town. The inside of my mouth thick as paste, I sat up
slowly, the aching pretty bad. I'd gotten almost seven hours of
sleep, though, and when I'd been up and around and moving
for a while, it would be better.

A cab dropped me a block away from the Tropical Motel—I
didn't want to pull up and be let out in front. I came around
through the alley, cutting through the parking lot. My rental
Chevelle was still in its slot by the outside door to my room,
and the slot next to Luann's door remained vacant.

My hunch was she'd still be around. I thought for a moment
about whether she'd be in her room or mine. Hers made more
sense, but mine had the better TV.

With my left hand, I knocked on the outside door to my room—the snubnose .38 was in my right hand, down along my side. Working my voice up as much as I dared, I said, "Luann! Me." Then I added: "Johnny."

She cracked it open. I could hear the TV going—*The Newly-wed Game*. She was barefoot in frayed jeans and a pink t-shirt. My nine millimeter was tight and huge in her small right hand. Her hair looked unwashed, her eyes red, her face sans make-up almost ghostly.

But seeing me seemed to transform her—she beamed, opening the door wider, and I slipped inside.

She hugged me and it ached like hell, but I didn't want to hurt her feelings so let her keep at it. Looking past the girl, I took in my room—no one seemed to be here but us. That left the bathroom, and I pushed her away gently and checked it.

We really were alone.

The door between our rooms was shut but not locked. Snubnose in hand, I went quickly in and found it (and its bathroom) vacant as well. I returned to my room, where Luann was shutting off the TV. She'd set my nine millimeter on the dresser. It had the safety on. I wondered if she knew how that mechanism worked.

I asked her, "Are you all right?"

"Yes. Oh my God, *look* at you! What did they *do* to you, Johnny?"

"You hit that tub pretty hard. Did it knock you out?"

"Yes, but…" She raised a gentle hand, not quite touching my face. "…oh, they hurt you *bad*."

I took her by that hand and we sat on the foot of the bed. "Have you been taking it easy? You could have a concussion. You should get checked out at an ER."

"What about *you*, Johnny? Your face, it's…"

"It's all right. I was lucky. They don't seem to have broken anything."

"What *happened*? How did you get away from them?"

"Honey, you don't need to know any of that. Let's just say an ER wouldn't help any of them at this point."

She squeezed my hand and nodded, her chin crinkling. "Good. Good."

"Have you been out of this room?"

"Just in here and mine."

"No one's tried to get in?"

"No. I put on the do-not-disturb."

If only I'd thought of that last night.

"Luann, that's not going to stop anybody who wants to come in and do you harm. Or me, if they know I'm alive."

"Who did this?"

"I think you know."

Her face hardened. "Mr. Woody."

I sighed. "I wish I'd done what you asked me to, like right away."

She nodded. "He called me."

"*Called* you?"

She nodded some more and pointed a thumb toward the door to her room. "Not too long ago. He wants me to come in to the club tonight, and do the last shift, seven to three."

"What else did he say?"

"That you were gone and the job was over. He meant me keepin' you company and servicin' you and stuff."

"Yeah. I get that. That's all he said about me, that I was 'gone?'"

More nods.

I thought about that. "Did he say anything about you clearing out of your motel room?"

"No. He probably hasn't thought of that. It's nothin' he'd check. I'm not important."

I got up and walked around a little, thinking. She was right. As far as Mr. Woody knew, Luann was just another employee. Just the little whore he'd provided me. He wouldn't even know—or it was very unlikely, anyway—that she'd been in my room when the Dixon boys and their helper barged in and dragged me away.

I went over and sat back down next to her. I took her hand again. "Luann, Mr. Woody doesn't have any way of knowing that we're…friends."

"Is that what we are?"

"I think so. I hope so."

She smiled. That seemed to be enough. "So he doesn't suspect me of anythin'?"

"What of? All you did was show me around town a little and stay on call for when I got horny. He knows nothing about you accompanying me to the Dixie Club. Or following me to the Fantasy Sweets and making those video tapes. Could have *no* idea that you approached me to make him go away."

"That's a good way to put it," she said with no irony. "But you know, it's typical."

"What is?"

She shrugged. "I'm nothin' to him. Nobody, just a nice little piece of ass. To sell or use any way he feels like. He doesn't know I have thoughts. Or feelings."

Now I was nodding. "Well, if he does, I promise he doesn't give a shit. But you're not alone, Luann."

"Huh?"

"He's been using me, too."

I was hungry. I'd bought a Snickers at one of the stops on the bus ride, but otherwise I was empty and my stomach was growling. The girl said she hadn't eaten either, hadn't even thought about it, but now that I was back "alive and everything," she was starving.

I had her order some room service for us, to her room, while I took a long, hot shower, after which I made a general inspection of the bodily damage. My eye wasn't so badly swollen now. My face had skinned patches where fist had met bone and skin, and my upper lip was a little puffy. Naked in the mirror I looked like Joseph's coat of many colors, if those colors were purple, blue, red, yellow and variations thereof. You will be glad to know that my dick and balls were in mint condition, and all my poking at my sides did not reveal anything that might be a broken or even cracked rib.

But I still had a general achiness that expressed itself with every breath, and I knew I could use some rest, even if my mind was too active to let me get any more sleep.

So after we ate our room-service meal, more Dockside grub (cheeseburger and fries for her, a rare steak sandwich and fries for me), we spent the rest of the afternoon and early evening just relaxing in the room. Most of the time we lay on the double bed with her snuggled next to me and watched whatever she wanted to on TV.

Around five-thirty, she started getting ready to go into the strip club, explaining that she did her stage make-up at work, just taking a shower and washing/drying her hair. That brought to an end a sleepy, lazy late afternoon, and you would never know that anything nasty hung over our heads but for the .38 on one nightstand and the nine millimeter on the other.

At one point I got off the bed and knelt by her canvas tote bag and removed the two bulky video cassettes; one had a label (blank) stuck on, the other didn't. Which brought something to mind.

I asked her, "Is there any way to know which of these is which?"

She knelt on the bed like a cat about to spring. "What do you mean?"

"One has Mrs. Woody bonking Mr. Killian, the other has me—you know."

"Oh. Yes. Actually, the one with the label is the one where you, uh, are doin' what you did. I stuck that on to know which is which."

"And why did you do that?"

"In case I needed to use the Mrs. Woody and Mr. Killian one on Mr. Woody."

So she'd had a plan B, in case I didn't come through for her. The kid did have a streak of the blackmailer in her, but in this instance I didn't mind.

"Might come in handy at that," I admitted.

Luann suggested applying some of her cosmetics to take the edge off my rough-and-tumble look. I said okay and, while the combination of pancake and liquid make-up seemed obvious under the harsh bathroom light, she assured me it would work just fine in the low-key lighting of a nightclub.

At six-thirty, I drove her within a block of Mr. Woody's, not wanting to be seen dropping her off at the club itself. I told her I'd meet her later, and she nodded and frowned, but didn't question me.

I did not feel like returning to the Tropical just now, so I drove over to the modernistic sprawl of the Broadwater Beach Hotel, where I treated myself to lobster in the Royal Terrace dining room. After that beating, I felt I deserved a decent meal, plus I was celebrating my imminent departure from this hellhole of a tourist paradise.

After a leisurely meal, I returned to my rental Chevelle in

the Broadwater parking lot and got the video cassette with the blank label from the floor of the back seat. I placed the cassette snugly against the left rear tire, then got in the vehicle, started it up, and backed over the rectangle of plastic with a satisfying crunch. I pulled forward slightly, bumping over it again, and the crunching became more of a crackle.

I got out and retrieved the smashed, flattened cassette, its video-tape guts squishing out, pieces of plastic flaking off. I tucked the object under my arm and strolled around to the marina in front of the hotel. The night was rather dark and there were few lights out on the waters. At the end of a dock, I tossed the mangled video tape long and hard. Its splash seemed nicely distant.

Just before midnight, I sauntered into Mr. Woody's as if I owned the place, and in a way I did. The big guy on the door frowned at me but said nothing as I moved into the smoky near-darkness. The stripper on stage was the short redhead with real breasts; this was early on in her routine, because both pasties and g-string were still in place as she worked it to Ike and Tina Turner's "Proud Mary."

Weaving around the occasional waitresses in their white shirts and black minis, I made for the door that said PRIVATE — NO ENTRY. The shaved-head Tony Orlando-mustached brute again stood watch in that same bored genie crossed-arms stance. He raised an eyebrow at me. I wondered if that came natural or had taken practice. Either way, Leonard Nimoy had nothing to worry about.

I gave him a near smile and said, "Tell Mr. Woody that Quarry is here to see him."

The raised eyebrow came down and a dumb-shit expression took over, indicating that maybe he was familiar with the name. But after a beat or two, he nodded, said, "Wait here," and went in.

I waited.

Maybe thirty seconds passed, as Mr. Woody decided whether or not he wanted to see me. I didn't blame him for needing time to think—after all, I'd had all afternoon to figure out how I would handle this.

The door opened and the big bald bouncer said, "I need to pat you down."

I opened my leisure-suit jacket and showed him the nine millimeter in the shoulder holster. "That's all I'm packing, and I'm not giving it to you."

He thought about that.

"But you're a big guy," I said. "You might be able to take it off me."

He thought about that.

"Look," I said, "I work for Mr. Woody, too. He *insists* that I be armed."

We were now officially dealing with concepts above his pay grade and all he could do was shrug and lumber back to his post while I headed down the hallway to the door marked MR. WOODY — PLEASE KNOCK.

I knocked, then went in.

He was already standing behind the steel desk. The room was as before, though the framed stripper posters were mostly gone, no doubt transferred to his new, nicer digs atop the Tropical. One remained, of Carol Doda, the girl who put fake tits on the map.

"My God, boy, am I relieved to see you," he said, gesturing to a waiting visitor's chair. "Sit! Please. Sit."

I did, and he did.

He was, as always, all eyes and teeth, the silver-gray comb-over rigidly in place; his leisure suit was about the green of the lower half of the Fleetwood I'd abandoned this morning in downtown Memphis. His shirt, a lighter green, was unbuttoned some to reveal tan skin, gray chest hair, and gold chains.

"I thought you'd left town on me," Mr. Woody said with a sideways grin. "I called and called your room at the Tropical, left message after message."

This of course was a lie: he hadn't considered that Luann would have been in my room to contradict him.

I said, "I had something of a narrow escape."

He frowned at me. "Is that…*make-up* on your face? What…?"

"I got pretty badly beaten up last night. I had to plaster this stuff on to make myself presentable."

He lifted his half-gone tumbler of Scotch in salute. "Can I get you somethin', boy? *Beat up*, you say?"

I waved off the drink offer and said, "Three guys rushed into my room last night, around, oh, nine? They pulled me out bare-ass and dumped me in the trunk of a car."

"What? Jesus! No! Go on."

"Well, it was an interesting car to get dumped in the back of—a two-tone green Fleetwood Caddy."

He squinted at me, as if seeing no significance to that. Sipped some Scotch, as he waited patiently for clarification.

"That's the drive-by car," I said, "from the Concort Inn. That nearly got the Broker and me?"

"Was it? Damn! Well, though, that makes sense."

"Does it?"

Mr. Woody waved a hand. "My word yes. Remember, I said the shooter you took down, there in Davenport, had a cousin in the moonshine bidness? A cousin he recruited as his wheel-man for the Broker run? Well, the cuz must've come *lookin'* for you."

"The man I killed didn't look like any moonshiner."

"You *killed* the man?" He shook his head. "What the hell happened, Quarry? Tell me your story."

So I told him my story. I didn't leave a damn thing out. I wanted him to hear what I'd done to Buck and Chuck and the man in Room 14. Every hammer blow, blowtorch swipe, and bullet in the back.

He finished his Scotch, got up, went to the liquor cart, and poured himself some more. "Jesus fuckin' Christ, Quarry. That is one harrowin' story. Sure I can't get you anythin'? If not hard stuff, how about a Barq's?"

"I'm fine." I shifted in my chair. "Is this all such a surprise? Didn't you hear what happened at the Dixie Club?"

He sat behind the desk again, nodding. "That the place burned down and some charred bodies turned up, yes. And that there's an unfortunate, as yet unidentified, shot to shit and floatin' in the motel pool."

"I kind of figured you'd know," I said, "since you mentioned to the sheriff yesterday how you'd made peace with the Dixons. Please tell me, Woody, that you didn't betray me to those *Hee-Haw* rejects."

He raised a palm, frowned in wounded displeasure. "Quarry, no. I am nothin' if not loyal to my people."

Just ask Jack Killian.

Mr. Woody was saying, "But I don't have to tell you how crazy them inbred state-liners can be. I guess they just didn't know who or what they was up against."

"I guess."

He swallowed. Rocked in his chair. "Well, you survived it, and that's what counts. It just shows to go ya that my confidence in your potential was damn well-placed. More than *ever* I want you to stay on here as my top man."

I shook my head. "No, Woody, I'm going to have to pass. When they start beating my bare ass senseless, and come at me with hammers and blowtorches, I draw the line. I'm heading home."

He sighed. Rocked some more. "Can't say as I blame you. You leave with my blessin', son, and do give the Broker my best regards." He extended his hand.

I raised a "stop" hand. "Woody, I'm not leaving just yet. We have a separate though related business matter to discuss first."

"We do?" The extended hand seemed to wilt.

I nodded. "I've been put through the mill, I guess you could say…"

"I guess you could."

"…and I feel I deserve some compensation."

Eyebrows that needed trimming rose above the goggle-style glasses. "Well, I don't know, Quarry—you pulled down some heavy bread from Jackie. I give you that little hooker on the house. Took care of your room tab, meals included. I'm sorry you got beat to shit, but that was not my doin'…if you're fishin' for some kind of severance pay, I don't think I can help. I mean, you only worked for me a day or so, and ain't done jack squat yet."

"Oh, you don't owe me anything in that regard."

"Okay. Good. Agreed."

I sat forward. "But I have something I'd like to offer you. Sell you."

"Sell *me*? I don't believe I'm in the market for much of anythin'."

"You are this. It's a videotape. One of those broadcast-type cassettes? Very high quality."

He frowned. "And why would I want that?"

"Because it has your wife fucking Jack Killian on it. In the Caligula Suite. The night he was killed."

His mouth pulled to the sides as if a smile was about to blossom, but instead froze in a fleshy-lipped grimace. Behind the thick lenses, the eyes were wide with the blankness that precedes rage.

"If," I said, "you're trying to decide whether to act surprised… maybe play cuckold or some shit…let me save you the trouble. It's obvious that *you* put your wife in bed with Killian that night."

"*What?* Why the *hell* would I—"

"To make it easier for me to get at him. She drugged his wine, too, didn't she? Later you sent her around to fuck with me *and* my head. Whether she's your partner in this or just your top whore, I wouldn't hazard a guess."

That round face went red as a ripe tomato.

"I guarantee you," I said, "there are no copies. I know tape copies *could* be made, but I don't know how, and don't have access to anything or anyone who could."

The red began to drain, lingering in his neck. I'd been hoping I might be treated to some nice deep purple, but this was more a whiter shade of pale.

He spluttered, "Who gives a diddly damn if you do have such a tape? Might be personally embarrassin' to me and my Wanda, this little peccadillo, but—"

"This tape puts your wife in bed with Killian just minutes before his death. That raises very embarrassing questions. Now, your friend the sheriff might not ask those questions, but the T.B.I. well might."

The Tennessee Bureau of Investigation. I admit that sounded a little like a TV show with a laugh track, but it got the right reaction out of Mr. Woody.

"How much, Quarry? How much?"

"Fifty thousand."

"You have a very peculiar sense of humor."

"I have a very keen sense of what I've been put through."

The fleshy upper lip formed a sneer. "You really think I keep *that* kind of money here at the club?"

"I have no idea what you do. Most of what you people down

here do in this fucking swamp eludes me. But that's my price. Fifty k."

He drank some Scotch, slowly. His eyes were narrow and moving behind the lenses. He seemed to be settling down.

Finally: "I will need till tomorrow mornin'. *Late* mornin'. This requires a visit to a safe deposit box."

"All right. You mind if I keep my room at the Tropical till then?"

He shrugged, overdoing it. "Why not? You're still my guest. I can meet you at your room with the money, if you like."

"Make it the parking lot. Noon?"

He nodded. "Noon'll be jes' fine."

I grinned at him, getting up. "Don't take it personally, Woody— it's just 'bidness.' After all, I did rid you of Killian. Think what kind of money and power'll come your way now."

He was breathing heavily through about the most strained smile imaginable, saying nothing.

I went out.

Luann was on stage, bare as the day she came into the world, but sharing attributes that had come along much later. Every chair ringside was filled, though only a few tables were. The sound system was blaring Three Dog Night's "Joy to the World."

I gave her a little nod and she gave me one back.

FIFTEEN

I waited in the Chevelle in Mr. Woody's parking lot until Luann came out in the short-sleeve Ole Miss sweatshirt and jeans. This was right before three and just after the patrons had stumbled out, some adjusting trousers, others doing their best to walk straight. She had stopped dancing at two-thirty—the bar's clocks were set ahead twenty minutes, not an uncommon practice—and had quickly gathered her things and hustled out.

"It went well," I said.

"Good." She seemed nervous but I could tell only because I knew to look.

I said, "There's time to take you back to the motel."

"No. I'll wait here."

"You can't drive. I don't see what good—"

"If I see somebody comin', I can honk the horn and warn you."

That actually made sense.

"Well, if I'm in there, and you hear shots and I don't come right out? You slip out of the car and run off somewhere. Just get the hell away, and hide till it seems safe."

"Okay. Can I have a gun?"

"Have you ever fired one?"

She shook her head. "But I know what to do. Point and squeeze."

Hawaii Five-O. Who said kids can't learn anything from television?

I showed her how the safety worked and handed the snubnose over.

Various employees poured out, the strippers and waitresses and female bartenders in a kind of pack, followed by the two bouncers, who were lighting up smokes. Luann had already told me there was no clean-up crew—that was done by day. I started the car and pulled around to the rear lot for the Lucky Seven casino, where employees were still trailing out. Took a little longer on this side. Money in windows that had to be balanced and so on. But by 3:45, the Lucky Seven was dark.

I got out, leaving her in the car back there, grabbed something from the back seat floor, and ambled around to the front, where I got a start: there were no cars in the lot.

Had Mr. Woody gone home while we were checking out the back?

I positioned myself along the side of the building, nine millimeter in hand, peeking around the corner, wondering if I'd blown it.

Within a minute, a two-tone brown Caddy swung in, kicking up gravel. Mrs. Woody was behind the wheel, and barely cut her speed till she was parallel to the front entry. Apparently she was picking up her husband, who came out on cue. He was locking up as she hopped out in a dark pants suit and heels, a little purse tucked under an arm.

They stood facing each other, the building to his back, the vehicle to hers, and began to talk animatedly. I couldn't hear what they were saying, in part because she had left the Caddy's motor running and its stereo, too—Barbra Streisand singing "Don't Rain on My Parade."

But they heard me fine when I stepped out and pointed the nine millimeter at them: "I don't think we should conduct business out here, do you?"

With my other hand, I held up the surviving video cassette and waved it just a little.

They made like a freeze-frame at the end of movie, then came to life in slow motion, Mr. Woody unlocking the door to the club and his wife studying me the way a spider does a fly trapped in its web. Only she had it backwards.

He led us through—like the Dixie Club's casino last night, Mr. Woody's was lit only by glowing beer neons—and his wife fell in alongside me.

She whispered, "If you stay and work for Woody, you and I…" And she raised both eyebrows and gave me a wicked half-smile.

So at least the job would have perks.

Then we were in his office. I tossed the video cassette on the desktop with a clunk, as if it were nothing special. I let him get behind there and his country-club wife towered next to him, tossing her purse on the desk with a smaller clunk.

I pointed the nine millimeter at him.

"I apologize about the indignities you suffered last night," Mr. Woody said with quiet sincerity. "How did you know that I was in back of it, anyway?"

"They had a key. It's your fucking motel. Woody, guy, fella—you sold me out to the Dixons. Come on, we went over this."

He folded his hands before him, as if to demonstrate he did not have in mind going for any gun that might be in a desk drawer or somewhere.

"I underestimated you, Quarry. Now, from the start I truly *was* impressed with you…that was never a lie…but now I see that you really are someone who could be of great value to me. Of enormous use."

He did love to use people.

"Here's the thing," I said. "I know this has been you all the way. *You* sent that prick in the green Caddy to take a shot at the Broker."

He stared at me agape. "Why in hell would I want to kill the *Broker*? He's my friend and colleague. That was *Killian's* doin'! You know that!"

"Only because you told me so. No. This is your doing. Anyway, you *didn't* try to kill the Broker—your man was told to miss. To just throw a scare into your 'friend and colleague,' to encourage him to send somebody down to kill Killian for you. Somebody like me. So you have Jackie out of the way, while taking no blame or credit for it…but Biloxi is all yours."

He began to say something, then just shrugged, and unleashed all those teeth in a big shit-eatin' grin, his eyes falling to the rectangle of plastic on his desk.

"What can I say, Quarry? I *really* did underestimate you. Now, as it happens, I *do* have considerable funds on hand here at the club."

"Fifty grand in funds?"

He almost seemed embarrassed. "Actually…I do. I was, uh… just putting you off to buy a little time. Would you mind if I had my lovely wife take down that framed poster of Miss Doda there? Wall safe's behind 'er."

"Fine."

Wicked Wanda gave me a flinch of a smile and I backed up, almost into the hall—I'd left the door open—and she went to the framed poster and removed it from its nail, rested it below. About the size of a 45 record, a gray metallic circle with a combination dial and handle was now exposed. Wanda glanced at me and I waved the gun for her to go back to where she'd been. She did.

Mr. Woody rose, slowly, and gestured toward the safe with an open hand, saying, "May I?"

I nodded. "If you come back with a gun, I'll shoot you both."

He paused to raise his hands as if in surrender, flashing all those teeth. "There is no weapon in that safe, son. Not that I truly *believe* you would shoot an unarmed woman."

"You never know."

He dialed the combination and swung the little round door open. He reached in and came back not with a gun, but with banded money—one at a time, stacks of hundreds each making ten thousand. As promised, there were five of these. He set them on the desk, near the video cassette he was buying, shut the safe, re-hung the Carol Doda poster, and resumed his place, sitting with hands again folded.

"I assure you, son, that if you stay on board and become a partner, *not* an adversary, this amount here, that must seem so considerable, will become triflin' indeed."

That didn't rate a response.

I turned to his wife. "Hey. Lady Macbeth. Hand me your purse."

She frowned just a little. "My purse?"

I just looked at her and she shrugged and handed it over. Shifting the nine millimeter to my left hand, I unsnapped the purse with my right, bracing the thing against my left forearm, and dug inside. As the clunk had indicated, a weapon was in there. I let the purse drop but held onto the little gun, a .25 automatic.

Mr. Woody frowned at me, making the hazel eyes behind the lenses smaller. "What the hell, man—"

But when I swung the little gun in his direction, those eyes got very big again and I put a bullet in his left one, spider-webbing the lens, his mouth open to express words of shock that would never come.

She lurched at me with bared teeth and clawed hands, red nails looking plenty sharp, but I sidestepped like a bullfighter and, the snout of her .25 flush to flesh and hair, shot her in the right temple.

She fell in an ungainly pile that seemed mostly legs and I put my nine millimeter away while I knelt to wipe off the .25 and press it into her right hand.

"Oh my," someone said.

I turned fast and there in the hallway was Luann, a hand to her lips. She had the .38 in the other hand, pointing down. Those almost invisible-blue eyes were wide.

She said, barely audible, "I thought you might need help."

I collected the .38 from her, stuffed it in my waistband, and took her by the elbow, walking her into the club where she'd danced so many times. I sat her down there in darkness and told her to stay put, not even taking time to scold her for not staying in the car.

So she'd witnessed another two killings of mine. This was getting to be a bothersome habit on her part. I'd deal with that later.

For now, I needed to check out the scene of the two latest killings and make sure things were staged correctly. The bodies didn't need any help in their positioning, and I hadn't touched much of anything. The wife had lost her grace in death, sprawled on the floor and taking up a lot of space. Mr. Woody slumped forward on the desk, his eyes open and surprised. No gore got on the money, the wall behind him getting a squirt of blood and brains. The currency *was* a little clumsy to deal with—I had to distribute packets to various pockets.

Then I looked everything over. Seemed fine. The video cassette on the desk would help explain this tragedy.

But I sure hoped Mrs. Woody had been right-handed.

SIXTEEN

I drove Luann back to the Tropical Motel. It wasn't dawn yet. The little cracks that were the .25 automatic's gunshots did not seem to have attracted any attention—doubtful they could even be heard outside the warehouse-like structure that housed Mr. Woody's and the Lucky Seven. The tragic homicide-suicide in the strip club office wouldn't be found for a while. No reason not to go back and check out. Or anyway, leave.

She had a few things to gather in her room, all of which fit into one light-blue suitcase and that canvas tote. I had a single suitcase, too, but also a garment bag courtesy of Godchaux's for the three black suits I'd acquired. Now I was ready for weddings and funerals, and job interviews, should I ever decide to change professions.

We each freshened up a little, and as sunlight began bleeding in around the curtains onto the parking lot, Luann and I—both in jeans and t-shirts now, an odd reminder that only a few years of age separated us—once again sat on the foot of the bed.

She had her interlaced hands in her lap and looked pale.

Without looking at me, she asked, "Why don't you kill me?"

"What, is that a request?"

Not surprisingly, she didn't smile at that. A sense of humor wasn't her long suit, and anyway it was kind of in bad taste.

Looking at the TV screen as she so often did, only now it was blank but for our distorted reflections on the curved glass, she said, "I saw you kill those people. It was so fast. They were alive and then...not."

"That's how it always is. Even when guns aren't involved. There's life in you and then there isn't."

She swallowed and looked at her folded hands. "Did she deserve it? His wife? Was she the mastermind or somethin'?"

"Pulling her husband's strings? Maybe. Anyway, she was in it with him. Doesn't matter."

"Doesn't?"

"No, and as for deserving it, hell, I don't know. She got involved in murder and that opens you up for things."

Her face turned toward me, eyes slitted, like she was trying to bring me into focus. "So you're not goin' to kill me?"

"No."

"But you'd probably say that if you were."

"Yes."

Strangely, that didn't seem to bother her. "When you drowned that man, it didn't seem real."

"Well, you saw it on a TV screen. It's different, close up."

She nodded. "I'm sorry."

"What for?"

"For askin' you to kill Mr. Woody."

"You're not sorry you're *free* of him, though."

She shook her head firmly. "No. No, I'm glad. And maybe there was no other way. Maybe I'm just sorry I saw it. So if you not gon' to kill me, Johnny, what do we do now?"

I patted her denim-clad knee. "You are going to go back to your life."

"Really?"

I raised a palm. "Temporarily. Not hooking, unless you want to. But dancing. Just kind of staying…under the radar."

She frowned at me. "I don't know what you mean."

"I mean, there's nothing to connect you to those killings. You're just a dumb little stripper who's going about her business. Other Dixie Mafia people will step up and take over, right? The clubs and so on?"

She nodded.

I asked, "Are you beholden to any of them?"

"No. Just Mr. Woody. He controlled my money."

"He doesn't anymore. You just keep an eye on the papers. You can read, right?"

She nodded. "I went to the seventh grade."

"Okay, good. Watch and see if what just happened goes down as a murder-suicide. If that's the case, you go to the bank where your money is. With Mr. Woody dead, you'll be able to get at it."

She smiled, nodded some more. "Kinda thought that might be the way."

No dope, this kid.

I said, "If they call it two murders, just sit back a while. You don't want to be a suspect. You might just wait for the bank to contact you."

"Will they?"

"Probably. If not, you may have to keep your head down and your body in shape and keep dancing a while."

"Easy on the cheeseburgers?"

"Maybe a little. In the meantime…"

I got up and went over to my suitcase on a little metal and canvas stand by the dresser. The nine millimeter was in there. I counted out three of the five banded packets of hundreds. I tossed them one at a time on the bed next to her. Her eyes went wider than Orphan Annie's.

"What's that for?" she asked.

"For you. Thirty grand. I'm keeping twenty for myself. That's what Mr. Woody paid us for the video tape of his wife fucking his partner. Don't declare it on your income tax."

"Mr. Woody always handled that stuff for me."

"Well, he won't be now. This is just your…get-out-of-town money. Which you'll do at some point. How much you got in the bank?"

"Eighty-seven-thousand-five-hundred-and-forty-two-dollars-and-fifteen-cents."

I whistled low and slow. "Nice nest egg. When you have that money, you add this to it. You can go somewhere and buy that strip bar you were talking about…just *not* in Biloxi."

She had a determined look. "If I do, I won't strip."

"That's fine. Make it just a bar then. Or some other kind of business. You know, you could get a night-school high school diploma and go to college and just make a whole new life of it. Future's a blank slate, honey. Don't keep doing what you're doing just because it's all you know. Learn something else."

Like maybe I should give up killing people and become a guidance counselor.

Her eyes sparked and now her hand was on *my* knee. "What if I went with you? You must live somewhere."

"But you know what I am and what I do."

"I don't care long as I don't have to watch. I bet you live somewhere nice. We could be more than friends."

The thought of her sharing the A-frame on Paradise Lake with me did not actually suck. But I didn't think what we'd had this past week was really something to build a life on. Of course, when your kid wanted to know how you met Mommy, you'd have some tale to tell.

"Luann, we need to go our separate ways. Together we might…get caught."

"Really?"

I nodded toward the money. "You may think you're a witness to crimes I committed, but you're not."

"No?"

"You're an accomplice. You were Bonnie to my Clyde at the Dixie Club when I killed three people. You hired me to kill Mr. Woody. Makes you as guilty of murder as me. Also, we blackmailed him with that video tape you made. We stay with each other, somebody might put the pieces together. Connect us with bad things."

This was part bullshit, part reality.

She frowned at the blank TV screen. "I thought you might have to kill me. Because I was a witness."

"No. You're an accomplice."

"Cool."

I had to laugh. "I don't know if that's how I'd put it, Luann."

She shrugged. "Well, it means we each know things about each other that we can't tell without gettin' both of us in trouble. If I tell, you tell. If you tell, I tell."

"Right."

"Means I can trust you and you can trust me."

The Jack Killian definition of trust again.

I said, "Yes it does, Luann," hoping they didn't teach her about immunity if she went to college. "Look, can I drop you somewhere?"

She studied me, nodded toward the bed. "You want to do it one last time?"

I gave her a kiss. Small one. "I don't think so. I think we covered that. We should go."

"Okay. We've probably made enough nice memories."

The funny thing was she was right.

On the way out of town, I would call the Broker and tell him I was on my way home, and that I had a hell of a story to tell. I figured he'd be happy with how I handled things and maybe even throw in some extra cash. That meant I'd have to edit out the twenty thousand I'd kept. And I would have to revise my report to leave Luann out. Didn't want her to be my next contract.

That memory I didn't need.

AUTHOR'S NOTE

Despite its period setting, *Quarry's Choice* is not an historical novel, and does not intend to suggest real people or events. Much of it takes place in the Biloxi, Mississippi, of the author's imagination, including among other things a loose interpretation of geography.

Though none of these works should be held accountable for any inaccuracies and excesses herein, I would like to acknowledge the following: *Biloxi* (Images of America series, 2009), Jamie Bounds Ellis and Jane B. Shambra; *Biloxi* (Postcard History Series, 2012), Alan J. and Joan C. Santa Cruz and Jane B. Shambra; *Dream Room* (2009), Chet Nicholson; *Mississippi Mud* (2010 edition), Edward Humes; and *The State-Line Mob* (1990), W. R. Morris.

Also, thanks to my pal Ron Parker for answering a couple of research questions.

WANT MORE QUARRY?

Try These Other Quarry Novels From
MAX ALLAN COLLINS and
HARD CASE CRIME...

The First Quarry

The ruthless hitman's first assignment: kill a philandering professor who has run afoul of some very dangerous men.

Quarry In the Middle

When two rival casino owners covet the same territory, guess who gets caught in the crossfire...

The Last Quarry

Retired killer Quarry gets talked into one last contract—but why would anyone want a beautiful librarian dead...?

Quarry's Ex

An easy job: protect the director of a low-budget movie. Until the director's wife turns out to be a woman out of Quarry's past.

The Wrong Quarry

Quarry zeroes in on the grieving family of a missing cheerleader. Does the hitman's hitman have the wrong quarry in his sights?

Read On for a
Sample Chapter From
THE WRONG QUARRY!

For a guy who killed people for a living, he was just about the most boring bastard I ever saw.

I had been tailing him for two days, as he made his way from Woodstock, Illinois, where he owned an antiques shop on the quaint town square, to…well, I didn't know where yet.

So far it had been every little town—on a circuitous route taking us finally to Highway 218—with an antiques shop, where he would go in and poke around and come out with a few finds to stow in the trunk of his shit-brown Pontiac Bonneville.

If it hadn't been for the explosion of red hair with matching beard that made his head seem bigger than it was, he would have been a human bowling pin, five-foot-eight of flab in a gray quilted ski jacket. He wore big-frame orange-lensed glasses both indoors and out, his nose a potato with nostrils and zits, his lips thick and purple. That this creature sometimes sat surveillance himself seemed like a joke.

I was fairly certain he was on his way to kill somebody—possibly somebody in Iowa, because that was the state we'd been cutting down on the vertical line of Highway 218. Right now we were running out of Iowa and the flat dreary landscape was threatening to turn into Missouri.

Soon there would be fireworks stands—even though it was crisp November and the Fourth of the July a moot point—and people would suddenly speak in the lazy musical tones of the South, as if the invisible line on the map between these Midwestern states was the Mason–Dixon.

Some people find this accent charming. So do I, if it's a

buxom wench with blonde pigtails getting out of her bandana blouse and cut-off jeans in a hayloft. Otherwise, you can have it.

Right now my guy was making a stop that looked like a problem. Turning off and driving into some little town to check out an antiques shop was manageable. No matter how small that town was, there was always somewhere I could park inconspicuously and keep an eye on Mateski (which was his name—Mateski, Ronald Mateski...not exactly Bond, James Bond).

But when he pulled off and then into the gravel lot of an antiques mini-mall on the edge of a town, I had few options. Pulling into the lot myself wasn't one of them, unless I was prepared to get out and go browsing with Mateski.

Not that there was any chance he'd make me. I had stayed well back from him on the busy two-lane, and when he would stop to eat at a truck stop, I would either sit in my car in the parking lot, if that lot were crowded enough for me to blend in, or take a seat in the trucker's section away from the inevitable booth where Mateski had set down his big ass.

This time I had no choice but to go in and browse. Had there been a gas station and mini-mart across the way, I could have pulled in there. But this was a tin-shed antiques mall that sat near a cornfield like a twister had plopped it down.

Mateski's penchant was primitive art and furniture—apparently it was what sold well for him back in rustic Woodstock. He didn't have his truck with him (a tell that he wasn't *really* out on a buying trip), so any furniture would have to be prime enough to spend shipping on; but he did find a framed oil that he snatched up like he'd found a hundred-dollar bill on the pavement—depicting a winter sunset that looked like your half-blind grandmother painted it.

I stopped at stalls with used books and at one I picked up a few Louis L'Amour paperbacks I hadn't read yet, making sure I was still browsing when he left. Picking him up again would be no problem. He'd be getting back on Highway 218 and heading for somewhere, probably in Missouri. Hannibal maybe. Or St. Louis.

But when I got back on the road, I thought I'd lost him. Then I spotted his mud-spattered Bonneville at a Standard pump, said, "Fuck," and took the next out-of-sight illegal U-turn I could to go back.

When I got there, he was inside paying. I could use some gas myself, so I turned my dark green Ford Pinto over to the attendant and went into the restaurant side of the small truck stop and took a piss. Mateski was gone when I got out, which was fine. I paid for my gas, bought gum and a Coke, and hit the road again, picking him up soon, always keeping a couple cars between us.

This is just how exciting yesterday and today had been. Not the Steve McQueen chase in *Bullitt*. But despite his fat ass and his thing for lousy art, Mateski was a dangerous guy. That he usually worked the passive side of a two-man contract team didn't mean he hadn't killed his share himself. The Broker had always insisted that the passive side of a duo had to take the active role once out of every four jobs. Keep your hand in. Use it or lose it.

The Broker had been the middleman through whom I used to get my assignments. I much preferred the active role, coming in for a day or two and handling the wet work, rather than sitting for a couple of weeks in cars and at surveillance posts taking detailed notes as to habits and patterns of a target.

Don't get me wrong. I don't enjoy killing. I just don't mind. It's something I learned to do overseas, as a sniper, where I developed the kind of dispassionate attitude needed for that kind of work. Killing is a necessary evil, as they say, although I don't know that it's all that evil in a lot of cases. War and self-defense, for instance.

On the other hand, there was one notorious asshole in the trade who specialized in torture. I mention him in passing now, but eventually it will have some importance. File it away.

As for me, my name is unimportant, but when I first started killing people for money—not counting Vietnam—I worked through the Broker. This tall, slender, dapper, distinguished-looking man of business, who might have been a banker or a CEO, recruited people like me, who had unwittingly learned a trade in the employ of Uncle Sam. He was something of a pompous ass—for example, he called me Quarry, which was a sort of horseshit code name, derived from my supposed cold-ness ("Hollow like carved-out rock," he said once) and also ironic, since the targets were *my* quarry.

So Broker's people that I worked with called me "Quarry" and I got used to it. On occasion I even used it as the last name of a cover identity, and as it happens, this was one of those occasions. John R. Quarry, according to my Wyoming driver's license, Social Security and Mastercard. So for our purpose here, that name will do as well as any.

I should probably clue you in a little about me. I was closer to thirty than forty, five ten, one hundred-sixty-five pounds, short brown hair, but not military short. Kept in shape, mostly through swimming. Handsome enough, I suppose, in a bland, unremarkable way. When was this? Well, Reagan hadn't been president long enough for his senility to show (much), and everybody was hurting from the recession.

Well, actually, I wasn't. Hurting. I lived quietly, comfortably and alone in an A-frame cottage on Lake Paradise near Geneva, Wisconsin. I had no one woman, but the resort area nearby meant I was rarely lonely. I had a small circle of friends who thought I sold veterinary medicine, but really I was semi-retired from the killing business.

"Semi" because I still kept my hand in, but not in the old way. After the Broker betrayed me and I got rid of him, I sort of inherited what today would be called a database, but back then was just a small pine file cabinet. Within it was what was essentially a list of over fifty names of guys like me, who had worked for the Broker—detailed info on each, photos, addresses, down to every job they'd gone on.

Since I was out of work, after killing the Broker, I'd had an intriguing idea. I could see how I could use the Broker's file, and keep going, in a new way, on my own terms. After destroying the information on myself, I would choose a name and travel to where that party lived and stake him or her out (a few females were on the list), then follow said party to their next job.

Through further surveillance, I would determine their target's identity, approach that target, and offer to eliminate the threat. For a healthy sum, I would discreetly remove the hit team. For a further fee, I might—depending on the circumstances—be able to look into who had hired the hit done, and remove that threat as well.

The risks were considerable. What if a target—approached with a wild story from a stranger claiming to be a sort of contract killer himself—called the authorities, or otherwise freaked out?

But I was well aware that anyone designated for death was somebody who had almost certainly done something worth dying over. Targets of hitmen tend not to be upstanding citizens, unless they are upstanding citizens with down-and-dirty secrets. And weren't they likely to be aware that they presented a problem to some powerful, merciless adversary? The kind of adversary who would be capable of such an extreme solution...?

From the start, I felt confident that such people would welcome my help. After all, their other option was to take a bullet or get hit by a car or have one of those accidental long drops off a short pier. And the fee I could charge—most people value their *own* lives highly—would mean I'd only have to take on these risky tasks perhaps a couple of times a year.

On the other hand, those "couple of times" required a huge amount of spec work. First, I always chose from the Broker's list names whose preference was passive, meaning I was guaranteeing myself a considerable amount of surveillance—but this was necessary, because if I followed the active participant to a kill, the passive half might already be in the wind, leaving a dangerous loose end. Both halves needed removal.

I had been lucky a few times, and staked out parties who within a few weeks had gone out on a job, minimizing my layout of time. But professionals in the killing game—again, because of the risk and the high fees—seldom take more than three or four jobs a year. At least the teams working for the Broker didn't.

That meant I could sit stakeout—renting a house across from a subject, for example, sitting in a car like a damn cop drinking coffee after coffee from paper cups—for literally months. This had happened several times. So I had begun to take measures to limit my expenditure of time.

Ronald Mateski was a good example.

Once I had determined Mateski was an antiques dealer, I began to call his Woodstock shop once a week from a series of pay phones in the Geneva area. If I got Mateski, I would ask for the business hours, or mutter wrong number. If I got a clerk, usually a female, I would say that I had an item I wanted to bring into the shop for Mr. Mateski to appraise—would he be around next week?

And when at last I'd been told Mr. Mateski would be gone for two weeks on a buying trip, going to estate auctions and the like, I thanked the girl, hung up, and smiled to myself…knowing that Mr. Mateski was heading out on a job.

And the length of time he'd be away meant that he was, as usual, taking the passive role.

That had meant a comparatively painless (if still painful) two days of tailing Ronald Boring Mateski to wherever the fuck he was heading—Iowa? Arkansas, God help me?—and determining his target: the person he would be gathering information on for the active half of the team, the killer who would be arriving at some indeterminate time in the near future.

Indeterminate because these killing teams—particularly now that the Broker was out of the picture—sometimes maintained surveillance for several weeks, and other times for as little as a few days.

My prep for this trip had been minimal. Select an I.D., pack clothes including a couple of nondescript sport coats and suits and white shirts and ties and the sweatshirts and polos and jeans I preferred, a few guns (my nine millimeter, a noise suppressor, and a back-up .38 snubnose revolver), a hunting knife in sheath, switchblade, lock picks, canister of chloroform, rags, several pairs of surgical gloves, some duct tape, a coil of clothesline. The usual.

And of course I'd driven a good distance from my home area to buy the 1980 Pinto, which cost a grand cash, the kind of nothing car that helps nobody notice you.

Around four o'clock, Mateski pulled off and drove twenty miles—longer than any previous antiques-buying detour—into Stockwell, Missouri, whose WELCOME TO sign included all the requisite lodges and an interesting designation: "Little Vacationland of Missouri."

We'd barely got past the city limits before he pulled into a row-of-cabins-style motel called the Rest Haven Court. It looked clean and well-maintained, and even had a small tarp-covered swimming pool. But it obviously dated back to Bonnie and Clyde days. Mateski stopped at the slightly larger cabin near the neon sign to check in.

Directly across the street was a modest-size Holiday Inn and that's where I pulled in, but for now I just sat in the lot, watching across the way in my rear-view mirror. Mateski must have had a reservation, because it took him under three minutes to register. Then he was back in the Bonneville to drive over to the farthest of twelve cabins, where he parked. Only three other cars were in the spaces at cabins. From his trunk, out from under the crap paintings he'd bought, he withdrew a small suitcase, and went over to the door marked 12 and let himself in.

I got out, stretched, yawned, making something of a show of it. Got my fleece-lined leather bomber jacket out of the back seat and slipped it on; I was otherwise in a sweatshirt, jeans and running shoes.

Was he in for the night?

Surely he would have to get settled. He might not even start surveillance till tomorrow. I decided to risk it.

At the desk, I asked for a second-floor room facing the street. The female clerk, a pleasant, permed platinum blonde in her twenties wearing big-frame glasses (much nicer than Mateski's and minus the rust-color lenses), informed me that I could have just about any room in the place.

"This is the start of off-season," she said chirpily. She had big brown eyes and a Judy Holliday voice—well, it was the Holiday Inn, wasn't it?

"An off-season for what?"

Very nice, very white smile. She might be worth cultivating as a source and, well…cultivating.

"Stockwell Park is the nicest fun spot this side of the Ozarks," she said. "People come from all over."

"Oh?"

She nodded and that mane of frizzy hair bounced. "Trails, trees, all kinds of greenery, so much space. Tennis courts, volleyball, playgrounds, swimming pool. Duck pond, too. Also, Stockwell Field is near there—we have a triple-A ball club, you know."

"In a town of twenty thousand?"

"Oh, Stockwell really hops in the summer. If we hadn't had this cold snap…and, uh, you know, the recession…we'd be doing land-office business, even now."

"Must get a little dull around here, then."

"It can be. We have live music in the lounge, on the weekend, if you're planning to stay that long."

This was Thursday.

"I might be here a week or more," I said. "Is there a reduced rate for that?"

"There is, if you pay a week in advance."

So we did the strictly business thing, and I got all checked in as John Quarry, but our eyes and mouths were being friendly. Maybe I could get laid on this trip. I already felt like I deserved it, after two days of Ronald Mateski. She seemed like a nice girl, and with her working here, so convenient.

I went up to the room, which I will not insult your intelligence by describing, and placed my suitcase on the stand, got my toiletries distributed on the counter in the john. Shower, no tub. The TV was a 21" Sony, which was nice, and they had a satellite dish, so I'd get a lot of stations. The double bed's mattress seemed a little soft, but I'd live. I went to the window, drew back the curtain, and *shit*, Mateski's car was gone.

I'd managed to fuck up already, making goo-goo eyes at the desk clerk. Someday maybe I would learn to think with the big head.

Not panicking, I took time to throw some water on my face, toweled off, brushed my teeth, decided on the luxury of taking a shit, during which I thought about my options.

Mateski was not here in an active capacity. He would undoubtedly watch the target for at least a week. Certainly nothing less than four days—the bare minimum to get patterns down. So I had no reason to lose my cool. I could wait till tomorrow and pick him up then, or I could drive around small-town Stockwell and see if I could spot his Bonneville. I decided on the latter.

It was a nice little city, well-off—the older homes well-maintained with big yards; numerous housing additions expanded the town's edges, with only one small trailer park to indicate anybody here would feel hard times. The downtown had a rustic look not unlike Mateski's Woodstock, but without a town square—four blocks of businesses faced each other across four lanes. Many businesses included the Stockwell name—STOCKWELL BANK AND TRUST, STOCKWELL INSURANCE, STOCKWELL TRAVEL, and so on. I spotted a large newish high school, tan brick with architecture that said late sixties, a smaller, older Catholic high school, a late fifties/early sixties grade school. A grand-looking county courthouse dated to the late 1800s, as did the similar city hall, just off the main drag.

The park area the desk clerk had extolled was on the west side of town, and I drove through it, winding around a vast expanse of green with the promised sports facilities, though at the far side there was an unexpectedly rocky and hilly area with a stream running through it. This section was mostly inaccessible by car.

This was the kind of all-American town President Reagan

mistakenly thought was typical for the nation, the kind of near-fantasy that Norman Rockwell painted for the *Saturday Evening Post* and that the Jewish moguls at MGM cooked up for Andy Hardy and his Christian audience during the Depression.

Also on the west side was a hilly area of mostly older homes, perhaps not quite as well-maintained but nothing to give the city fathers fits. I cruised this neighborhood and that's when I spotted him.

He was, as is good surveillance practice, sitting in the back seat of the Bonneville. That was wise a couple of ways—people who saw Mateski would assume he was waiting for somebody, and those who glanced at the vehicle, seeing no one in front, particularly after dark (which it was), would not notice him at all.

He was almost directly across from a big black cement-block building that sat on the corner atop the hill with two terraced levels that cement stairs with railing climbed. Across the front of the building, above windows and doors, in very white bold letters, were the words VALE DANCE STUDIO. Lights were on in the building, glowing yellow like a jack-o'-lantern's eyes.

I drove around the block, which required going down the hill, and came up behind the building, where a cement drive taking a sharp turn to enter was labeled VALE DANCE STUDIO PARKING — PRIVATE. What the hell. I pulled in.

Maybe twenty-five cars were waiting there, most with motors running—an interesting mix that included a good share of high-end numbers, Lincolns and Caddies. Men and women, sometimes couples but mostly not, were sitting in the vehicles, a few standing in the cold, smoking.

I pulled the Pinto into a space and got out and walked over in the cold to a woman in a full-length mink coat; her oval face was pretty, with bright red lipstick and jeweled glasses. She was my age, maybe a little older. She was smoking, her hands in leather gloves.

"I'm lost," I lied, my breath making as much smoke as her cigarette. "Can you point me to the Holiday Inn?"

She gave me directions that I didn't need with a smile that I didn't mind. Then I made a move like I was heading back to my car, only to stop and give her my own smile, curiosity-tinged.

I asked, "What *is* this place?"

"Can't you read?" she said, blowing smoke, not bitchy, just teasing.

Big letters saying VALE DANCE STUDIO were across the back of the black cement-block building as well. It was an odd squat-looking building, like a hut got way out of hand, not quite two stories with all the windows fairly low-slung.

"I'm gonna take a wild swing and say it's a dance studio," I said, grinning, my breathing pluming, my hands tucked in the pockets of my fleece-lined jacket. Wouldn't she be surprised to know my right hand was gripping a nine millimeter Browning.

"Yeah," she said, breathing smoke, nodding, clearly chilly, "I used to go come here all the time as a kid."

"You're a dancer, huh?"

"Not really. It was a skating rink when I was in school. We came here all through elementary and junior high."

"Sure. All skate. Ladies' choice. The ol' mirrored disco ball, before they even called it that."

She smiled and laughed and it was smoky in a bunch of ways. "Skating's gone the way of the dodo bird, I guess."

"Except for roller derby."

"Ha!" She nodded toward the building. "It's a dance studio, as you've gathered. Students are junior high and high school girls."

"Oh, you're here to pick up your daughter?"

"Two of them. One I think has a real chance."

"Chance for what?"

"Mr. Roger is working with both my girls, the younger for Miss Teenage Missouri, the older for Miss Missouri. But it's my young one who has a real chance."

"Beauty pageants, huh?"

"They're mostly just called pageants now. You know." She shrugged shoulders thick with mink. "Times change."

"Sure do. They fired Bert Parks, didn't they? So, did you say Mr. Rogers? Like on TV?" I knew she hadn't, but I was milking it.

"No, Mr. Ro*ger*. Roger Vale. It's his studio. He is *so* gifted. And I don't care what anybody says. We stand behind him. Look at all these cars."

"What do you mean?"

She waved at the air and her cigarette made white trails. "You know how it is. People always talk. It's because he's different. That's all I'll say about the matter....*Oh*, there's Julie and Bobbi!"

She dropped her cigarette, toed it out, and waved. Out the back of the building's two rear glass doors, teenage girls in fall and winter coats were emerging, chattering, smiling, laughing. They had a small flight of cement stairs to come down, about a third of what was in front of the building.

"Nice meeting you," I said to the mother, though neither of us had exchanged names.

"You, too," she said, and beamed.

Maybe I should have got her name. That desk clerk wasn't a lock, you know.

I got in the Pinto.

Soon I was heading through the intersection of this otherwise residential neighborhood and could see the brown Bonneville parked in the same place. A few daughters were coming down those front steps with parents picking them up on this side. But not many.

I drove on through and took a left down the other side of the hill, and came around the adjacent block to park on the opposite side of the street, down a ways but with a good view of the Bonneville, its engine off, just another parked vehicle. Me, too. I sat there in the cold, the Pinto's engine off too, wishing I'd grabbed something to eat, but unlike Mateski, I remained in the front seat. I wanted to be able to take off quickly, if need be.

Was he shadowing one of these wealthy parents?

That seemed a good bet. This was a money town, and these were money moms and dads, for the most part.

For whatever reason—maybe some parents had gone inside to have a word with the dance instructor—it was a good hour before the lights in the big black building went out. All the daughters, all the parents, were long gone by now. I started the car up, drove slowly past the parked Bonneville, and again went around the block, down the hill, and came up around and into the parking lot.

Only two cars remained on the gravel—a baby-blue Mustang and a red Corvette, parked very near the foot of the small slope behind the building. Not Lincolns or Caddies, but two very choice automobiles, it seemed to me, especially driving a fucking Pinto.

But no parents or kids were around those vehicles. Everybody was gone. No mink-coat moms, no dads in Cads. Only one light on in the building now, and that had been around front.

The dance instructor?

Did he *live* on the premises, as well? That seemed unlikely but not impossible.

I again nosed the Pinto out of the lot, turning left, heading down the hill. I turned around in a drive and came up and parked opposite the dance studio's parking lot entrance. I had barely done this when another car pulled in just ahead of me and parked.

The Bonneville.

Shit fuck hell, as the nun said when she hammered her thumb.

I just sat there with my nine mil in my hand, draped across my lap, wondering if I'd screwed the pooch already. The Bonneville's driver's side door opened and the big red-haired red-bearded quilt-jacketed apparition that was Mateski—still in those tinted glasses!—got out, and my hand tightened on the nine mil grip. Then, once again, he climbed in the back of the Bonneville.

I waited five minutes, five very long minutes, then pulled out and drove off. When I parked next, after doing another circling-around number, I was just around the corner from Mateski, parked a few spaces beyond where his Bonneville had originally been, where I could just catch a glimpse of the Pontiac's grillwork.

Perhaps three minutes later, a car's bright headlights made me wince—*brights in town? What the hell!* The vehicle was going fairly fast, probably pushing forty, and as it roared through the residential intersection, I saw two things—a pretty blonde teenager behind the wheel, and that she was driving that baby-blue Mustang.

Would Mateski follow?

Was the blonde, or maybe one of her parents, the target?

I started the car, just in case. Anyway, I could use the heat.

But the Bonneville stayed put.

So did I, and I left the motor running because I was cold and hungry and tired, and gradually getting to be not cold anymore was about all I could do about any of that.

He was still parked there at three in the morning when I left, heading to the 24-hour delicacies offered at Denny's. Like I said, I was hungry, and I would then head to the Holiday Inn, because I was tired. These are the things we settle for when we are hungry and tired.

Anyway, I'd had a busy day.

I'd bought some Louis L'Amour paperbacks, and I'd flirted with a desk clerk, and had a pleasant and illuminating conversation with a mom in a mink coat.

I'd also, almost certainly, figured out who Mateski's target was.

A dance studio instructor.

Mr. Roger.

No "s."

Don't Let the Mystery End Here.
Try These Other Great Books From
HARD CASE CRIME!

Hard Case Crime brings you gripping, award-winning crime fiction
by best-selling authors and the hottest new writers in the field.
Find out what you've been missing:

DEADLY
BELOVED

by **MAX ALLAN COLLINS**
SHAMUS AWARD-WINNING AUTHOR

Marcy Addwatter killed her husband. Shot him dead in the
motel room where he was trysting with a blonde hooker. Shot
the hooker, too. But where the cops might see an open-and-
shut case, private eye Michael Tree—*Ms.* Michael Tree—sees a
conspiracy. For Ms. Tree, digging into it could mean digging up
her own murdered husband's grave...and maybe digging her own.

Based on the longest-running private-eye comic book series of all
time, *Deadly Beloved* brings you the first-ever prose adventure
of the legendary Ms. Tree—the groundbreaking female P.I. who
put the 'graphic' into graphic novel.

> *"The big, bloody bouquet one would expect
> from the author of* Road to Perdition.
> *Sharp and satisfying."*
> — Publishers Weekly

Available now at your favorite bookstore.
For more information, visit
www.HardCaseCrime.com

The Final Crime Novel from
THE KING OF PULP FICTION!

DEAD
STREET

by MICKEY SPILLANE

PREPARED FOR PUBLICATION BY
MAX ALLAN COLLINS

For 20 years, former NYPD cop Jack Stang has lived with the memory of his girlfriend's death in an attempted abduction. But what if she didn't actually die? What if she somehow secretly survived, but lost her sight, her memory, and everything else she had…except her enemies?

Now Jack has a second chance to save the only woman he ever loved—*or to lose her for good.*

ACCLAIM FOR MICKEY SPILLANE:

"One of the world's most popular mystery writers."
— Washington Post

"Spillane is a master in compelling you to always turn the next page."
— New York Times

"A rough-hewn charm that's as refreshing as it is rare."
— Entertainment Weekly

"One of the all-time greats."
— Denver Rocky Mountain News

Available now at your favorite bookstore.
For more information, visit
www.HardCaseCrime.com

A Collaboration in Suspense From
Two of Crime Fiction's Biggest Stars!

The
CONSUMMATA
by **MAX ALLAN COLLINS**
and **MICKEY SPILLANE**

"FRIEND, YOU'RE TALKING TO A GUY
WITH A PRICE ON HIS HEAD AND
THE POLICE AT HIS BACK..."

Compared to the $40 million the cops think he stole, $75,000 may not sound like much. But it's all the money in the world to the struggling Cuban exiles of Miami who rescued Morgan the Raider. So when it's snatched by a man the Cubans trusted, Morgan sets out to get it back. A simple favor—but as the bodies pile up...dead men and beautiful women...the Raider wonders what kind of Latin hell he's gotten himself into, and just who or what is the mysterious Consummata?

Begun by mystery master Mickey Spillane in the late 1960s and completed four decades later by his buddy Max Allan Collins (*Road to Perdition*), *The Consummata* is the long-awaited follow-up to Spillane's bestseller *The Delta Factor*—a breathtaking tale of treachery, sensuality, and violence, showcasing two giants of crime fiction at their pulse-pounding, two-fisted best.

**Available now at your favorite bookstore.
For more information, visit
www.HardCaseCrime.com**

The Lost Final Novel by the Author of
MILDRED PIERCE and THE POSTMAN ALWAYS RINGS TWICE

The
COCKTAIL
Waitress

by JAMES M. CAIN

The day Joan Medford buried her first husband, her fate was sealed. For on that day she met two new men: the handsome schemer whose touch she'd grow to crave and the wealthy older man whose touch repelled her—but whose money was an irresistible temptation...

This never-before-published novel by one of crime fiction's most acclaimed authors will remind you why Cain is considered, together with Hammett and Chandler, one of the true giants of the genre.

*"Here, long after anyone would have expected it, is
the voice of James M. Cain, as fresh and as relevant as ever.
The Cocktail Waitress will involve you, and then shock you
with an ending you'll never forget. This is a true rarity:
a reader's novel that's also a literary event."*
— Stephen King

*"How considerate of the postman to ring a third time,
delivering Cain's final gift to us thirty-five years
after his death."*
— Lawrence Block

**Available now at your favorite bookstore.
For more information, visit
www.HardCaseCrime.com**